Nick J. Brown was born in Salford sometime between the death of Elvis Presley and the release of *Never Mind the Bollocks, Here's the Sex Pistols*. He lives in Manchester with his partner.

Twitter: @NorthernMailman
Bluesky: @northernmailman.bsky.social

Also by Nick J. Brown

To Rise in the Dark

HUNTER

Nick J. Brown

ÍNCENDIARY BOOKS

Copyright @ 2025 by Nick J. Brown

Independently published.

The moral right of the author has been asserted.

All characters and events in this publication, other than those clearly in the public domain, are fictitious and any resemblance to real persons, living or dead, is purely coincidental.

All rights reserved.

No part of this publication may be reproduced, stored in a retrieval system, or transmitted, in any form of by any means, without the prior permission in writing of the publisher, nor be otherwise circulated in any form of binding or cover than that in which it is published and without a similar condition including this condition being imposed on the subsequent purchaser.

ISBN: 9798311369350

Cover image by Jessica Key / iStock by Getty Images

For my mum and dad

1

The client in his office was verging on distraught. Her voice spoke of trying times, her accent moneyed Cheshire. She welcomed an offered tissue with thanks, but not the glass of supermarket brand Irish cream. Even in anguish the lady had standards.

Blonde locks ended at narrow shoulders; navy pinstripes ran neck to ankle. What she had on her feet he could not say, they were somewhat beyond his scope. Neither podiatrist, nor fetishist, nor even a cobbler, he was merely Hunter.

She was Delamere Forest, solicitor with a Manchester firm, and someone dear to her, one Doctor Dickie Shrub, was missing. Not yet at the stage of involving police, she had chosen Hunter to find him. Hunter, though, this October Monday was having quite enough trouble locating his notebook.

He had his pen, that had been in an old mug whose sole purpose now was keeping the biro in easy reach, but where was his notebook? He had no mug for that. While he searched, Ms Forest made her predicament clear.

'Doctor Dickie Shrub is unfamiliar with the city, and so I'm concerned. I don't believe he could have gone far because of his legs yet he seems nowhere to be found.'

As one of only two surfaces in Hunter's office, his desk attracted detritus like stains to a fresh shirt. It housed, in no particular order: a laptop; the aforementioned tissues, set aside mainly for clients but also autumn's inevitable assault on Hunter's nasal passageways; a days-old free newspaper full of days-old free news; a bottle of water; the old mug-turned pen holder, royal blue in colour and bearing the Everton crest; a stack of puzzle books; a comb; his landline; a second comb he had bought to replace the first only to recover the original sometime later; and a copy of The Complete Dramatic Works of Samuel Beckett of which Hunter had yet to really crack the spine. Most of this he would have put away in a drawer, but his desk only had the one and that was already in a state beyond full.

He found his notebook inside the newspaper, opposite the headline HORSE PROFANES ROYAL SEAL, and opened to a fresh page. Under the name *Doctor Dickie Shrub?* he began to scribble thoughts. *A colleague? An older lover? Her father?* Hunter tried to imagine the man. A serious individual. Pipe smoker, perhaps. If there was a leg issue, he might walk with a stick, one with an eccentric handle, some silvery face fashioned and polished to a toothy snarl.

'Do you have a recent photo?' Hunter asked.

Delamere Forest lifted a smartphone from her handbag, tapped and swiped then passed it to him. In the picture Ms Forest sat with a small dog on her lap and a man stooping next to her.

She was laughing, he was not, the canine's tongue lolled between them. Hunter zoomed in on the man. Tall, dark hair, and on the sullen side. Not old, however. Similar in age to Ms Forest, around the thirty mark he would guess.

Hunter returned the device and with it a question. 'You've called him, I take it?'

'Yes, of course. Repeatedly, in fact. All around our building. On each and every floor. Even out onto the street.'

Hunter tapped his biro on the page and rephrased his enquiry. 'But you've phoned him?'

'Phoned him?' Something in the client's tone suggested incredulity.

'Yeah, is his mobile switched on? Have you checked your voicemail?'

'*Voice-mail?*' Delamere Forest's level of perplexity seemed over the top for what Hunter deemed a reasonable ask.

'Ms Forest,' he said sitting forward, placing notebook and pen on the crowded desk, clasping his hands, and affecting a most serious expression, 'I understand a lot of this seems obvious or pointless to you. You may've gone through it all in your mind already. But the thing is, I find it's the obvious or pointless that can help, that can really break a case open. If his mobile is switched on, we might be able to trace it. Or could an errant voicemail be waiting with a simple explanation to all this? Every piece of information, no matter how small, can help.'

Delamere Forest stared at Hunter, appraising him. Most likely debating how much "help" this man might provide.

'Mr Hunter,' she said at last, 'Doctor Dickie Shrub has no mobile phone.'

The cogs in Hunter's brain slipped into a position of

enlightenment, and he sat back, safe in the knowledge progress was being made. 'Well, it's certainly a stance I can agree with. I'm not all that keen on the things either.'

To forgo the digital revolution was an attitude Hunter admired, though not one he, in his line of work, could fully commit to. Parts of his day were indeed made easier by having the online world at hand: locating obscure destinations; obtaining background information on persons and businesses; checking bus timetables. He did not, however, like to share his mobile number as he had noticed a direct correlation between doing so and the number of calls he would then receive.

Hunter had no interest in permanent contact. He much preferred a buffer, the ability to reply at leisure. Weighty in his pocket, the phone gnawed at him, so he kept the device streamlined. In need of no extraneous messaging services or constant news updates, his applications could be stored upon a single home screen. The sole notifications Hunter received were goal alerts from Everton matches, a form of interruption he embraced but which did not happen in a positive sense anywhere near often enough. To possess no mobile at all, however, showed serious commitment.

Delamere Forest leant toward him, carefully placing a hand on the cluttered desk.

'No,' she began, 'you misunderstand.' Ms Forest was speaking slowly now, as if breaking the spell of some childhood myth to an eight-year-old. 'The reason Doctor Dickie Shrub has no mobile phone is because he's a dachshund.'

*

On her lunch hour, Delamere Forest had left the offices of Waite, Tarry and Holding to return home where she discovered the front door of her apartment ajar.

'Of course, this troubled me, Mr Hunter. I know for a fact I locked it, I'm fastidious about such things. So, I stepped away and went to enlist the concierge.'

The concierge in turn collected the hand pump from his ten-speed bicycle in the hope any intruder might be fought off with small but persistent blasts of air.

'We went inside,' she continued, 'it was as if we were in a film, moving from doorway to doorway. He went first, of course, the concierge, he was the one with the pump. We searched each room but found no one. No burglar, but also no Doctor Dickie Shrub.'

There was nothing missing from the apartment bar the dachshund.

'We checked the building, then checked it again. The staircases. The corridors. The lifts. We knocked on each neighbour's door at least once.'

After an hour's fruitless probing it was suggested she might want to call in a professional. After a further hour, she had contacted Hunter.

His office was on New Mount Street, inside an old red brick and sandstone building flanked on all sides by recently erected apartment complexes. Hunter's door bore the motto *Recoverance of Things Lost* across its frosted plastic window, and inside was one room and a toilet. This one room contained little: the desk; two chairs; and an obligatory filing cabinet with old cardboard box on top. All was enclosed by four blank plaster walls.

Hunter asked to see the photo again, zooming in this time on the canine. Its elongated body, its dangling tongue like a half-eaten slice of processed ham, its squat limbs. The issue with Doctor Dickie Shrub's legs Hunter had taken to be mechanical, not simply a matter of length.

'Doctor Dickie Shrub,' he began. 'Is that not a little...'

'A little what, Mr Hunter?'

'A little… time consuming?'

The lawyer was sitting back once more in her seat, brushing blonde strands behind an ear. 'It's only five syllables.'

This was irrefutable and Hunter moved on.

'Ms Forest,' he said, 'I've every confidence I can find your dog. In my experience, most things just turn up.'

'Really, Mr Hunter?'

'On the whole, yeah. Well, except those that don't.' He returned the phone across the desk. 'Can you send me this picture?'

Seconds later the photograph was on Hunter's own mobile screen.

'What do you mean,' Delamere Forest asked, 'about those which don't?'

'Well, the thing is,' said Hunter, 'this is where mystery comes in. Even as a civilisation thousands of years in the making, we still only know so much. There are and will always be stuff out there which, despite the best efforts of a well-recompensed industry professional, continues to defy explanation.'

This speech was a disclaimer Hunter trotted out for every client, a way of putting failure down to forces beyond his control as opposed to simple incompetence. While some listened and endured, others – Delamere Forest among them – were curious for more.

'What kind of mysteries?' she asked.

'All sorts, really. The Bermuda Triangle, for example. The ongoing and unfathomable success of certain music acts. And then, you have the local phenomena.'

'Local phenomena?'

This was a part of his spiel Hunter enjoyed and he made himself comfortable, settling into his chair, clearing his throat. He would have put his feet up were he not in polite company.

'Do you know the Shudehill tram stop?'

Ms Forest nodded.

'Well, one day I was there at Shudehill, and it was a normal day, there was nothing to suggest anything odd might happen. Anyhow, there I was, and the electronic board clearly stated a Manchester Airport tram was due in 3 minutes. A little later, it read Manchester Airport, 2 minutes. Later still, Manchester Airport, 1 minute. Well, sixty seconds pass with no sign of this tram, so I look back at the board and what does it say?'

Ms Forest was leaning forward again, a manicured hand hovering an inch above Hunter's desk. 'What did it say?'

'It says,' said Hunter, 'Manchester Airport, 12 minutes.'

Delamere Forest sat back and crossed one pinstriped leg over the other. As a reaction to Hunter's tale, it was inscrutable, and he felt obliged to carry on.

'So, where did that tram go, you might ask? One second, it's on its way, then suddenly gone. But where? And this wasn't some isolated incident; I've witnessed it plenty of times over the years. This is a regular occurrence. And what happens to the passengers already on these trams? And the drivers, where did they go? It's quite the conundrum. Not to mention worrying. It's why I never get on a tram at Victoria.'

Hunter brought himself closer to his desk, placing elbows on closed laptop shell, hands beginning to gesticulate. 'There's no great distance between these two stops, and the Airport line only starts at Victoria. So, if the electronic board is to be believed the tram is at Victoria and then the tram leaves Victoria and onto Balloon Street, but somehow it doesn't reach Shudehill. At the speed a tram glides it should take no more than a minute yet somewhere in those sixty seconds the unexplainable takes place. Now, Balloon Street. What is so special about that short thoroughfare?'

Here, Hunter paused. He was not a man for extended monologues. He liked the client to get involved and Delamere Forest did not disappoint.

'And what is so special about it?' she asked.

'Well, I don't want to be the one to say, discrepancy in the fabric of time and space, but…'

Hunter paused. Again. He would have to be careful not to overdo these breaks in the narrative. There was always the risk of losing the audience, one who was not sufficiently engaged in his words. But Delamere Forest was no longer at such a distance from him, she had moved incrementally to the edge of her seat.

'Do you think Doctor Dickie Shrub may have wandered into a discrepancy?'

Hunter shrugged and stood. 'Well, Balloon Street isn't far from your apartment and if he was in the wrong place at the wrong time…' He headed for the filing cabinet. It took him two strides. 'The thing is, I did once see a peregrine falcon round that area, which makes you think doesn't it?'

The lawyer's features sank into confusion. Also, her tone. 'Is this relevant?'

They had moved beyond relevancy and into a zone Hunter enjoyed far more. That of buffing his client's confidence in him with obscure knowledge and tales picked up during his forty-five years of life.

'It's relevant,' Hunter said, 'if you consider the cat.'

'The cat?'

'Are you sure you wouldn't like a drink, Ms Forest?'

'I'm sure and please, call me Dela.'

From the top drawer of his filing cabinet Hunter removed the bottle of supermarket brand Irish cream and a lowball glass. He filled the latter and returned the former to the drawer.

'Well, Dela, before Balloon Street was Balloon Street, before the tram tracks, the paved road, the buildings, it was a garden, and from this garden one of this country's earliest successful flights took place. A bloke called James Sadler lifted off in a balloon of his own design. Have you heard of James Sadler?'

Ms Forest's head shook in the negative.

'Few people have,' Hunter said, filling his mouth with cut-price liqueur. 'He was big in his day but soon forgotten. Anyhow, he'd come up from Oxford.'

'The university?'

'Not quite. He was a pastry cook in his dad's shop. Was without formal education but did have a keen interest in chemistry and aeronautics. Most likely,' Hunter said, sitting down, 'he was an autodidact.'

'Oh, really?' said Ms Forest. 'How sad. I imagine there's a cure for that now, right?'

Hunter lifted his glass to enjoy the soft burn of £4.79 well spent. 'Not yet,' he replied, 'but the search goes on. Anyhow, the French lads, the Montgolfiers, had been attempting to smoke their way into the skies, but Mr Sadler made the connection that it was hot air which made a balloon rise and so he rose up from this garden and landed somewhere out in Radcliffe.'

Dela Forest was quiet a moment, then asked where the cat figured in all this.

'Well, the cat went with him.'

'What?'

'I assume as co-pilot.'

'And this is important?'

'Well,' Hunter stood once more, returning to the filing cabinet, 'it's a cat, isn't it? Doing something genuinely impressive. It's a cat taking part in a revolutionary flight.'

'It is not the cat, I'm speaking of,' stated the lawyer, 'it's this entire tale.'

Hunter was in danger of losing her. He opened the second drawer of the cabinet and took a sugar free ginger crunch from an open pack. 'Well, it's unnatural, isn't it. Man isn't meant to fly. He's meant to arse around on terra firma. So, could this unnatural act have created something equally unnatural?'

Despite her suspicions, Delamere Forest made the leap without hesitation. 'You mean, the discrepancy?'

Hunter closed the cabinet and returned to his desk, noting her use of "*the* discrepancy". This was now a "the" situation. He dipped his biscuit in the Irish cream and nodded. 'There are more things in heaven and earth, Geraldo, an' all that.'

'And you believe this possible?'

'What, do I think a wormhole of some description is swallowing up these trams, and maybe spitting them out seven miles to the north?'

It was the lawyers turn to nod, while Hunter admired his sodden biscuit.

'Not, really, Dela. No.'

'But you've looked into this?'

Hunter shook his head. 'No one's ever thought to hire me for the job and office space round here doesn't come cheap.'

'But you've been to Radcliffe to check?'

'No.'

'Why not?'

'Well, Dela. I'm essentially a rational man. And the more I thought about this business and believe me I've really put a lot of thought into this, the sillier it sounded. The less sense the whole thing began to make. The cat, the peregrine, the balloon. For what reason would this anomaly divert the Metrolink all that way? Why, Dela, why? Because the thing is…' Hunter bit off a portion of steadily disintegrating ginger crunch and let the spicy mush sit on his tongue before swallowing. '…the tram already goes to Radcliffe. It's on the Bury line.'

Delamere Forest was too upset to return to work and so went home to her apartment in the Ancoats area and Hunter walked with her. He was ready to start his search and hoped the trail may still be fresh. At her block, a converted mill, the client left Hunter on a backstreet which he inspected for signs of Doctor Dickie Shrub. A lost collar, maybe. A freshly chewed bone. Some stray turd upon the cobbles. If Hunter was a dog, where would he roam? Which way through these narrow old streets might he go?

At the first intersection Hunter veered instinctively left – there would be ample time to try the opposite later. He passed along Gun Street and Cotton Street, Blossom Street and Loom Street, then stopped and in the interests of thoroughness retraced his steps. Now Hunter went right, strolling Henry Street and Jersey Street and Murray Street to the Rochdale Canal where he paused to consider the aquatic skills of your average dachshund. Was it too early in the investigation for such negative thinking?

He put his back to the water and recanvassed the area. After ten minutes milling up and down Karl Marx Alley and Engels Passage, Hunter took himself into the nearby hostelries to enquire behind bars and check fireplaces for resting sausage dogs. With no lead in sight, Hunter returned to New Mount Street and his office.

Hunter was indulging in some professional arts and crafts when his landline began to ring. Partway through the construction of a missing dog poster, he was convinced the caller could only be Delamere Forest with the glad news Doctor Dickie Shrub was safely home. He would bill Ms Forest for an afternoon's work and rejoice at being rid of this animate quarry. Hunter picked up the receiver.

'The Co-operative Printing Society, Hunter speaking.'

This was the sort of ploy he enjoyed using on those who interrupted the lazy flow of his days. To put them on the back foot. To make them think twice about calling again. Sadly, it never seemed to have much effect.

'Recoverance,' an unknown female voice said in reply, 'is that an actual word?'

Hunter put down the poster and picked up a ginger crunch. 'Definitely. I believe it was a great favourite with Beckett.'

'Was it now?'

As a question, Hunter deemed this of the rhetorical variety and held his tongue. The honest answer here was no.

'Recoverance', the voice repeated. It was a voice of costly education and the south.

'Re-coverance', Hunter countered.

'Re-coverance?'

'Recover-ance'.

If they carried on in this fashion the terms of common usage would soon render their conversation moot.

'No matter, Mr Hunter. I came across your website. It's rather austere.'

'I like to describe it as clean.'

Others would call it neglected.

'You don't have many testimonials on there.'

'Well, if it's feedback you want, I could tell you what my PE teacher said about me in 1994.'

The voice replied with a no, then introduced herself. She was Estella de Fenestrate, a literary agent in the capital, and she had an offer for Hunter.

'Your website says you find that which is missing. Well, I may require your services, yet mine is a delicate situation and not one I wish to discuss over the phone. Would you be willing to come down to London? Say, tomorrow?'

'Tomorrow?'

'You will be paid for your time and any expenses.'

'I'll just check my diary. Give me a moment.' Hunter reached for the free newspaper on his desk, leafing its pages close to the handset. 'Yeah, I think I could fit that in.'

It was raining by the time Hunter got to Balloon Street, yet he inspected each side of the road with care. He was diligent in his work, no matter the weather. Hunter walked down to Corporation Street and then back up to Dantzic. He witnessed trams pass in both directions, but no cats, no falcons, and no dachshunds. He saw no sign whatsoever of curious phenomena, so went to stand on the Shudehill platform.

On a fine day he would walk home, to his rented apartment on the other side of the city centre. He enjoyed the exercise and fresh air. He would not enjoy twenty minutes in a downpour, so three stops on the Metrolink it was to be.

Hunter looked up at the electronic board.

Manchester Airport, 3 minutes.

He had begun the day with an empty workload and now had two cases. One definite and one prospective for which he would charge a day rate plus costs incurred.

Manchester Airport, 2 minutes.

He had finished his missing posters, but they remained back at his office. Doctor Dickie Shrub would have to wait. Tomorrow, Hunter would go to London.

Manchester Airport, 1 minute.

Technically, it would be work, though Hunter would make of it what he could, take in a museum, a gallery, make a tour of the record and book shops, wander by the Thames. It would be nice to get out of the city for a time. Even if only to go to another city. A larger city. A busier city.

No tram had appeared, and Hunter looked back up at the electronic board.

Manchester Airport, 12 minutes.

2

On Tuesday morning Hunter woke in good time to make his train. He slapped at the button to silence his alarm, returned his head to the pillow, kept one eye open to avoid slipping back into sleep, and did just that. He rose properly sometime later and dressed in a rush. There was no time to walk or take the tram, only a hurried taxi ride would get him to the station and his pre-booked carriage. In a silver hatchback on the ring road, Hunter sat checking his watch and worrying if the day was lost as news headlines aired over the vehicle's radio:

> *'Select committee connects summit sommelier.'*
> *'Probe into Height-based death cult to be scaled down.'*
> *'United fans split as forward regresses.'*

Three hours later, Hunter was within the headquarters of a noted publishing house and being shown into the office of one Zora

Liu. The room was four times the size of his own and the voice which asked him to take a seat was pure New York. This was not who he had spoken with over the phone. Zora Liu was around forty and Chinese American. She wore a charcoal suit and her black hair was tied up in some form of complex bun.

As Hunter settled into a cushioned chair, Zora made her way over to the window. After reaching past a row of plants to let in some air she turned, a small silver pistol flashing in her right hand.

'My apologies. I realise this is somewhat impolite.'

No one had ever pulled a gun on Hunter before, and he did not quite know how to feel. The directness of the firearm clashed with the lavish comfort of the chair. Was he shocked by this opening? Was he shocked by anything anymore?

It took all of fifteen seconds for Hunter to regain his composure, to connect the open window to a cigarette obscured behind the pistol and the pack of twenty Zora Liu was hiding now inside a cactus pot.

'Oh, it's a dirty habit, you don't have to tell me. It was my teenage rebellion until I realised how disgusting it was and quit. But every now and then it assails me in the dark times, you know. Three weeks I've been in this country and I'm almost back on a pack a day.'

She put the cigarette to her lips, lighting it with a flame from the mock gun, then took a drag and turned to exhale a long grey plume out into the capital air. 'My unpaid intern already suspects. I've caught her sniffing around the office. I've been given *the look*.'

'Well, if anyone asks,' said Hunter, 'I'll say I brought the stench down with me from the industrial north.'

'I appreciate that, Mr Hunter.' Zora Liu took another hit of nicotine and glanced at a clock on the wall. Hunter could no longer see the pistol. 'I'm afraid we're waiting on a third party. Estella? She called you, yesterday.'

Hunter nodded.

'She may arrive at any point in the next hour. Estella has an interesting theory about time. She believes it only elapses in her presence. These minutes, for her, are not ticking away. She thinks we're all trapped in a kind of stasis waiting for her to walk in the door, you know. Each second not passing. Our lives not wasting. This cigarette not moving to my lips.'

In an act of small talk, Hunter enquired about Zora's move to the UK and was given the lowdown. After a career in Big Apple publishing she had been offered the London office of P&P, the position having become free following the sudden demise of an editor, one Leslie Organ.

'An act of God, you might call it. Leslie was struck by lightning. What I heard was he was playing golf with friends when a storm began. They insisted on finishing their round and then, somewhere on the thirteenth hole…'

While Zora Liu smoked, Hunter was left to wonder just what he had been summoned to find. Something inanimate, he hoped. A missing manuscript if anyone still produced manuscripts these days. Some great shabby mass of paper with a masterpiece inked upon it, now sadly misplaced. That, Hunter could handle. What he could not handle was another Doctor Dickie Shrub.

Hunter had been in this game long enough, the better part of a decade now, to know when it came to recovering that which was lost, the inanimate were always preferable. Unmolested by high winds, steep gradients, or children with a stick, the inanimate tended to remain in place. Their recovery no more than ticking off each place in turn. Yet the animate, those with legs, well, legs could carry them across the world and back. Legs, and wheels. Legs, and wheels, and hot air balloons.

'Estella was the one who found your website,' Zora Liu told him, interrupting his reverie. 'I don't do online anymore. I can't. I'm a recovering addict.'

Hunter took a moment, then asked, 'an addict of what?'

'The internet. Is digital sobriety not a thing over here yet? Because believe me, it's coming. What do they say about Britain and America?'

'The special relationship?' Hunter reviewed his mental archive. 'When America farts, Britain ends up with shit on its face?'

'Something like that. Anyway, I can't be around the internet. Look at my desk. Not even a computer. I'm a woman of analogue. I have a cell phone, but it's vintage, text and calls only, you know. Even my mom has a more up to date device. I can't email, my unpaid intern takes care of all that, plus dictation and correspondence. These are exactly the kinds of things we don't pay her for. The point is, I had to stop. The thing was giving me headaches.'

'From staring at the screen all day?'

'From staring at the screen with clenched teeth. I was tense, you know. In the end, I found myself getting IRATE.'

'That's understandable,' said Hunter.

'No. IRATE. The Internet Recovery and Technological Emancipation people. I had to take a step back. Make a change in my life. That said, I may have just gone and replaced it all with a different habit.' Zora Liu brandished the cigarette; its smoke rose as ash tumbled. 'Are you online much, Mr Hunter?'

'Not if I can help it. My life feels like one long struggle against the creeping onset of technology and mildew.'

Hunter could at least switch technology off and ignore it, but the mildew grew no matter how often he aired and sprayed and wiped his apartment. It permeated all corners, flourishing where he dared not look. Or was that still technology?

'I know the feeling,' said Zora. 'That's why I'm embracing the real again. Especially books. No more of this electronic business. I love the feel of a real novel in my hands, you know. The heft of all those words. A permanence that can't be wiped out in a keystroke. Oh, material goods are indulgent given the state of the world, the likelihood of catastrophe. But in the event of some terrifying disaster, they'll find me in the foetal position clutching my *Beloved*.'

'Your partner?'

'No. The Toni Morrison hardback. It's a signed first edition. Do you read at all, Mr Hunter?'

'When I can. I find I prefer a good book to most people.'

'That sentiment is doubly true in my line of work as half the people I deal with are writers.' She looked at the clock again. 'The other half being agents.'

Hunter enquired after her writers; if there were any he might know.

'I should hope so, Mr Hunter. Carlton Gas, Rosetta Stone, FYI Crisp.'

Hunter nodded; it seemed the thing to do.

'Wonderful novelists,' Zora went on, 'but all a little on the needy side, you know. What I'd really like is a nice recluse.

Someone you only hear from one year in five when they cycle courier their latest straight to your desk. But then the problem with recluses is they're so difficult to find. The chances of one presenting themselves at your door are slimmer than *The Crying of Lot 49*. The world demands so much from us all now. It's not quite so easy to pull a Pynchon anymore. But Harper Lee, she had a good run. Salinger, too. Though, once some ass with a camera has you incensed behind a shopping cart, the mystique tends to dissipate. Recluses should not be seen frequenting their local supermarket.'

Hunter watched as she tapped ash into a teacup on the sill.

'A recluse or two would be very welcome. That, or a nice dead one. Excuse me a minute.'

Zora Liu balanced her cigarette on the cactus pot and walked to her desk where she pressed a button on her landline. 'Is Ms de Fenestrate even in the building yet?'

Hardbacks were stacked on a coffee table beside Hunter:

Just Saying - The Oral History of Oral Histories by CS Gas
Holy Sheet - a Turin Shroud Adventure by Rosetta Stone
Stories I Believe Are True by FYI Crisp.

Hunter picked up the latter to occupy himself, inspected the front, the back and then flipped to the writer bio:

FYI Crisp was born in 1951 and attended the University of Michigan. Denied entry into the Weather Underground on account of his asthma, he laid down his placard and picked up a pen. He is the author of twelve novels and lives in the Buffalo area with his wife, a German Shepherd, and an inhaler.

When Hunter closed the book on FYI Crisp, Zora Liu was already back by the window, cigarette in hand.

'We better make a start,' she said. 'Tell me, are you familiar with Thornton Pyle?'

Hunter recognised the name. A writer of some distinction, though distinctly not a favourite of his. 'I've read him up to a point,' he told her.

'Oh, really.'

'Yeah, it's usually around chapter three.'

Zora nodded. 'He's not to everyone's taste. Give me Didion any day. The dry humour, the nice clean sentences, a wacky obsession with the California State water apparatus. Where were we again?'

'Thornton Pyle.'

'Yes, we have a proof of his new book somewhere if you'd like a copy?'

Hunter would have preferred to regurgitate a live cat. A feeling he translated for the occasion as a simple, 'no.'

'Thornton Pyle,' Zora began, 'his father was Earl Pyle.'

'His dad was an Earl?'

'No, well, yes. An Earl of sorts. It was his name. Earl Pyle. A fellow American. Captain of industry. One of the Boston Pyles. He married an English woman from some well to do family and settled over here in the sixties, I think. Anyway, you may have seen Thornton has been involved in a situation.'

Hunter had not seen.

'He said the unsayable,' Zora Liu informed him.

'The unsayable?' Hunter asked.

'Well, No. Not really the unsayable because he actually went ahead and said it, you know. But, possibly, unrepeatable.'

'Unrepeatable?'

'Yes.' She took a long drag and exhaled. 'Would you like me to repeat it for you?'

Hunter shook his head, his enthusiasm for the day's controversy being even less than for the free proof.

'He was up in Manchester,' Zora continued, 'on a radio show when it happened, some topical argument thing, and he got carried away. There were complaints, articles, a whole furore. You must've heard about it.'

Hunter had not.

'Anyway, through some hard work by me and my team, we arranged a television appearance the next day for him to perform his penance, you know. So, we could all move on with our lives.'

'And that didn't go well?' Hunter asked.

'It didn't go at all,' said Zora. 'Thornton was in his dressing room right up to the moment when he wasn't.'

'He disappeared?'

'Gone, Mr Hunter. Out there. Loose among your dank, sardonic mills while we attend to the damage. It's really quite distressing. My unpaid intern has been dealing with angry messages online all day. Twitter. Facebook. All the socials. She's barely had time to go out and collect my lunch.'

Hunter sank further into the seat. There was to be no manuscript, then. 'Have you reported him missing to the police?'

'No. The police represent a step we don't wish to take right now. He's not missing in the grand sense. He's just… beyond our reach, you know. As it stands, he's a grown adult male we haven't heard from in less than twenty-four hours. That does not make it a police matter. Plus, it's not only his welfare we're concerned about, there's also the company's investment. P&P

have no wish to cut Thornton Pyle loose. Both parties have enjoyed a long-running, successful relationship. P&P would like this situation resolved quickly but without the man himself we don't currently see a way to do that.'

'And you want me to find him?'

'Yes, Mr Hunter. P&P will write you a blank cheque to do so.'

If the phrase 'blank cheque' was a little out of date, it was no less enticing because of that. Hunter's bank balance was comfortable enough, but would he say no to an extra influx of cash? One more case now could mean one less later, at which point he could take time off and travel. A nice payday could take him anywhere. To America, a place he had never been. Or a winter following the England cricket team around the Australian summer. He did not need to take the job, he could have said no, yet his notebook was already in his hand, his biro clicked to a primed state.

'When did you last speak to him?'

'Late Sunday evening.'

Earlier that day the interview in which Pyle made his unrepeatable remark had been nationally broadcast to a modest audience. Calls of complaint were made to the radio station, online objections received on its social media accounts. The latter seen by a few at first, then shared and seen by more. Rival radio stations had picked up the story, TV channels also. Newspaper journalists quoted odd-named Twitter accounts. Pyle's original remark only alluded to by some but echoed verbatim by many. On a quiet Autumn Sunday, a medium-sized storm had built which had bypassed the news-shy Hunter.

'Thornton sounded fine,' Zora insisted. 'He'd been flustered in the afternoon, you know, what with the initial panic, but once things were in place for the television show on Monday, he relaxed. We told him to keep his mouth shut until then and work on what he was to say. It was a nice, comfortable daytime slot. There was never going to be an interrogation.'

From the corridor came a voice, and then the office door opened. A tall redhead strode into the room talking on her mobile, the device held canape style, a sleek metallic cracker before the woman's industrious jaws. 'Must go, Jacinta. Speak tomorrow. Ciao.'

Zora Liu stubbed out her cigarette, closed the window and was moving toward her desk. 'Well, Mr Hunter, would you look who it is.'

The redhead ignored this and put her phone away. Approaching Hunter, she unbuttoned her long green coat. 'I do apologise, Mr Hunter. What can I say? Life! There really is so much of it, isn't there? Estella de Fenestrate, we spoke yesterday? Thank you so much for coming down.'

'You know, Mr Hunter,' said Zora, 'every time I meet Estella, I feel like I lose an extra hour of the day on top of that which my unpaid intern has blocked out for the pleasure.'

'Oh, the pleasure is all hers, Mr Hunter.'

'She wants me to publish a book by some effluencer she represents.'

'It's influencer, Mr Hunter, as *she* well knows.'

'Is *she* sure, Mr Hunter? Because as someone who used to spend 18 hours a day scrolling through other people's crap, believe me, effluencer seems far more apt.'

There was something off about the conversation. Neither of the women had looked at one another, each staring instead at Hunter.

It was rare for Hunter to feel like the only adult in the room. It was a state of affairs which terrified him. 'Can we get back to the Pyle case?' he pleaded.

Soon, all three were seated around the desk.

'I imagine Zora has explained the situation,' Estella began. 'Thorn, you see, is an artist and the weight of his creative process rests heavy upon him. As do misunderstandings such as this.'

Hunter's pen was poised. 'And you last heard from him when, Ms de Fenestrate?'

'Estella, please. That would be yesterday morning. About an hour prior to the interview. He seemed in good spirits. Thorn greatly appreciates the chance to speak about his art.'

'And what about the chance to make televised apologies?'

The agent's expression tightened. 'Perhaps, less so.'

'Nothing since?'

'His phone appears to be switched off.'

'And the hotel we're paying for,' added Zora Liu, 'tell us he hasn't returned to his room. They last saw him Monday morning before he headed over to the studios.'

'Did he take anything with him?' asked Hunter.

'They say not. All his belongings are right where he left them.'

As Hunter made notes, Estella de Fenestrate leant over to tap him on the arm. 'We would not be having this discussion, Mr Hunter, had a certain person not thought a live radio discussion good promo for Thorn.'

'It would've been good promo, Mr Hunter, for anyone not an idiot.'

'I really think, Mr Hunter, that is uncalled for.'

Mr Hunter could only apologise.

'With such a great many negative reactions online,' Estella told him, 'I fear this may become too large to pass off with a mere show of remorse. This situation cannot, *must* not, continue. The harm could prove irrevocable, and not just for Thorn. Careers are on the line, here.'

'Sales, also,' added Zora.

A muffled classical theme began to play, and the agent reached into her handbag. 'That's all for me I'm afraid. Ciao.'

Estella de Fenestrate was in the office barely ten minutes. It had not really been worth unbuttoning her coat. When the door closed, Zora Liu was already halfway to the cactus, and Hunter put away his notebook and pen. The meeting appeared to have reached its end.

At the plants, the editor turned. 'For my crankiness,' she said, 'I can only apologise. This is not how I saw my first weeks in England turning out. They say any new job is a stressor. They say moving to a new home is a stressor. And then, you add someone like Estella de Fenestrate. You may have felt a tension between us?'

'I sensed a little something.'

Zora reached into the cactus pot. 'I'm sure a man in your line of work is naturally discreet, but I should make it clear you were never in this office.' She reopened the window. 'This meeting never took place.' She took out her pistol. 'And I'm certainly not about to light up another damn cigarette.'

3

With business done for the day, Hunter gave himself a few hours off. He strolled by the Thames, meandered shop aisles for records and books, admired an exhibition of Bob Dylan needlework but not the Bacon retrospective at the Tate. The sky was becoming unfriendly and time slipping away, his train at Euston would not wait.

Hunter worked on the journey home. He had a media contact from the television world at Salford Quays and the task of persuading this man into an evening rendezvous; the subject of which Hunter was coy about. Somewhere around Stoke his contact finally succumbed leaving Hunter free to delve into Thornton Pyle.

He searched social media sites he would normally avoid but found no presence of the writer whatsoever. Had they been hastily deleted or, with Pyle's fame having come before the online world was born, did they ever even exist? All Hunter discovered were arguments he would rather stay out of. He had a job to do. He should remain above the commotion.

A switch to Wikipedia was more helpful. Thornton Pyle. Aged 58. Born in the Home Counties. Raised in a capital townhouse. Three years at Cambridge studying Applied Metaphor. Two in a publishing company before discovery by well-regarded literary agent Tomkin Soup – Estella's predecessor and Pyle's maternal uncle. Beside all this was the author's photograph; expensive attire below a face flushed with success, broken capillaries and the smug grin of inherited wealth.

Hunter felt something in him rise and it was not a reaction to the quick sandwich he had eaten while hurrying back to Euston. As the son of a dock worker and dinner lady, as someone whose education had ended with college, this man seemed a natural enemy to Hunter's class. A part of him would take great pleasure in running Thornton Pyle to ground, yet Hunter was a professional and impartiality a key skill in his work. He pushed those feelings of resentment deep, put away the mobile phone, and emitted a sly performative burp before leaning his head on the window and closing his eyes.

Once back in Manchester, Hunter took a taxi from Piccadilly station to Wilmslow Road and the Tastetanbul kebab emporium. He stood at the counter and ordered, received his food in a tray, then sat down in the corner furthest from the door, alert for each customer who came and went. Three teenagers in puffer jackets. A man in overalls.

After ten minutes, another man walked in, dressed the smart side of casual, and a little younger than Hunter, similar in height but thinner and black. His hair was close cropped, his beard small and well-tended. The man spotted Hunter and gave a subtle nod before focusing on the high menu wall. Hunter shovelled sustenance into his mouth as he waited. His contact had arrived.

'Is this place new?' Hunter asked when Ahmed Said Ali was finally seated across from him.

'Only the management and the name,' replied Ahmed. 'They've rebranded. It used to be Chompstantinople.'

The five-syllable mouthful brought back a memory for Hunter, one softened by booze and illuminated by neon, which he now relayed.

'We'd get a cab down here after a night in town. Head the opposite way from home just to come to Meat Meat Meat before going back to the Height.'

'Meat Meat Meat?' Ahmed's plastic fork halted in mid-air, a strip of spiced lamb unspooling, disapproval etched around his eyes. 'Mate, do you know how often that place got shut down? I mean, the health services were in and out of their kitchens that much they might as well have called it Meat Meet Mice.'

Such talk put neither of them off their food.

'I can't be out long, Hunter. Unlike you, I've a life beyond work.'

'That's a bit harsh, Ahmed.'

'But true though, eh? I need to be back before eight. I'm watching the United game with my boys.'

How would Hunter be spending the rest of his evening? While Ahmed returned to his wife and two sons, Hunter would go back to the rented apartment where he lived alone – unless you counted his rubber plant, which for obvious reasons many did not. Hunter's boisterous upstairs neighbours were the most prominent sign of life. He could hear their television set, their laughter, even their preparation at mealtimes. Vegetables chopped so loudly they must be using an axe.

'How do you think they'll get on?' Hunter asked. It was a League cup encounter and United were away to Spurs.

'Let's just say I don't like midweek matches,' Ahmed told him, 'As it generally means double the pain and misery of a normal week. Who're Everton getting beat by?'

'Luckily for me,' said Hunter, 'I've a night off from all that.' Everton had been knocked out in the previous round.

Ahmed glanced at the other customers, then lowered his voice. 'Let's get to the point, shall we.'

To anyone listening, Hunter and his TV researcher contact would simply be two men enjoying an eat-in takeaway and discussing football woes. Yet their meetings were clandestine affairs in never the same kebab venue twice.

'This writer,' Hunter began, 'the one from yesterday at the studio. Do you know what happened?'

'Pyle?' Ahmed looked up from his tray. 'Why do you ask?'

'How about we say I'm not asking.'

'I imagine you'll still want an answer, though?'

'It'd be nice.'

'And what's in it for me?'

'Nothing, you owe me one.'

'No, mate,' Ahmed gestured with his fork, 'you'll find it's you that still owes me.'

'Are you sure?'

As much as Ahmed was a source for Hunter, Hunter was likewise for Ahmed. They had traded favours so often it was difficult to recall who was in whose debt.

Ahmed had helped Hunter by providing a backstage pass for a client's daughter to stand within some bulky minder's arm-length of an Antipodean pop starlet following a studio performance.

Hunter had helped Ahmed by tracking down the errant children's show presenter giddy on imported narcotics who had ridden his programme's resident alpaca off the set and into the Salford environs. Hunter discovered the unlikely pair queueing at the salad bar of a nearby gastropub.

Ahmed had helped Hunter in a convoluted case of wrongful dismissal, pointing him in the direction of a disgruntled former colleague. An incident which ended in an embarrassing reprimand for Ahmed's producer.

Hunter had helped Ahmed by never again coming to the attention of the producer.

'If I tell you what I know,' said Ahmed, 'it won't be for free. I'll want something in return.'

'Fine,' Hunter said. 'What is it you're after?'

Ahmed checked the time on his phone. 'We'll get to that.'

'Ok. Tell me about this Pyle business?'

'Well, one minute your Pyle is sat in make-up, the next he's gone.'

'And?'

Ahmed shrugged. 'And not much more. The make-up girl was called out of his dressing room for a moment and when she came back, he was wandering away up the corridor talking on his mobile. She assumed he'd just stepped out for a second and waited. Only she was waiting for nothing. Cue mild panic and a search of the building, the other studios, the toilets. No Pyle anywhere. Finally, they checked with reception, who said he'd wandered straight out the front doors.'

Hunter considered this. He himself was not much of a public speaker and the thought of making an apology in front of a studio audience was even worse. And what of the phone conversation, might that hold some significance?

'So, what happened?'

'Luckily, we had a back-up segment ready to go. A video of a cat wandering up and down the keys of a piano. With a little imagination and discounting every third note, you could convince yourself it was tinkling out a classical concerto. What's your interest in Pyle?'

It was Hunter's turn to shrug, and he stared out at the busy street. 'This call, did he make or receive it?'

'Couldn't tell you, mate. Now, what can you tell me?'

'What do you mean?'

"Come on, you're not here just out of curiosity. And I doubt it's for the kebab, either.'

'I'm a hungry inquisitive man and nothing more.'

'Look, Hunter, this Pyle thing is something I could really work with. I mean, it's classic Opinion Sphincter Industrial Complex territory.'

Hunter's attention was piqued. 'Opinion Sphincter Industrial Complex?'

'It's industry jargon.'

'Jargon for what?'

'Mate…' Ahmed began and then stopped. After a moment he lay down his fork, while Hunter continued shovelling. 'Look at your sphincter.'

'I'm not sure I'm that flexible.'

'Any will do, your body's full of them. They're, what, a valve? They open and close to let things move around your system when piss or shit or bile needs to be released. You receive some impulse along the nerves telling you it's wee time and, thankfully, this is one of the ones you can control but there's others you can't. You've no power over them. They just do their thing.'

'Where are you going with this?' Hunter asked between mouthfuls.

'Stay with me. Now, think back to how it used to be. If something in the news moved you enough, the only way to air your views would be writing a letter or phoning in with the hope you might end up on the radio.'

'Or boring everyone down your local.'

'Exactly. The level of interaction was virtually nil. Nowadays, though, interaction is the point. It's the only thing that's keeping the industry from dying on its arse. The People aren't just your audience, they're your unpaid publicity department. They see a story and it's easier for them to just fart out some reaction than it is to say nothing.'

The bell of the shop rang, and Hunter instinctively looked up. A young couple had walked in. He returned to the conversation. 'And this is the Opinion Sphincter Industrial Complex?'

Ahmed nodded and picked up his fork. 'The People are hungry, mate. The People must be fed. We need shite to comment on, to laugh at, to argue about. We gobble up each 240-character opinion and 500-word think piece, toss out the first thought that comes to mind and then move on to the next. I mean, It's like you with that kebab. Look at you, you're not taking the time to chew, to appreciate the flavours; you're just filling your belly. Let the thing sit on your tongue a while.'

'This chilli is a little hot for that. And besides I'm hungry. I've had a busy day, London and back.'

'London?' Ahmed sat forward. 'You are working on this Pyle thing, aren't you? The Opinion Sphincter Industrial Complex would love your Pyle thing. I'd love your Pyle thing.'

'It's not my Pyle thing.' Hunter paused to chew, simply to prove a point, only for his stomach to send a message to hurry the next bite along. 'What's so special about it, anyway?'

'It's grabbed a lot of attention online.'

'Sprayed all over Shitter?' For Hunter, few words or concepts were unimproved by having some variation of a vulgar term inserted within.

'Hunter.'

'Shit-stagram?'

'Please.'

'Faecesbook?'

'Just, what is your problem with the internet, anyway?'

This Hunter did sit with, but with no real breakthrough beyond a shrug. 'I'm not sure I see the fuss in it. There's nothing online I wouldn't rather get out in the real world.'

'You could have a kebab delivered right to your door.'

'Why would I want anyone coming right to my door, kebab in hand or not. I live in an apartment block for the very good reason I don't get people coming right to my door. I like a buffer.'

Ahmed checked the time, once more. 'Let's get back to the point here, mate. This Pyle thing. It's special and I'll tell you why. When the printed word was King, an editor might've gone big on the front-page headline but beyond that they'd fill their paper with stories to appeal only to the people who'd buy it. Now though, because of the internet, everything needs a front-page headline because everyone can see it. Half the job is pandering to your core audience and the other half is boiling the piss of those who wouldn't wipe their backside on your words never mind spend a penny on them. They turn out articles knowing they'll wind people up and in frustration and anger, those people then share them. And I'm not judging anyone, because I'm terrible for it. Could be United, could be politics. I know all this, and I see cynical decisions made every day at work but come evening, I'm right there online falling for it all.'

'Why?'

Ahmed sat back, pondering this. 'You engage a couple of braincells. You wiggle your thumb a bit, and thirty seconds later someone you've never met tells you you're a genius. That, or a communist.'

'Never both?' asked Hunter.

'Another thing is your Pyle business has something for everybody.' He began to count on his fingers, gesturing with the fork. 'For those who're appalled at what he said. For those who agree with what he said. For those who can turn it into a funny meme for the numbers. For those who can turn it into an opportunity to further whatever agenda they have. But it also brings something new to the table.'

'Like what?'

'Like where the hell is he? I mean, your standard public fuck-up usually plays out in one of two ways. An ill-advised comment is made, and you get an apology. The sorry episode runs its course. The People eat, but it's a very prosaic meal.'

'Can we stop saying "The People" as though it accounts for everybody?'

'Fine, Mr Pedantic. *Some People*. Is that better?'

Hunter assented.

'The other way is an ill-advised comment is made and there is no apology, they choose instead to style the thing out. Well, *Some People* take these incremental chunks until a meal more filling comes along, but real satisfaction is never achieved. It's like a taster menu.' Ahmed leaned forward, elbows on the table, fork dancing as he made his point. 'To disappear though, Hunter, on the verge of a very public grovelling. Well, that's not part of the accepted narrative. That's dishonouring the narrative. I mean, that's tickling Some People's balls and running away.'

'You paint quite the image.'

'Dessert hasn't even been served yet and your Pyle has skipped out on the bill.'

'I've told you, he's not *my* Pyle.'

'Come on, Hunter. Help me out here. This has flavour. I could do with something like this to show my producer.'

'The shouty man?'

'Yes, the shouty man.'

Hunter felt a moment of paranoia. The producer had made his feelings about him clear, and Hunter scanned the kebab emporium for eyes directed his way. No one immediately stood out, yet an alias was primed and ready should anyone require his particulars. He was Ken Bingsley, a man of unspecified employment and unprovocative nature.

'Something like this could really push my career along,' Ahmed continued. 'There's only so many feline Mozarts a man can serve up before he begins to question his life choices.'

'I can't promise anything from this,' said Hunter.

'Why? Because you're not asking?'

'Exactly.'

'What can I expect then?'

'I dunno. A favour down the line.'

'I'm not keen on favours down the line. The line is a fuzzy concept. I mean, how long is this line? How wide, mate? Is it liable to blow away in a stiff breeze?'

The pair had reached an impasse and ate in silence before Ahmed switched the conversation back to the less complicated subject of football. 'Do you think your mate will score tonight?'

'My mate?'

'O'Connor. He's from your way, isn't he? Irlams o' th' Height?'

'Yeah, but I don't know him.'

Connor O'Connor was a United striker twenty years Hunters junior. Their paths had crossed only once.

'Do you get back there much?' asked Ahmed.

'The Height? Why, are you after an autograph?'

'Just wondered if you kept up with the gossip.'

Hunter stopped eating. 'What sort of gossip?'

Ahmed was chewing, chewing some more and then finally swallowing. 'What do you know about this death cult?'

At first, Hunter was baffled then recalled a headline from the taxi radio that morning:

Probe into Height-based death cult...

'I heard something, but assumed it was your standard slow news week nonsense.'

'Not for the Opinion Sphincter Industrial Complex it isn't. A shadowy ring of evil is right up their alley. My producer won't stop going on about it and if I can't distract him with your Pyle thing, I'll need something to show him and soon.'

'Does he know you're asking me about this?'

'Does he bollocks. The only way he'd have you in on this is if you turned up as a corpse.'

'Have there been any bodies?'

'None that we know of.'

Hunter toyed with his remnants of döner meat and naan. 'Is there actually a story here, or is it just rumours?'

'Mainly the latter so far, that's why I want you looking into it.'

'But is there anything at all to back it up? A highly placed informant? A secret note? Bog wall graffiti?'

'Look, mate, this death cult. Confirm it, debunk it. I mean, we can work it into something either way. My producer gets a segment, Some People will be satisfied for a time and…

Hunter lifted his plastic fork to interrupt, 'we're all five minutes closer to the grave.'

4

Hunter was up at seven on Wednesday and straight to work. He sat by the window next to his rubber plant with a bowl of cereal, a large coffee, and his landline, eating and drinking and practising the call he was about to make. He had not forgotten Doctor Dickie Shrub. The missing posters had been completed and waited on New Mount Street for Hunter to distribute them around the area. First, however, he had to update Delamere Forest.

Since Monday afternoon all communication regarding the case had been via a series of convoluted voicemails. On Tuesday morning Ms Forest had called Hunter's office and left a message requesting news of the canine quest. Hunter, at that point on a train speeding to the capital, had checked his landline voicemail remotely and having arrived at Euston called the lawyer's home number from a payphone, safe in the knowledge she would be at work. He pretended not to have received the client's message and gave her answering machine a detailed but mostly fictional rundown of his progress.

Later, after returning to her apartment, Dela Forest had once more rung Hunter and left another voicemail which Hunter had picked up after his kebab with Ahmed Said Ali and now, after a mixed night's slumber, he rang the offices of Waite, Tarry and Holding, gambling correctly she would not start work this early, thus leaving him clear to update her machine, free of questions to which he had no answers. The call made, Hunter watered the rubber plant and returned to his breakfast.

With stomach filled, nature attended to, and caffeine reserves at maximum Hunter opened his laptop to delve once more into the life of Thornton Pyle. Following on from his previous search, he began on the P&P website which informed him Pyle's first novel, *The Sweet Boy and the Wet Nurse*, had won the Blunderbuss Gadget prize for fiction, while his second, *Adolf and the Bulge*, was awarded the prestigious Count Fladj Iron Donkey. Further books brought similar acclaim.

Yet this was not what Hunter was after, this was no more than the veneer of an existence, a life's self-satisfied grin. Hunter wished to go deeper, to scratch away and uncover anything rotten hidden behind, and so moved on to newspaper archives. This, at least, was an aspect of the internet Hunter could approve of. Recorded history at his fingertips while he lay on a leather two-seater in a level of undress he would not inflict upon the world.

The release of each Pyle tome had brought glowing assessments, plus interviews with the same three or four outlets. Hunter read these interviews and then reread them, assuming he had missed something first time around. Ample column inches were given over to tours of the writer's palatial London home: portraits of Pyle's noted lineage; antique furniture graced by prominent buttocks; his extensive collection of Third Reich tableware. There was little mention, however, of contemporary issues. Here, it seemed, was a man of no strongly held beliefs.

A toppling of sorts came in the late nineties. His novels *The Elder Bonaparte Brother*, *The Missionary's Position*, *The Life and Grime of Frank Reactionary* were not well met. To describe their reception as mixed would be to embrace a level of kindness most critics did not. This appeared to slow Pyle down, his output reduced to a book every five years or so. He had no secondary career imparting wisdom to students, but he was not a recluse. Hunter found scores of pictures: Pyle smiling for the cameras at gatherings or premieres; Pyle treading the novelist's circuit; Pyle being Pyle. Also, the same old interviews with the same old outlets, the author's answers as anodyne as ever.

Hunter, though, had no real yardstick for judging this man. He loved books but knew little of their creators. Did not know a writer. Had never even met one. Theirs was a world Hunter only engaged with via the page.

Manchester was unusually warm for autumn. The day offering a last flash of heat which would fade quicker than a holiday tan. Hunter left his apartment on Little Peter Street and crossed the city centre in bright sunshine, stopping briefly to pick up a free newspaper and read the front-page headline: IDIOT IN ROOM FULL OF IDIOTS MAKES IDIOTIC REMARK.

At New Mount Street, Hunter collected the posters from his office then headed for Ancoats. In the centre of each photocopied appeal was a black and white Doctor Dickie Shrub, tongue a-lolling, cropped from Dela Forest's picture. Details were filled in around him. A short description of a shorter canine, plus last known whereabouts. Hunter had added his work landline but decided it wiser to leave the dog's name unmentioned. Experience told him certain facts were best held in reserve.

As he made a circuit, sellotaping each A4 plea to a lamppost, the force of passing vehicles down narrow roads fluttered the papers in his hands. Hunter was in no hurry, the day had yet to get going, and he had ample time to get started on his other cases.

By Cotton Street he was down to the last half-dozen posters, his mind thinking ahead to a return to New Mount Street, when he became aware of a trailing presence. A duplication of steps as he walked and silence when he stopped.

Hunter continued, maintaining a slow pace and outward display of calm, yet inside his breathing had quickened, his armpits dampened by more than weather warmth. He bypassed Karl Marx Alley and Engels Passage, made a right and then a left and another right and was on Gun Street. Halfway up, he paused in front of a shop window.

Behind his own reflection in the glass, a distant figure loomed over his shoulder. They were maybe twenty feet back on the opposite side of the road, features obscured by flat cap and the upturned collars of a long coat unsuitable considering the hot spell. Whoever this was had dressed for chill October, yet the day was far more August.

Questions about who and why would come later, Hunter's first thoughts were of evasion. He walked on and at the Blossom Street cobbles made an exaggerated show of crossing safety, looking both ways and catching the figure on the edge of his peripheral vision.

Nearby, a taxi was beginning to pull away but before it could gather speed, Hunter darted out into the road, greeting blasted horn with apologetic raised hand, then carried on along Gun Street. He did not look back and moved faster now, heart rate climbing – his doctor, at least, would be pleased.

Hunter had almost reached the safety of George Leigh Street when a white transit began to reverse. The van's mournful beeps imitating Hunter's alarm as it blocked his exit. With no wish to head back the way he had come, to face his pursuer, Hunter saw his only opening, an underground car park, and in a moment had ducked under the barrier and into the gloom.

Hunter crouched in a damp alcove, waiting as cars came and went: a bright red hatchback; some dark saloon; a sporty number in tasteful meringue. Hunter's passageways thickened with exhaust fumes and the less than subtle reek of piss. It was not an ideal spot to catch one's breath.

Who could be following him? He had no enemies, had upset no clients. None he was aware of, anyway. Was this linked to a case? The dog, the writer, the death cult?

Hunter allowed ten minutes to pass and then noticed a couple walking to their vehicle, opening the doors, starting the engine. As their silver SUV moved toward the exit, Hunter slipped out alongside them, seeing no long-coated figures as he grew reaccustomed to the light.

5

Hunter was back at the office on New Mount Street, budget Irish cream calming his nerves as he stood staring out his window directly into a larger one across the way. This larger window's occupant appeared gainfully employed during daylight hours and so Hunter was not forced to watch them go about their activities. Instead, he enjoyed the still life tableau of a most likely rented existence: the matching black leather two-seaters; the carefully selected art prints of minimal outlay and imagination; their habit of leaving the lights on.

An insistent drumbeat returned Hunter to his office, where the postman, Claude, filled the doorway.

'Don't mention the football,' were the deliveryman's first words.

'Why?' Hunter asked, moving toward his desk. 'What happened in the football?'

'I told you not to mention it.'

Bald and bespectacled, Claude Horn also hailed from Irlams o' th' Height, had gone to the same schools as Hunter, had grown up only a street away. The pair were old friends.

'A little early for a tipple, isn't it?' asked Claude.

'Strictly medicinal purposes,' said Hunter, taking a further mouthful. He sat down, placed the booze on the desk and set about changing the subject. 'Have you noticed anybody acting strange out there this morning?'

'Strange, you say?'

Hunter nodded.

'Do you know how many people I run into of a morning?'

'How many?'

'Hunter,' the postman began, 'I see all of life out there. And when they need directions, they see me.'

'Yeah, but anybody strange though?'

'To be fair, pal, I consider all people strange until they prove otherwise.'

Hunter was getting nowhere and let the topic slide, passing over two sheets of paper. 'What about these?' One was a recent picture of Thornton Pyle. The other a missing dog poster.

'Together or on their own?'

'Either or really.'

'That'd be neither then. I see so many faces they all blur into one and as for man's best friend, I try to steer well clear. You know what they're like around posties. Must be the uniform. All that starchy cotton.'

Claude gave the papers back, and with them a handful of letters for Hunter. 'New cases, are they?'

Hunter gave his friend vague outlines of each. 'I'm told this Pyle character is all over social media.'

'Not on my feeds he isn't. All I get is football, old music and older shots of Manchester and Salford. If I spot them about though I'll let you know.'

Hunter then made a tentative enquiry about his third and most recent case. 'Any news off the Height?'

Claude still lived in a terraced house a short walk from both their parents. 'Like what?' he asked.

'I dunno. The usual. Or maybe, the unusual?'

'Spit it out, pal.'

Hunter picked up his glass and took a generous slug before proceeding. 'Alright, what've you heard about this death cult?'

'Death cult?' Claude leaned on the client chair; a playful grin aimed at Hunter. 'Are you sure you're pronouncing that right?'

'That's what they called it on the radio.'

'I don't listen to the radio. Other people talking and playing their music is my idea of hell.'

'You're drifting, Claude.'

'We're all drifting, pal. It's the human condition. Don't you think a death cult on the Height sounds a bit far-fetched?'

'Not been approached to join, then?'

'Ha, I doubt it. You know how I feel about group activities. I've not the correct level of enthusiasm.'

With no fresh clue at hand, Hunter began to flick through his post. There was a bill, an offer of credit – *you have been invited to accrue debt for the benefit of our non-tax-paying parent company* – a further bill, and a rival offer of credit. 'The enthusiasm about death?' Hunter enquired.

'The enthusiasm about most other members of the human race. Do you think all this might be connected?'

'To what?'

'The dachshund and the fella.'

Hunter paused. 'Well, I didn't until now.' Could there be a

connection, other than the fact these events all entered Hunter's life in the same short period of time? It could make things easier for him. Or more difficult. One of the two, certainly.

'Anyhow, what did happen with the football?' said Hunter. United had been away to Spurs, it was the match Ahmed Said Ali had hurried home to watch.

'I told you not to mention it. But for your information, pal, we lost. 1-0. Shouldn't have though. And wouldn't have, but for a certain so-called goal scorer.'

Connor O'Connor. The United striker was struggling through a prolonged barren spell, and Hunter had taken a call from him, or a voice claiming to be him, last week asking for help in finding his lost touch. Hunter had explained that was not quite his field and suggested O'Connor try a sports psychologist.

'I thought you were a fan of his?' said Hunter.

'To be fair, I am,' Claude stopped to consider this. 'Well, I was. I know he's a Height lad an' all, but if it carries on like this, the next time I sing 'Oh, Connor O'Connor' I'll be chucking in a few expletives.'

'And what does your Phil think?'

Claude and his sibling were regulars at United. 'Our kid doesn't sing at the match. He swears a lot, but he doesn't sing. He says O'Connor gives the ball away too much, that he's short a yard of pace. Says he's not a United player.'

'Really?'

'Yeah. That, and he doesn't like his beard.'

Among Hunter's post was a bill for a previous resident, a Mr Elvis Love. Hunter crossed out the address on the front, circled the one on the rear, wrote in clear capitals, ELVIS HAS LEFT THE BUILDING, then passed the letter back to Claude. 'How is he, these days, your Phil?'

Claude smiled at the letter before replying. 'He's not been the same since what happened with the Dog.'

'The dog?' A spark flared in Hunter's synapses, and he took a further swig of cheap liqueur. Was this another missing canine? Might there be a link after all? 'What happened with the dog? Do I know your brother had a dog?'

'Not *a* dog, pal. *The* Dog. And Partridge.'

The Dog and Partridge was a Height pub their families had long drunk in, but which had called last orders for the final time. The building now renovated and home to a doctor's surgery.

'They still go in there,' Claude said, 'my mam and our Phil, but it's just not the same. There's no atmosphere. Or, to be fair, there is, but it's not a pleasant one. Too many posters on the walls asking grim questions. Too much daytime telly. I was in there the other week, actually.'

'How come?'

'I was having a DRE.'

Hunter looked up from his glass. 'A DRE?'

'Digital rectal examination.'

Hunter looked down again. 'This is about where you lose me.'

'Don't worry, pal. It's really not all that high tech.'

6

Hunter had devoted a good few hours to pursuing Doctor Dickie Shrub, had made an initial enquiry regarding the death cult, and now his attention returned to the missing writer.

Zora Liu had given him details of Thornton Pyle's hotel, The Snooze Inn. It was close to Piccadilly Station, though perhaps too close. Such a location put in Hunter's mind the thought Pyle might be long gone by now, having performed some railway flit home to the capital or across a border to Scotland or Wales. The author had last been seen or heard from on Monday morning. It was now midday Wednesday.

The Snooze Inn was of the low-end chain variety and Hunter thought the place an odd choice for someone like Pyle. Yet if the publishing company were footing the bill, this may have been nothing more sinister than cost cutting.

At reception, a young woman flashed her best minimum wage smile.

'I'm here to look at a room,' Hunter told her.

'Certainly,' said the young woman. 'Is this any room in particular?'

Unsure how much she knew and how much he should share, Hunter leaned closer and lowered his voice. 'I was told you'd be expecting me.'

The young woman was tall with glasses and behind her frames wore the embattled stare of one who must bend to the whims of a species she clearly despised: the terminally ungrateful city break enthusiast. She matched Hunter's conspiratorial lean and hushed tone. 'We expect people every day, sir. That's why we have the rooms.'

Hunter cleared his throat, raised his volume and introduced himself. 'I'm Hunter. Someone should've called about me.'

'Someone should've called about *me* a long time ago,' the receptionist countered, 'but, like Diana Ross, I'm. Still. Waiting.'

Hunter gave her about a mile's worth of slack and explained the situation.

'Oh yes,' said the young woman, 'I dealt with this myself. The lady sounded a bit on edge.'

'Was that before or after she spoke to you?'

'Very good, sir.'

'Couldn't you have told me this five minutes ago?' Hunter asked.

'Yes,' she replied, handing him a key card, 'but then we'd have so much more of the day left, wouldn't we. Enjoy your stay.'

On the fourth floor a Do Not Disturb sign was in place outside Thornton Pyle's room, and Hunter paused in the corridor, bracing himself for whatsoever lay inside. The receptionist had not seen the writer in days. No one at The Snooze Inn had, and

Hunter considered how he might react to discovering a corpse, the air of two-day rot. Most likely he would vomit, but then he would only be a stride or two from the bathroom. Unless the body was in the bathroom. Hunter put the key card to the door and entered.

There were smells alright, but none of rancid decay. Hunter scented stale coffee, staler food, and a toilet insufficiently flushed. The room was of standard layout: double bed; table by the window; wall-mounted flatscreen. In one corner was a suitcase, in another a plastic bag containing worn clothes, shirts hung in a tall cupboard. The initial reading Hunter took from the scene was nothing more than Man in Hotel Room, and he set about a more detailed examination.

Under the table was a drawer and in the drawer a Bible and in the Bible a small vintage dirty magazine wedged deep in the Psalms. A quarter of an hour later Hunter shut the drawer and moved to inspect the table.

There were takeout coffee cups and used room service plates, tram tickets and crumbs of varied size and hue. Below the table and its drawer of delights was a half-full bin which Hunter probed with care and more than a little foreboding.

Among used tissues and serviettes was a leaflet scrunched into a ball. Hunter flattened it out on the table. Salford Museum and Art Gallery, it read. Bar having been used as a coaster, abstract Olympic Rings printed on it in a single shade of brown, the leaflet conveyed to Hunter a sense of nostalgia. He had not visited there since childhood, on school trips or summer days out with his mother. What interest might Thornton Pyle have in the place?

The sole other clue Hunter found in the room had been a

sticker on the cover of the vintage magazine for Bhatt's Tomes, a bookshop on the other side of the city centre. He made a note of this for professional purposes.

Hunter left the Snooze Inn and headed toward New Mount Street. Progress had been minimal, but then it always was. That was the job, and he enjoyed it. Hunter saw every case as a puzzle, and he did so love a puzzle. Those with words, those with numbers, even the humble jigsaw. He kept a stack of puzzle books on his desk containing crosswords compiled in the 90s, when Hunter's interest in popular culture was at its zenith.

A case would present him with an avenue to follow and follow it he would, either to illumination or a dead end. Patience was the key. Methodical patience and no distractions from your task. Hunter always marvelled at how slow time went by if you just sat alone appreciating the length of a minute, concentrating on a single problem. How much was possible in an hour, in a day, if you eliminated the unnecessary. Soon Hunter would be back on New Mount Street, in glorious silence at his desk with nothing more stimulating than a low-sugar ginger biscuit, enjoying each second of each sixty and pondering his next move.

As he paused on Dale Street, noting a newsagent sandwich board headline – SALFORD YOUTH FOUND FALLIBLE – Hunter felt once more he was not alone.

A van was parked nearby, and Hunter pretended to take an interest in the business advertised across it – Assmann Gas, plumbing, heating, etc – but really scanning the window for reflection. He soon saw that same long coat with collars upturned. That same flat cap. That same figure across the road a short distance back.

Hunter adopted his most indifferent air, a leisured amble, slow and without purpose, then suddenly took a sharp turn down Mangle Street, upping his pace to brisk among the industrial bins and ancient fire escapes.

He emerged on Back Piccadilly in the shadows and rear exits of firms, and neither looked back nor broke into full pelt – a runner not head-to-toe in lycra attracted attention and Hunter already had enough of that. He moved across Newton Street, remaining on Back Piccadilly where more bins greeted him but no glass panes to search for his stalker. The only faces were those of graffiti leering from aged brickwork.

A right turn put him on Little Lever Street and soon he was back on Dale, crossing before a double decker could gather speed. A further right and Hunter stopped to crouch behind a transit. He was on Lever Street proper now. His heart rate pumping and breathing erratic, armpits drenched in sweat.

In time, body and mind relaxed, panic subsided; fatigue and a sense of elation hit him. He would have laughed had he the energy. It was only then Hunter became aware of a shadow growing over him and the fear returned.

He looked up to see not his pursuer but a rotund man in a yellow vest, carrying a large cardboard box under his arm. Hunter smiled and pointed down to a booted foot. 'Shoelace.'

7

An interest was being shown in Hunter, an interest he did not care for. He had been followed twice already and had yet to even pause for dinner. He could have gone home to his apartment on Little Peter Street, but there was no guarantee whoever was shadowing him might not show up there, to molest his intercom, or worse, gain entry to the building and accost Hunter on his very doorstep. Now seemed a good time to remove himself from central Manchester, so with no calls received as regards Doctor Dickie Shrub, Hunter stayed on the trail of Thornton Pyle and took the bus to Salford.

Hunter rode the V2 beyond the River Irwell, and the sign welcoming visitors to the other City – *You are now IN Salford, home of the best Scrooge, the best Poirot, the best Jesus, and the best Gandhi*. He alighted on the Crescent by the old fire station and Working Class Movement library and crossed the busy main road, where beyond the grass stood the red brick Museum and

Art Gallery with its dual entrances, neither of which Hunter had stepped through in two decades.

He started in the gallery. With walls painted dark green and a ceiling Hunter guessed to be art deco, this was not your average art space. Hunter had the feeling he had stumbled onto a Kubrick film set, the palpable sense Leonard Rossiter might emerge from some secret doorway at any moment to converse with Hunter in his best Russian.

Life-size sculptures dotted the carpet, paintings busied the walls, yet Hunter paid both little attention. His interest was in the visitors and searching their faces for his quarry. There were older couples, a loner here and there, schoolchildren with pads making sketches of the works. No Pyle, though.

Then, glancing past a pair of alabaster buttocks, Hunter experienced a flash of recognition. He saw not the author but, in the far corner, something familiar to him.

Hunter approached and was soon stood before a landscape. John Charles Dollman's *Famine* was a sight he knew well; in the centre was a tall, hooded form, attended by carrion crows, directing an endless wolfpack over the land. Hunter had first discovered it as a teenager, having never seen this sort of thing represented in art until then. There were no flowers, no important figures, nor concubines of important figures with or without flowers. This was not some idyllic vision and the youthful Hunter had been fascinated by the piece, had bought a print and pinned it to the bland woodchip of his bedroom wall. Some weeks later, he had noticed the two or three wolves closest to the mysterious leader, their heads turned outward toward the viewer, and staring straight at Hunter. Their eyes not necessarily bright, just lighter than the intense darkness surrounding them.

With no sign of Pyle and in need of more cheery fare than *Famine*, Hunter left the gallery and moved into the museum, heading downstairs to Lark Hill Place, the 19th century moment frozen in time. When precisely in the 19th century, Hunter did not know. At the time of the Peterloo incident? Or when Marx and Engels were over the road in the Crescent ale house, drinking and fomenting?

Before stepping back in time, Hunter took a moment to make a donation and dress in the period attire provided for visitors. Disguises were part of his job as was the adoption of a pseudonym. Hunter chose a baggy cap and beige shop coat, then admired himself in the mirror while deciding on an alias. He mind-flicked his cerebral Rolodex, adjusted the cap, and settled on Ellis W Lowryder. A moment later, he was standing on the cobblestones of an age long ago.

The street was murky, his path lit by lampposts and shop windows aglow. Hunter half expected a fog to take hold. It was nighttime in the past.

The area had many businesses but few people. There was the corner shop with provisions of sweets and groceries, a music store with its display of instruments. Another seller sold books, toys and games. There was a tobacconist, a chemist and druggist, a bleeder replete with leeches. A blacksmith shod the feet of horses, a clogger did likewise for bipeds. The dressmaker, milliner and haberdasher attended to the rest of the human form.

Under a lamppost Hunter saw someone waiting, and headed that way, boot heels ringing on the cobbles. The someone was a child, a barefoot chimney sweep whose bovine stare suggested one too many cramped dark places. Hunter would have engaged the child in conversation, given him sixpence in exchange for information, even Sherlock Holmes had his urchins. Yet the sweep remained mute, no more than a soot-faced mannequin.

To complete this slice of Victorian life was a one-up, one-down artisan's cottage and, Hunter was pleased to note, The Blue Lion Tavern inside which he found a corseted barmaid, her dark hair tucked under a bonnet. Unlike the chimney sweep, she appeared pure flesh and blood.

Hunter watched her dry glasses, feign interest in non-existent customers, and adopt the classic pose of the trade – arm resting on bar, light but measured grip on beer pump. She was good. Hunter might almost believe it was an actual pub. He sat awkwardly on a stool – comfort not being so readily available in the 19th century – and tried to ease his way into conversation.

Hunter had not been down this way in a long time and told her this.

'And is it just as you remember?' the barmaid asked, scanning a far empty corner where no one was causing a commotion.

'Not really, because back then I believed it was real.'

She gave him a quick glance. 'Oh right.'

'Yeah, you know, excavated while they dug out the plumbing for the museum above.'

The glance became a full-blown stare. 'Am I not real, then?'

'Well, yeah, but you're…' Hunter searched for the correct word, settled on 'inauthentic,' and regretted it at once.

'Inauthentic? You really know how to make a girl feel special.'

'No, it's just I used to believe this had been an actual street. The thing is, I'd read books about the discovery of ancient ruins, previous civilisations. So, why not here?'

'Early Salfordian man?'

'Exactly. Everything built on top of what came before. The literal foundations of a world to come. Every time they expand the Rome metro they uncover more and more. Ancient barracks. Tools and pottery.'

'Nero's fiddle,' the barmaid offered, no longer looking at him.

'Yeah. Under the paving stones, earlier, less sophisticated examples of the form.'

Her interest had returned to the far corner. Hunter was losing her and decided to get to the point.

'Do you get many out-of-towners in?'

She gave Hunter another glance. 'We get all sorts in here.'

He took out his mobile with a recent picture of Thornton Pyle saved in readiness and laid it between them. The barmaid's attention flicked to the device, and the picture. Her practised indifference slipped, revealing a state of nerves.

'Put that away,' she said, hushed and serious.

'What?'

'Quick, before someone sees.'

'Why?'

'They're forbidden. Put it away.'

Hunter watched her expression expecting this new mask to fall and a joke revealed but saw only earnestness. He slipped the phone back into his pocket.

'I'm not supposed to talk about anything contemporary.' Her voice was still low. 'I have answers for you, but not here. Here, I can only tell you about the 19th century. At a push, the build-up to the First World war, but that's about it.'

Hunter did not know what to say. He could be on to an important clue and had no wish to make a misstep.

'We're not allowed to break character,' she told him. 'We have to stay in the roles we've been assigned.' A man and woman walked into The Blue Lion and the barmaid reassumed her classic pose, though kept her words quiet. 'Do you know the Bargemen?'

Hunter nodded. The Three Jolly Bargemen was an old school city centre boozer on Big Peter Street.

'I'll be in there tonight,' she said. 'Come after eight.'

8

Above ground, and out on the grass, Hunter returned himself to the present by checking his messages. He had three.

The first was Delamere Forest replying to his earlier call and requesting an update. The second was in response to the missing dog posters. A low, male voice enquired whether a reward was in play and if so, how much. The third message informed Hunter he had recently been involved in an accident and compensation could be his if only...

With hours to kill before his meeting at the Bargemen and seeing as he was already in Salford, Hunter thought it a good time to drop in on his parents. They still lived in his childhood home, and he had not seen them in a week. Hunter would call in and listen to their tales, of ailments their own and their friends, and pick up any other gossip which may or may not include local death cults.

It was a thirty-minute walk, but a pleasant enough day on which to take it. The journey passed quickly enough as did the university, the high rises, and the precinct. Hunter was soon on the Height and passing familiar shops on Bolton Road: the vets; the funeral home; The Red Herring fishmongers; and the Taste of Hungry sandwich bar.

Back on Viscount Drive, his old street, that row of semi-detached abodes he had rushed to or from more times than he could count, Hunter opened the old gate at number 49, then rapped lightly on the old door.

At the nearest bay window, a woman's face loomed: late-sixties, grey hair, an expression of deep confusion. The confusion became a smile and soon she was greeting Hunter at the front door.

'This is a surprise,' his mother told him. 'But you should've called before coming over. We might've been out.'

'But, mum,' said Hunter, removing his boots in the hallway and then following her through to the kitchen, 'you're not out.'

That Mrs Hunter had been a dinner lady at his school was a source of great embarrassment for her son. To have a parent so close by while he was trying to find his way in the world, while he was hoping to project a certain image to his peers, a different Hunter than he was at home. Yet great embarrassment, he found, could often be balanced out by an extra dollop of buttery mash.

'I thought you were the man,' she said.

'Which man, mum?'

'The meter man. Your dad's at war with the water people, again. He's out in the yard, calming down. Do you want a drink?'

Hunter ignored all this information and went straight to asking after his parents' wellbeing.

'Oh, we're fine. Are you sure you don't want that drink? I'm making a brew.'

Hunter declined. 'I don't know how you two sleep at night with all that caffeine inside you.'

He had already had his regulation single jolt of caffeine this day and dared not risk a second. Though Hunter would not quite term himself an insomniac he had definite problems regarding slumber. It might be biological: a late coffee; too much sugar; an alcoholic imbalance in his bloodstream. Or it might be his neighbours: slamming doors; guffawing at volume; striding their wood block flooring so loudly he assumed they must be wearing clogs.

Other times the problem was Hunter's mind. He had difficulty in shutting off his brain. It waited in standby mode, a tiny red LED glowing at the edge of darkness, ready for the slightest thing to wake it. One night, he could be poring over facts of cases searching for the link which would bring the whole thing together. The next, he may just as easily be replaying some perceived slight on public transport from a good six hours beforehand.

And then, in the times when he did sleep, came the dreams. Sometimes, personal; a face from the past waylaying him with some cryptic memory. Sometimes, sexual; a body from the past waylaying him with some classic mammaries. On occasion, Hunter would even be visited by the downright surreal.

One recent evening he had watched back-to-back documentaries on Hemingway and Picasso, pausing only for an intermission consisting of a heavy plate of macaroni cheese. When dozing later, under the influence of industrial strength cheddar, Hunter had found himself in Paris and seated around a table in a bar the only entrance to which had involved clambering through a window.

At the far end of the table was the famed writer, at the near the feted painter. Hunter witnessed the two artistic titans locked in silent confrontation. Walrus-faced literary landmass versus cue ball headed Cubist, neither wishing to look away and show weakness. Alcohol was imbibed, nicotine and more smoked, tension built until the diminutive Spaniard overturned the table and many a drink, stood as tall as possible and bellowed in an unexpected Salfordian tone, 'are you looking at my Andalusian machismo?'

In these moments, Hunter would snap awake to the pulsing of blood throbbing round his brain and an urge to urinate.

'So, what's happening round here?' he asked his mother as he sat at the kitchen table. 'Any big news?'

'Like what?'

'Like anything, mum. No unusual gossip?'

'Let me see.' Mrs Hunter filled the kettle, then apportioned instant coffee into mugs, and readied the milk. 'Sally Clare got married.'

'Should I know Sally Clare?'

'If you didn't, it's too late now. The Williamson brothers have started up a window cleaning service.'

'The twins?'

'Of course, the twins, do you know any other Williamsons? Oh, and your friend Claude, he had one of them digital rectal examinations.'

None of this was the sort of gossip Hunter had expected or indeed wanted. 'How do you know about Claude?'

'His mother told me; I saw her in the butchers. Have you ever thought of getting a digital rectal examination?'

'Why, so you'd have something to tell Mrs Horn when you're out shopping?'

'She's not Mrs Horn, anymore.'

When Hunter was a child, she was Mrs Horn, a nurse at a local hospital. When Hunter was a teen, she was still Mrs Horn and still a nurse. Then, when Hunter was in his twenties, Claude's father had died and three years later Mrs Horn became Mrs Cornet, though remained working at the hospital. When Mr Cornet, a local carpet impresario, passed a decade after that, Claude's mother left nursing and threw herself full time into carpets. She was now married to Jack Euphonium, a market trader, who traded in stock dependent on the inclinations of his suppliers and Salford market's customers. To Hunter, though, Claude's mother would remain Mrs Horn.

'All that's just normal gossip, mum. Has there been nothing out of the ordinary?'

'There was Mrs Ted. Do you remember Mrs Ted?'

He did recall Mrs Ted. Tall and gaunt, a greying spectre even back when Hunter was a child. 'She's still going?'

'She almost wasn't. The poor woman had the fright of her life when the police smashed her front door down at six in the morning.'

'Really?' Hunter sat forward; this could be something.

'They went rampaging about her house. Overturned the beds. A young constable rifled through her drawers.' His mother spoke the next line in a whisper. 'They thought she might be one of those cannabis farmers.'

'And was she?'

'No, they had the wrong street.'

The kettle boiled, and Hunter watched his mother pour and stir.

'Have you heard anything about…' he paused, sensing the doubt in his own voice, '…a death cult?'

His mother turned; her eyebrows rose. 'I beg your pardon.'

Hunter repeated his question with increased volume and care.

'Oh, that. You'd best ask your father about that.'

'Why, he's not took up any strange hobbies has he?'

'No, but his ears aren't as bad as mine. And before you go.'

'I've just got here, mum.'

'I know, but before you go, your dad's lost his keys again. Can you have a look for him?'

'Certainly,' Hunter replied and then mumbled, 'If he asks nicely.'

'Don't be like that.'

'You heard that did you?'

'Not completely but the pair of you are predictable enough for me to guess.'

Hunter was directed through the back door into the yard with a hot beverage for his father. He found the old man corralling fallen leaves.

'Alright, dad.'

The elder Hunter stopped and leant on his brush, staring at his son and then the mug and then his son again. 'Would you look who it is. The searcher. Found your way to anything of interest lately, like a real job?'

To his father, Hunter was nothing more than a hired lackey to those with more money than sense, and the old man went back to his sweeping.

'You know you can get people to do that for you,' Hunter offered.

'Do I look like I'm made of money?'

He did not. The close-cropped beard was grey, so too his eyebrows and what was left of his once black hair, now hanging on only above his ears and at the rear of his dome. He looked even paler than usual. The only part of him to retain any original colour were his eyes, still blue, still sharp. The docks at Salford where he had worked closed when Hunter was a toddler, but he always associated the old man with that job. He was a staunch trade unionist. Someone with a view on the world.

'I hear you've lost your keys again,' Hunter offered.

'They're not lost. I've just put them down and can't remember where.'

'Sounds pretty close to lost if you ask me.'

'And did someone ask you? Because I told her not to.'

Hunter searched for a different topic. 'What's this about the water people?'

'The bane of my bloody life,' his father looked up, 'that's what this about the water people is. But I'm not getting into that right now. I'm out here for a bit of peace.'

While his father went back to his leaves, Hunter felt relief at not being dragged into any labyrinthine utility grudge and enquired instead about the death cult.

'I've heard things,' the old man told him as he swept, 'rumours about the library. Hushed talk and that.'

'It's a library, dad. Hushed talk is the only kind they allow.'

'This is different, so I'm told. It's lower than hushed. Lower than a whisper.'

Hunter stared at the man who would not meet his eye. 'A deep whisper?'

'Yes. A lot of deep whispering round the library.'

'Deep whispering about what?'

'Well, murder, apparently.'

Hunter watched his father continue to work his brush, premeditated killing not being enough to distract him from this task. Murder. But of whom? Hopefully not dachshunds, disgraced literary types or hired lackeys to those with more money than sense.

'And you heard all this, did you?' Hunter asked.

'No,' his father replied. 'Pat MacGuffin told me about it in the fishmongers.'

'Pat MacGuffin?'

'Aye, I was in there buying some mackerel.'

If Hunter had already suspected this case to be nothing more than a joke tale, he was now convinced.

'Seriously, dad. Pat MacGuffin?

'I said, aye.'

'Would this be the same Pat MacGuffin also known as Bullshit Pat MacGuffin?'

The brush stopped moving, the elder man turned to his son. 'No, it's a very different Pat MacGuffin. He's a changed man. Pat's a pillar of the community these days. Helps out with anything for anyone. Drives people to appointments. Chips in at the food bank. He runs The Red Herring now.'

'You are joking, aren't you?'

'I'm deadly serious, son.'

'Pat MacGuffin? The Pat MacGuffin who reckoned he once stood at a urinal next to Bowie in full Ziggy Stardust garb?'

'Even alien celebrities have to take a piss, son.'

Upon hearing this claim as a music-obsessed youth something had not sounded quite right to Hunter. He had seen pictures from that bygone era in magazines, clips on TV of David Bowie's early alter ego, and never once did Ziggy's jumpsuits appear designed to accommodate such practicalities.

'The Pat MacGuffin,' Hunter continued, 'who said he was at the Hand of God game in '86? Yet somehow was back on the Height from Mexico the next morning.'

His father shrugged. 'Air travel's a modern miracle.'

'Don't you remember that summer he's supposed to have worked for MI5?'

Mr Hunter resumed his brushwork. 'Doesn't ring a bell.'

'Well, dad, I remember. I remember that for a man supposedly away on classified operations he was seen an awful lot in the Co-op.'

'Doesn't mean anything. The Tories might've thought the place a front for some Marxist coup.'

'So, you're happy buying your mackerel from a bloke who might've been a class traitor?'

His father stopped and met his gaze. 'Son, I'd never go so far as saying I was happy about anything, and you've hardly a leg to stand on bearing in mind you'd work for Satan if he paid you enough upfront. But if I only bought from people I agreed with, I'd be out here empty-handed and in just my underpants.'

Hunter stood chastened but only for a moment. 'Ethically sourced, are they?' he enquired.

'Ask your mother, she washes them.'

'A Marxist plot, though, dad? In the Co-op?'

Mr Hunter returned to his leaves. 'I don't talk politics in the yard, son. I come out here to sweep.'

'Dad!'

'Don't have a go at me. You're the one who brought all this up.'

'Yeah, and you're the one who seems to believe a lot of nonsense.'

The man stopped once more; the brush handle gripped tight. Hunter saw knuckles about to burst his papery skin.

'No, son. You never asked me what I believed. You asked me what I'd heard. And I told you.' The elder Hunter was breathing heavily and allowed himself a moment of calm. 'Asking the right questions is important. Meaning is important. Remember that.'

Hunter felt like a small boy again, rebuked for some immature act, often in this very yard. A ball hoofed too close to a window. Action Man figures buried up to their necks in soil. His investigation into the magic of fire which almost set ablaze their weekly refuse.

His father was a serious man, not prone to the flights of fun and games other parents were. He and Hunter clashed regularly, and there were times when the son felt he could trace their schism back to a May afternoon in 1985. The FA Cup Final was on television and his father, an ardent United supporter, had set all else aside to watch the build-up. At kick-off, Hunter in an act of childish rebellion made the decision to support their opponents, Everton.

It was a tense ninety minutes plus extra-time and not just on the field at Wembley. The Hunter household was divided. In the end, a single goal decided the match, delighting his father and saddening Hunter. Yet he had made his decision and from that day on had stuck with it.

The problem, in fact, was not so much this decision as the force which had directed the young Hunter to it. Some inner devil compelling him not fall in behind his father. Not to fall in behind anyone. To push back. Hunter had the mark of the provocateur, even at the age of five.

Now in his forties, Hunter still found himself occasionally beholden to that inner devil, yet had also learned to suppress it when needed, as he did in the yard with his father.

'What do you believe then, dad?' he asked in his most respectful tone.

The old man shrugged, a particular angle of shoulder making its presence known under the cotton of his shirt. His father was only seventy, but retirement had seemed to age him fast. After the docks had shut he continued in manual jobs, seeming to require some level of activity to keep himself alive.

'Believe?' Mr Hunter was staring at something his son could not see. 'I don't know. I sometimes wonder if I believe anything anymore. Beyond this yard, beyond the gate, beyond your mother. It's difficult to say.' The man went back to sweeping.

'Let me do that for you, dad.'

'No, I can do it myself. And it's not just the money, it's the noise. I don't need to pay someone to make a racket outside my window. The neighbours'll do that for nowt.'

Hunter watched his father and wondered how different the pair of them really were.

'All this science and technology in the world, eh dad. You'd have thought they'd have come up with a quieter leaf blower by now.'

'But they have, son. It's called a brush.'

The Height library was smaller than Hunter recalled but then his eyes were so much higher than they used to be. As a child he was a regular visitor, accompanied by a parent or his grandmother who lived on a neighbouring street. Books were found to be a good way to distract the young Hunter, to calm his inner devil, so long as it was he who chose the books. Later, Hunter would visit on his own, intrigued by stories of ancient civilisations and spy novels calling to him from the shelves, until his teenage years when time became increasingly devoted to music, alcohol and an apprenticeship in lust.

Now Hunter returned to walk the single floor building and, as at the museum, he gave more attention to people than the creative endeavours on show. A pensioner or two, a young mother with child. No one around raised his suspicions. No one discharging an air of tension pushed to grim acts. Except, perhaps, the young mother.

The place had many windows and not a single bulb in disrepair, it seemed a little too well-lit to host nefarious dealings, yet Hunter proceeded with caution. He could not walk up to a stranger and drop the phrase 'death cult' into idle conversation. The right questions, Hunter knew, were important. He would have to be subtle. He would listen and observe.

While observing and listening Hunter explored the shelves for sign of Thornton Pyle's work. He located Fiction and followed it all the way to P, scanning the spines into Q and R to be thorough. He went back and scanned them again. There was nothing.

While pointless in many respects, this act was useful to him in one. It offered Hunter the beginnings of a normal interaction which could then be steered into stranger territory. He waited until the librarian had finished dealing with an elderly man and begun staring into space, then approached the counter.

'Excuse me,' Hunter began, politeness always a handy tool, 'do you have anything by Thornton Pyle? There was nothing on your shelves.'

The librarian smiled. 'I'll just have a look for you.' She was mid-fifties, short and had blonde curls, her fingers danced across the keys of a computer. 'No, sorry. We had two of his but they're both out on loan. I could reserve them for you if you'd like.'

'No, that's alright. Can I ask who loaned them out though, and when?'

'Certainly, you can ask.'

There came a pause, and it took Hunter a second or two to realise this may not be as straightforward as he imagined.

'Ok,' he said, 'who loaned them out, and when?'

The librarian inclined her head to share a sorry smile. 'I'm afraid I can't tell you.'

'Why not?' asked Hunter.

'I can't just give out information to anyone.'

'Isn't that how a library works, though?'

'For members, yes.'

'But I am a member.'

'You are?'

'Yeah.'

'Well in that case, I could tell you when they're due back in, and you could track back from that date.'

'But not who loaned them out?'

'I'm afraid not.'

'Fine,' said Hunter, 'that'll have to do.' This would be something at least. A tiny seed from which to begin.

'Excellent. I would be more than happy to share this information with any member upon production of the relevant identification.'

As beginnings went, this seed was not for growing. Hunter stared at the librarian behind her counter. Under the tight curls and overabundance of poplin, she was not the mild-mannered keeper of knowledge he had taken her for. Might her leanings stretch to murder?

'The relevant identification?' Hunter asked.

'Yes,' she said, 'a library card. *Your* library card.'

'And if I didn't have my library card with me?'

'Well then I think you'd be in for a disappointment.'

Hunter decided she was not the person to ask about any death cult and thanked her for her time. He continued to listen and observe around the library, passing monitors and keyboards, the talking books. With progress non-existent and exit on his mind, he stumbled across the notice board. Its wooden edges and corkboard backing were barely visible under a mass of paper and card. Offers of help for the infirm, advertisements for local businesses, a twenty-four-hour delivery service for any item human urges might conjure a need. Under a taxi company flyer, the corner of something black stuck out, and Hunter moved the flyer until a rectangle was fully visible. Printed on the black in deepest red was DEATH.

Hunter checked over his shoulders to make sure no one was watching, then unpinned the card and flipped it over:

Height Library. 19:30. Refreshments provided.

To which day this referred was not stated, and Hunter rechecked the vicinity for unwanted attention then slipped the card into his jacket pocket. He pondered a return to the counter. Should he ask the librarian about this? Would it be worth his time to do so? It mattered not for the librarian was gone.

9

Hunter traded the old haunts of Salford for Manchester and his rented apartment. He ate and put on a clean shirt as the upstairs neighbours crushed garlic with a shoe. By the time he left for The Three Jolly Bargemen, temperatures had fallen, the sky turned dark, and lamp light showed Hunter his path.

The Bargemen squatted halfway down Big Peter Street among taller, newer buildings closed for the night. Metal bars clung to the pub's windows, keeping hoodlums out or patrons in. Hunter arrived early and made a circuit of the rooms to see if the Lark Hill Place barmaid was present. She was not and Hunter's nerves tingled. This type of clandestine enterprise he always found a strain. The step into the unknown to meet a person whose name he did not even possess. Would she even show?

At the bar Hunter was served by a buxom blonde. He took his pint and placed himself on a stool not centre stage yet not in the wings. He had no wish to stand out nor appear to be hiding. Experience taught him the middle ground was always the way.

A principle which also applied to school classrooms and riding a bus.

This was an ale house Hunter had only been in a few times and not for many years – when out in town, he and Claude usually did their drinking in The Skull and Crumpet – and the Bargemen appeared to have changed little from what Hunter could tell. The walls were damp woodchip paper, the carpets sticky enough to affix you to the spot should you stand around too long.

A voice he recognised came from the direction of the bar and Hunter turned to a woman neither buxom nor blonde. She was a slim brunette with heavy eye shadow, and it took Hunter a moment to place her. She was the Lark Hill Place barmaid and introduced herself as Vicky Park.

'You seem surprised,' she said. Her 19th century outfit had been replaced with vest top and faded blue jeans, yet her vocation remained unchanged. 'Did you expect a hot date?'

Hunter shifted on his stool. 'A lukewarm one, maybe.'

A man approached the bar and their conversation paused until he went back to his table juggling three pints.

'So,' said Hunter, 'you work in a mock pub in the day and a real one at night?'

Vicky Park assumed her familiar pose, one arm resting on the bar, one hand on a pump. 'That would depend where you believed reality ended and escape from reality began.'

She reached for an empty glass. 'Is this real?'

She indicated a prowling Alsatian. 'Is that real?'

She gestured behind Hunter. 'Is he real?'

An elderly gent was shuffling past on his way to the lavatory but stopped, confused by the slur and on the verge of a conniption. 'It's alright, Eric, I know you're real enough. I'm just making a point.'

The gent resumed his shuffle and Hunter smiled. They appeared to be picking up a thread from hours ago, one buried deep under the Salford Museum and Art Gallery. 'What about those pies,' he asked, noticing a nearby glass dome. 'Are they real?'

The barmaid shrugged. 'Buy one and find out.'

Hunter did buy one and found it tasted real enough. Perhaps, a little too real and by as much as three days.

An interruption came from over Hunter's shoulder and a shadow was cast over him. 'Is this fella bothering you, Vicky?'

'No more than you do, Joe.'

'That's harsh, Vicky. Harsh! I might have to go home and rethink my life.'

'But you'll have another pint for the road first though won't you.'

'It'd be rude not to.'

While Vicky Park poured his drink, the man introduced himself to Hunter with an extended hand. 'Joe Dimly.'

Joe Dimly was taller than Hunter, and heavier set. The branded polo shirt of his employment obscured beneath a denim jacket; a few dark hairs lingered around his pale orb.

Joe pointed to the stool where Hunter sat. 'Pete Moran used to sit there.'

'Pete Moran?' Hunter vaguely recalled the name.

'Yeah, you know, the singer. The dead one.' Again, Joe pointed. 'That very stool.'

'Did he now?' replied Hunter, in a tone of fake interest.

Vicky placed a dimpled glass on the bar. 'Let the customers drink in peace, Joe,'

Joe Dimly nodded. 'Yeah. That very stool.' He picked up the glass and inhaled half its contents. 'Or sometimes the one down by the dartboard.'

'Joe?' Vicky said, her tone rising.

'Occasionally, he'd be sat up the other end entirely. If the karaoke was on, that is.' The second half of his beer disappeared in a single gulp.

'Joe.'

'And then,' he put the glass down, 'every once in a while,' an immense hand smeared foam from his lips, 'he'd just lean.'

'JOE!'

'He was a bit of a maverick.'

Joe Dimly faded into the pub interior, and Hunter waited to make sure he and the barmaid were alone, then brought out his mobile and the picture of Thornton Pyle. 'This is the fella I was asking about.'

Vicky Park pressed her fingers on the devices screen to zoom in, and Hunter noted her black painted nails, also the lack of a ring.

'I've seen him,' she said, nodding. 'He was at Lark Hill Place last Saturday, asking lots of questions.'

'About what?'

'About everything. Lark Hill Place. The local area. The standard of pastries in the museum café. Not seen him since, though. Who is he?'

Hunter gave her a brief rundown. Name, occupation, current level of notoriety.

'Oh right.' Vicky Park's shadowed eyes narrowed. 'He never said he was an author. And he told me his name was Stephen.'

'Stephen what?' Hunter's notebook was out of his jacket, biro clicking into action.

'I didn't ask, and he didn't say. I thought he might've been a lecturer at the university. Or he might've told me that, I don't remember exactly. We get a lot of visitors.'

'Did he say why he was there?'

'Not really. He might've mentioned some project he was working on, but that's about it.'

Hunter's notes so far consisted mainly of question marks. *Stephen, question mark. Project, question mark.*

'So, you're a bit of a detective, then?' the barmaid asked.

That did rather sum up his work life. 'I find things for people,' he replied. 'Anything that's lost, really.'

Hunter could never quite pin down when he discovered his talent in this regard, he just seemed to possess the knack for locating the missing and mislaid. Objects did not simply disappear; the concepts of spontaneous combustion or theft by otherworldly beings were not ones he embraced.

All Hunter had to do was go through each case practically, as he did with his puzzles, and he believed a thing would turn up. It helped that there was a stubbornness in him, Hunter had never been one to give up easily. He would carry on his searches beyond the point when many would have lost hope. And if people were happy to pay for him to indulge this stubbornness, then all the better. Hunter's guiding principle for every case, be it lost soul or sentimental heirloom, was simply, *it has to be somewhere.*

Hunter took a generous swig from his pint. 'I'm not just after this writer,' he told the barmaid, 'I'm also on the lookout for a dog.'

Before him, Vicky Park's mouth opened yet the words came from the opposite direction.

'There's one over there,' the voice behind him said. He had not heard Joe Dimly approach.

Hunter followed Joe's finger and saw the Alsatian once more prowling the area, weaving between furniture, pausing to sniff every third crotch.

Hunter left the Bargemen and commenced his short walk home from Big Peter Street down to Little Peter Street, a ten-minute sojourn at the most. On his way he picked up a discarded free newspaper and scanned the headline, PM ZOO VISIT HELD UP BY CROSS PORPOISES, before putting it in a bin.

Cushioned against the world and its ills by an alcohol buzz, Hunter considered his progress as he ambled. Thornton Pyle seemed to have a fascination with Lark Hill Place. A fascination which ended once his troubles in the so-called real world began. Was there a project Pyle was working on or was "Stephen" merely trying to impress a young woman?

Hunter had left his number with Vicky Park in case Pyle returned to the 19th century street. A number which, he now realised walking the quiet night-time city centre, was that of his mobile rather than the office. Had he done this by accident? A little drunk, perhaps, and outside business hours. Or had there been a design in this? An amorous intent? Vicky was attractive, a similar age to Hunter and never mentioned a significant other. Not that their talk had strayed into the personal.

Hunter was allowing his mind to wander back over the memory of eye shadow and tight jeans when he heard a noise to his rear. He turned to scan the long alleyway he had taken a short cut down whilst in his erotic reverie. It was too full of darkness to pick out anything beyond the sizeable industrial bins which might provide excellent hiding places for those who preferred to carry out their abominable deeds unseen.

Only now did Hunter recall the figure who had trailed him that morning. This long-coated stalker had slipped from his thoughts, yet the figure had likely not forgotten him. And who might that stalker be? Was it Pyle or someone who wished Pyle not to be found? And what of DEATH? Their card was still in Hunter's jacket pocket. If *They* knew Ahmed was on to them and had followed him to Tastetanbul, could *They* now be after Hunter? And who were *They*?

Hunter carried on the way he had been heading but saw no immediate exit left or right. He caught a thick stench of days-old urine and the light of a distant main road lamppost flickering, transmitting its call to him in municipal morse. Hunter estimated escape to be at least a hundred yards away.

He heard the noise again, nearer this time and certainly clearer. A sharp rattle. Some piece of refuse dislodged by a pursuing foot. An empty glass bottle slowly rolling out alarm.

In the battle of fight and flight the latter response kicked in and Hunter was away, moving fast, maybe too fast. Fixed on that far-off luminosity and not minding his step, he felt his boots slide on slick ground and almost fell, maintaining his balance with the help of a large plastic bin. Hunter turned and walked backwards, breath and pulse pounding hard through his body, eyes searching alleyway murk. At the same time Hunter saw movement his heel caught the kerb and down he went, landing heavy on his backside, a sitting duck for whosoever was coming for him. He tried to stand only to slip and fall into panic.

10

Panic was not something Hunter felt all that often. Bar the occasional shadowing by unknown assailants, his life held little to induce the feeling. Childhood had been a happy time, he was the sole offspring of two well-adjusted, capable parents. The years were stable. Calamity bypassed 49 Viscount Drive.

Death only came into Hunter's life through the demise of his pet Supergerbil and was dealt with by a simple act of cloning. A trip to the Height pet shop with his mother for a replacement who was duly christened Supergerbil II. There would be no passing of cherished family members until later; the only great losses he felt in those early years were by Everton and in FA Cup Finals – 1985, 1986, 1989. He learned of trauma via TV screens and the page. The news and dramas, the novels he read in his teenage years; terror and heartache remaining always at arm's length.

Then, in Hunter's late twenties his grandmother died, and he was sad but not distraught. She had been at the high end of what many considered "a good age" and he had witnessed her becoming less and less the woman he knew and loved. Her world diminishing, her body curling in on itself until she was no more. Hunter had finally been introduced to death and had dealt with it.

The closest he had come to real trauma was back in the nineties, one breaktime in a Salford school playground where Hunter made a small misjudgement. On this day he had not blended in with the masses, he had stood out from the crowd, he had put a target on his back. On this day Hunter had worn his Everton cagoule.

He had been minding his own business attending to some gravel with a foot, when suddenly he noticed his surroundings appeared different. The sky above had closed in, the nearby bricks that much closer. Two boys had Hunter cornered. Older boys. Taller boys. Boys with early-stage facial hair framing their grimaces. One of the boys brought out a long, sharp item from his pocket. As the item moved toward Hunter's face details came into focus.

He noticed the ridges, the curl of a descending circular stairwell. It was a screw, and a rusty old one at that. The intention of these malevolent rascals was then made clear: Hunter should remove the offending article or have this ancient unhygienic item introduced violently to an ear.

Hunter felt not so much terror as curiosity. He had questions. He wondered at the timeline of events. Which had come first, the screw or the cagoule? Rust, of course, would indicate the former. But had the boys picked the screw up a while ago and pocketed it for some future heinous act or had they seen the cagoule and become enraged, searching about for a weapon they might brandish?

And where had they found it? Were long rusty screws lying fallow in the northern earth awaiting their chance to be repurposed, though with little expectation of such dire usage? It was, perhaps, a remnant of the city's industrial age. This seemed plausible, and Hunter's mind was eased, another of life's mysteries had been solved – one thing he could never explain, however, was how so much pornography found its way into bushes; some questions are simply too complex for the human mind.

Later, Hunter would have an epiphany regarding the cagoule incident. He would see where the boys had failed, would smile over their youthful ignorance. Their mistake had been to threaten him physically, the screw being intended to pierce his lobe. Yet Hunter as a youth had, like many of his peers, no concept that human beings were susceptible to such things – his gerbil had certainly not died because of an errant screw. Hunter had survived countless scrapes. Hospital visits for him were an adventure, a day trip somewhere out of the ordinary. He had hung upside down from many a climbing frame and woken, hours later, in just as many infirmaries.

Hunter's eureka moment was to realise that if the boys had threatened violence upon the cagoule rather than himself, he would have folded immediately, sunk to his knees and begged them to spare this polyester wonder. It was Hunter's most treasured possession and finding another in the shops of Manchester and Salford would have proven difficult for his parents. To dig out even this one had been a majestic find in those days. But an ear? As far as Hunter was concerned, that would have been fine. He had two of them, after all.

*

Back in the alley, under its wretched air of stale piss and distant streetlight SOS, the bottle continued to rattle. Hunter's backside was still flat on cold stone and youthful fearlessness nowhere to be seen. The years had eroded such cockiness. Should he ever require spectacles that second ear would prove invaluable.

With fear of bodily harm now a real concern, his mind was on its knees imploring leniency in his assailant. But who approached? Hunter hoped a rough sleeper on the hunt for sustenance or urban fox doing likewise.

The bottle's roll ended, and there was a moment of dread silence before Hunter heard a fierce growl, followed by the small pop of a fart – provenance unknown – followed by another fiercer growl. Out of the shadows waddled a dachshund.

Hunter would have laughed were his throat not so dry. He gathered up his resolve, coughed and spoke. 'Doctor Dickie Shrub, I presume.'

Doctor Dickie Shrub responded with a yap in a tone Hunter would call derisive, and before he could set himself, the pocket canine was scampering his way. About a foot or two in front of him, the dog twisted to his left and Hunter tried to dive after him but was not used to operating at such reduced elevation. He lacked sufficient technique to propel himself after the hound. His hands caught nothing but urine-tinged air. Doctor Dickie Shrub was gone, and Hunter left splayed upon the ground.

Safely home in his rented bed, Hunter was dreaming. The scene was Lark Hill Place, and he was being chased across cobblestones in the jumpy flickering motions of bygone cinema. Behind him he heard heavy panting yet dared not look.

Out of breath, Hunter paused and caught his reflection in the window of the streets toy shop. He was the chimney sweep. The soot-faced urchin. A cheap top hat wedged upon his adult skull and chimney brush in hand. Beyond the glass he saw a figure. A man. Was that Pyle in the shop, stood leafing through some book or annual?

The panting was closer now, and Hunter resumed his escape. He made it into the Blue Lion just as a mammoth dachshund the size of a medium dinosaur halted outside, its stinking tongue filling the doorway. Hunter was secure, for now. He turned away from the canine's lolling mouth meat and there was Vicky Park, the barmaid in her period dress but with modern eye shadow. Hunter's hands gripped his grimy brush.

Vicky sat on the bar and crossed her legs, Sharon Stone *Basic Instinct* style. The ruffled cotton skirts too long to tell if she was wearing underwear or not but flashing Hunter views of heavy black boots and deep red stockings.

She crossed her legs again. And again. And then again.

With each repetition the movements became faster and faster. More exaggerated, more performative. No longer filthy demure but increasingly the domain of 1980s bearded television fool Kenny Everett. The scene somewhat Lynchian in its mundane horror and in the sexual ballpark of an iron lung.

11

Hunter woke on Thursday hoping for a less eventful twenty-four hours. Wednesday had been long and curious, though progress was made on all fronts. Effort exerted, steps taken, boot soles worn down. Enough perhaps to convince his father he held a proper job, though most likely not.

The DEATH card was still in his jacket, waiting to be passed along to Ahmed Said Ali. He had good news too for Delamere Forest, her dog was alive and well enough to put the fear of God knows what into Hunter. His Pyle case, however, was troubling him. He had gained information regarding the writer's timeline before his disappearance yet nothing after that. Three whole days left unaccounted for.

The morning was wet, Manchester's weather reverting to type, and with the makings of a hangover pawing the edges of Hunter's brain, he took the tram across the city. He had drank three or four pints in the Bargemen, then a few bottles when home to steady the nerves after his alleyway encounter, and that was enough these days for Hunter to feel the next morning as if he was operating under some invisible cloak of lead. Movement sluggish, energy lacking, brain function that of primitive man.

At his office on New Mount Street, Hunter struggled to push open the building's heavy doors, then struggled to push them shut again, and as the outside world disappeared, and all daylight was sucked from the antechamber, a hooded figure emerged out of stairwell gloom.

Hunter reeled; this was happening rather too often of late. Flashbacks of the previous evening assailed him. The darkness, the cobbles, the thick urine stink. But for the doors behind him he would have ended up once more on his arse, and vulnerable to far worse than the short limbs of a sausage dog. The figure was raising an arm, and, in another flash, Hunter saw the hooded spectre from his art gallery landscape. *Famine*. Was this his death?

Hunter need not have worried. The arm raised only to bring the hood down and reveal a bearded face Hunter knew but did not really know. Connor O'Connor, United's misfiring striker and former Height resident.

The pair were soon up in the office. The footballer apologising for his unorthodox entrance, and Hunter pouring himself a glass of bargain Irish Cream. It was not yet half-nine.

'This might sound like an odd question,' Hunter began as he closed the filing cabinet, 'but you weren't about looking for me yesterday morning, were you?'

O'Connor shook his head. 'We were travelling back from London. Then the gaffer had us in at the training ground. The little sadist made us watch the game from the night before.'

Hunter filled his mouth with liqueur and swallowed. A sweet silky burn ignited in his pipes. 'I did say over the phone this isn't really my sort of thing.'

'I know, mate. It's just I'm getting desperate.'

Hunter sat down. The man across the desk from him was a Premier League star, sometime England international, and a millionaire several times over. If he really believed Hunter could help him, he truly was desperate.

And he did look it. His hood was up once more covering his slicked back hair. The heavy top stated PUBLIC ENEMY in bright yellow on black. O'Connor glanced over his shoulder at the door. 'I don't suppose you could lock that, could you?'

Hunter opened his mouth to speak and instead filled it again with low proof booze.

'I know I sound paranoid, but what it is is everyone's a paparazzo these days. I can't seem to go anywhere without getting a camera shoved in my face. That's why I was hiding under your stairs.'

Hunter put his glass down, stood and went over to flick the door latch. Only then did O'Connor feel safe to remove his hood again. 'What should I tell anyone if they ask why I was here?'

Hunter was back in his chair, drink in hand. 'Tell them the truth, or as close to it as possible. Tell them you've lost something.'

'Like what?'

'I dunno. Anything. What do you spend your money on?'

Hunter wondered how much the footballer earned. He had read the rumours, seen the astronomical sums thrown about in the press. He could not imagine looking at his own bank balance and seeing all those extra zeros.

'Lately, I've been getting into NFTs.'

Hunter was not fluent in abbreviation and felt no shame in admitting so.

'Non-fungible tokens,' O'Connor explained. This did not make the issue any clearer.

'Is that a euphemism?' asked Hunter.

'It's like crypto, mate.'

After a five-minute lesson, Hunter, still under his leaden cloak, remained none the wiser and they moved on to O'Connor's troubles.

'It's fifteen games now,' the striker told him. 'It's getting embarrassing, is what it is.'

'Fifteen?' Hunter was sure Claude had said sixteen. Sixteen games without a goal, the stretch made even longer by the three-month summer break.

'There are some who've started saying I didn't even score that last one.'

'Why?'

O'Connor paused and looked away to stare out of the window. Hunter did not like to rush his clients, he preferred to let them get to the point in their own words and time. Their time also being his, which he duly billed them for.

'Because,' the footballer began, 'it kind of went in off my arse.'

'And you claimed it?'

'Course I claimed it, mate,' O'Connor said, almost offended. 'I'm a goal scorer. I score goals. If that ball doesn't hit my bum, it doesn't end up in the back of the net and we don't win that game.'

As the striker recalled it, from an injury time United corner the ball had bounced around the penalty area, many legs thrown its way until a defender managed to get a clear kick. A kick which only sent the ball toward O'Connor and his behind, which subsequently deflected it back the way it had come, to slip past a bemused goalkeeper, and give United three points.

'I was doing their right back a favour. No one likes an own goal on their record.'

'But now people are saying it's not yours?' Hunter asked.

'Idiots, mate. That's all. Tedious online banter merchants and jealous old farts trying to stay relevant. It's not my fault their knees don't work anymore. No matter what they say, I'm the one whose arse it went in off.' O'Connor tapped the slogan on his chest. 'I'm the one with a bruised bum cheek for a fortnight.'

Hunter swilled his glass, thinking out loud. 'But what's the etiquette for this kind of thing?'

'Etiquette? Mate, the panel ruled. My arse, my goal.'

'But you haven't scored since?'

'Can you stop saying butt, mate? I told you I'm getting paranoid.'

The footballer stood up to prowl the office and Hunter took another mouthful. He let the liquid sit on his tongue, pondering what someone more qualified might make of the situation.

'It's possible,' said Hunter, mouth now empty, 'that claiming a goal you didn't score, has upset some form of balance.'

O'Connor stopped his pacing. 'Balance?'

'Yeah,' Hunter replied, not quite knowing where he was heading. 'This imbalance is why it feels like there's so much chaos in the world. Bad things draw more of our focus, and we forget about the good.' Was this true? Did it make sense? It sounded plausible enough to Hunter. The lead cloak was loosening its grip. 'We end up, I suppose, being unable to see the, er, good for the, er, the trees.'

'The trees, mate?'

'Metaphorical trees. A forest of shit that the good gets lost in. An orchard of excrement. Anyway, don't worry about the trees. In fact, forget about the trees. The metaphorical ones, anyway.'

The footballer leaned on the filing cabinet, itching at his beard. 'So, I need to do what, precisely?'

Hunter began to shrug then turned it into a shoulder rotation. He needed to appear to know what he was talking about. 'Redress the balance. Appreciate the good. *Be* good. Accrue some… karma?' He was babbling now, yet O'Connor seemed to understand.

'Karma's a collectible?'

'Yeah, definitely. Think of it like one of your NFTs.' Hunter's grasp of all these concepts was shaky yet he felt sure a confident tone would see him through. 'Your non-fungible shites.'

The younger man was no longer scratching but nodding. Hunter did not understand much about O'Connor, and O'Connor knew just as little about him, yet they appeared to have found common ground. A fee was agreed, though Hunter made a reasonably convincing show of waving it away, and as Hunter unlocked the door and O'Connor replaced his hood, readying himself not to face the world, the striker paused. He had noticed the stack of photocopied pleas for the safe return of Doctor Dickie Shrub on the cardboard box atop the filing cabinet.

'Nice dog. I like it. Low centre of gravity, just like me.'

'Well, if you see him about out there,' Hunter said, 'do give my number a call.'

'You know, they said I was too short to make it when I was a kid.'

Hunter did not know this.

'But look at Messi. Look at Maradona. Not now, obviously, but as he was years ago. Undersized. Underestimated. Turn your weakness into a strength. 'There's more than one way to play this game', that's what my uncle Pat always told me.'

A sudden burst of tinnitus exploded in Hunter's ear. 'Uncle Pat?'

'Yeah.'

'Off the Height?'

'Yeah.'

'Uncle Pat off the Height?'

'Yeah.'

The tinnitus was now at a hellish level.

'Not...' Hunter paused, hoping the old streets were home to many a Pat. '...Pat MacGuffin?'

'Yeah,' replied O'Connor. 'Do you know him?'

'Pat MacGuffin? As in...' The word 'bullshit' was a hair's breadth from slipping free.

'As in Pat MacGuffin off the Height, yeah.'

'He's your uncle?'

'Yeah. Well, no, he's not really an uncle. What he is is more a family friend. He used to work with my dad but runs the fishmongers now. Do you know The Red Herring?'

Hunter felt his mouth go dry. Words seemed difficult. His lead cloak had tightened.

'I can put in a word for you, if you like, mate,' O'Connor went on. 'Get you a discount on some mackerel.'

'No.'

'Prawns?'
'Maybe.'
'Whatever you want, really.'
'Thanks.'

Hunter's mobile rested at his neck and by the time his father picked up on the fourth ring, his glass was refilled and then his mouth. He was feeling more composed.

'Alright dad, how's it going?'

'*It* is going to be very dry around here from now on, that's how it's going.'

'You're quitting the booze?'

'I've told your mum we're not using any more water until this business is settled.'

'The water people, again?'

'Always the bloody water people, son. The water people and their systems.'

'Right. Well, anyway, the reason I called was, did you know Bullshit Pat MacGuffin knew Connor O'Connor?'

'Yes,' said his father, without pause.

Hunter waited, hoping for more which never came.

'That's it?' he asked. 'Yes?'

'Well, it was a simple yes or no question, wasn't it?'

Hunter could not argue about the nature of his enquiry yet wondered what the answer meant. Did knowing O'Connor somehow validate MacGuffin, negate his past tall tales? Was Hunter going to have to pay another visit to the Height, to call upon The Red Herring?

'And you never thought to mention this to me?'

'I didn't think you'd be interested.'
'Why not?' Hunter asked.
'Well, it's United, isn't it?'

12

Hunter sat with Beckett's *The Complete Dramatic Works* in his hands. Ten minutes had elapsed since speaking with his father, and the morning appeared to have reached a lull. With time to kill, he could have tried an outdated crossword from his puzzle books, but no. Hunter decided to read.

He found the opening play, *Waiting for Godot*, and took a deep cleansing breath to empty his mind. Hunter cleared his throat, loosened his shoulders, and then the landline began to ring.

'The Harp and Shamrock,' he said upon lifting the receiver, 'Hunter speaking.'

'I've got your dog,' a male voice informed him from a place of deep echo.

'That's great news,' said Hunter, laying the book down. 'Where was he?'

'You don't understand. I've *got* your dog.'

This subtle emphasis changed all. The man had not found and wished to return but was holding and likely required ransom.

Hunter sat back, pondering a refill of the tumbler on his desk.

'Is he Ok?'

'For now. And he'll stay that way if you follow my instructions.'

'Which are?'

'I want a grand.'

Hunter found his notebook and began to write. 'Non-sequential used notes, I take it?'

'What else. And put them in a jiffy bag.'

'That'll mean a trip to the Post Office. How about I put them in a plastic bag and wrap it with masking tape?'

'A. Jiffy. Bag.' The man was insistent.

'Fine. And how do we make the exchange?'

'Top of Market Street, there's a bin outside the old Debenhams entrance, on the Arndale side, just before the tram stop. At five this afternoon, you drop that jiffy bag in the bin and keep walking. I don't want any funny business. If you want to see your dog again, you won't look back.'

Hunter was scribbling the most salient points, *Debenhams, bin, five*. 'That all seems satisfactory. There's just one thing, though. I'd like to speak to my dog, please.'

'What?'

'To make sure he's Ok, that sort of thing.'

'What?'

'Yeah, you know,' said Hunter. 'This is how these things normally work. I'm not gonna ask him any questions or anything. Nothing about who or where you are. I just want to hear him. It would put my mind at rest.'

'That's not happening.'

'Go on, let me hear a growl.'

'No.'

'A whimper?'

'Stop talking.'

'What chance a plaintive howl? A mournful whine? Some earnest display of suffering condensed into a single heartfelt lament. Hello?'

Distracted from attempts to read, Hunter switched to rearranging his office, seeking the best spot on a wall to affix the souvenir he had picked up from the Bob Dylan needlework exhibition in the capital. Hunter tried it opposite the window and either side of the door. Behind him seemed pointless.

He heard footsteps and turned; Claude the Postman stood in the open doorway. Bald head damp, glasses in dire need of windscreen wipers, the letters he pulled from his satchel were the only part of him not drenched.

'You look like you've been in the Irwell,' Hunter told his friend.

'Thanks for that, Mr Basic Observation. Tell me something I don't know.'

'Ok.' Hunter was beginning to feel more human. His hangover now a distant memory, the leaden cloak removed and resting over his seatback. 'How about that your mum's broadcasting to all and sundry about your DRE?'

'Oh, I know that alright, pal,' Claude said, as rainwater accumulated under him, 'I think she's disappointed they didn't give me a certificate she can frame and hang in the front room. To be fair, I doubt she's entirely clear what's involved.'

'Struggling to put her finger on it is she?'

'Aye. Unlike that doctor. Actually, she was in there for a check-up herself the other day.'

'In the Dog?'

'Aye. She's got restless legs.'

A spark went on in Hunter's brain. 'Wrestlers legs?'

'Restless. Legs.'

Hunter began to imagine Claude's mother in spandex pinning her third husband to some floodlit four-poster combat square, then quickly erased the image. 'Wrestlers legs?'

'Rest-less. Legs.'

Claude now appeared to be stood in a puddle and Hunter began to wonder where he might source a mop. In the meantime, he had a question for his old friend. 'Do you ever go in The Red Herring?'

Claude shook his wet hairless pate. 'I don't do fish. No matter how much I hear the stuff's good for me, I can't get past that honk. All those tiny bones, an' all. Stink plus jeopardy in one slimy package is not my idea of a pleasing culinary experience.'

'But you know Pat MacGuffin?'

'Sure, Bullshit Pat.'

'And did you know he knew Connor O'Connor?'

'It's common knowledge on the Height, pal.'

'How do I not know then?'

'Well, to be fair, you're hardly ever on the Height anymore, are you.'

Hunter began to bristle, and the postman switched topics, asking how his cases were getting on.

While Hunter laid out his progress, Claude did a passable impression of interest, before stating, 'You don't half deal with some funny folk.'

'They're not that funny.'

'Funny strange, I meant.'

'They're not that strange,' said Hunter.

'That bloke downstairs was.'

'What bloke downstairs?'

Surely O'Connor was not still hiding in the stairwell. If he was, Claude should have recognised him even under his hood. Hunter asked for a description.

'Beyond soggy it's difficult to say, pal. Had his cap pulled down and his collar flicked up. Wore a big coat. He asked me to give you this.'

The envelope the postman passed bore no stamp and only *Mr Hunter* written in neat flowing script. Inside was an appointment card and an address for a dental surgery on Peter Street. The appointment was in three hours' time. The practitioners name, Richard Shrub.

Hunter was up out of his chair and racing through the door past the postman Claude. He had no wish to wait almost half his working day to discover why this man had been following him. The stairs were taken in leaps, and Hunter was outside in seconds, onto a wet Ludgate Street, where he moved at a hustle under the heavy shower. With breathing laboured and shirt soaking, he turned onto Old Mount Street. Of the long-coated figure there was no sign beyond a silver hatchback pulling away in the distance.

The rain had eased by the time Hunter met Ahmed Said Ali at Döner Summer, a pop-up takeaway opened on Oxford Road for the city's warmer months which had found popularity and put down more permanent roots. The pair sat under a drooping canopy, each with their kebab of choice.

'Did your lads enjoy the United game?' Hunter began.

'Mate, they're still sulking about it. I've told them every defeat is a good lesson for life. I don't think they believe me.'

'How old are they again?'

'Seven and nine. What do you have, Hunter?'

He handed Ahmed the card with DEATH upon it.

Ahmed flipped the card and read its cryptic message aloud, ' '*Height Library. 19:30. Refreshments provided.*' Is this it? I mean, what else do you know about them?'

Hunter shrugged. 'That they're considerate enough to put on tea and biscuits is about as far as I've got.'

'Considerate,' began Ahmed, 'would depend on the standard of the tea.'

'And the biscuits.'

Thoughts of sustenance caused Hunter to fill his mouth, as Ahmed turned the card over and over.

'It doesn't say what day,' the TV researcher mused with a frown.

'I know,' Hunter answered through lamb and naan, 'I'm working on that.'

After prolonged consideration Hunter had decided he would visit The Red Herring, though it would mean returning to the Height for the second time in two days, a ratio Hunter felt somewhat extreme.

'D-E-A-T-H.' said Ahmed. 'What does that mean?'

'The eternal question.'

'This is something, Hunter, but I need more. The Opinion Sphincter Industrial Complex is getting restless. If nothing happens soon Some People will start to drift. Attention is everything these days, the last great commodity. You don't need to take your audience's money off them anymore, only their time.'

'No one is getting any time out of me that I don't get paid for.'

'Mate, all this *will* come for you.'

'It can try.'

'You just wait. You think you're immune to the zeitgeist, to the controversy of the hour, but there'll be something and before you know it, you'll be just like the rest of us. A slave to our appetites.' Ahmed paused to wind a length of meat around his fork. 'And Some People's appetite is incredible. For news, for media. I mean, the phrase "the media" still gets tossed around, but it means nothing anymore because everything is media. Every tweet, every blogpost, every video. All is media these days and all is news. There're no time specific slots or set pages to fill. It's all just out there waiting to be interacted with; for the right impulses to be fired up. The only limitations are the number of hours in a day to consume it all.'

Ahmed wrapped his mouth around the fork, emptied it of food and chewed calmly. Finally, he swallowed. 'Did you know that in America they're already experimenting with a 36-hour news channel?'

'36-hours?' Hunter paused; kebab just shy of waiting teeth.

'Yes. 36-hours of news in a single day.'

'How's that supposed to work?'

'No one's sure yet. Our best guess is it'll be like those legal disclaimers they race through at the end of adverts. Only all day, every day.'

'They can't do that.'

'Mate, course they can. It's simple. They either relay the broadcast at one-and-a-half times the speed.'

'Or?'

'Or everyone will have to talk a lot faster.'

'Are you taking the piss?' Hunter asked.

Ahmed wiped his mouth with a serviette. 'I don't really know. You make a sarcastic remark in a corridor and before you know it that remark is looking out your TV at you from a prime-time slot.'

'Starting next week,' Hunter announced, his voice booming, 'The Great British Pubic Topiary Challenge.'

'You say that as a joke, but these kinds of things don't take as long as you'd think to develop.'

Hunter took a bite, chewed once and gulped. 'I have questions about this 36-hour thing. Logistics and that.'

'Course you have questions, mate. This whole development is big news in itself.' Ahmed was back on the card. '"*Height Library. 19:30. Refreshments provided*'. When you find out the when, who knows what you'll uncover at the meeting.'

'Me?' asked Hunter. 'I'm not going to a meeting of any organization with the name DEATH.'

'Course you are.'

'Fuck that. I was on the Height yesterday and I'm going there later. That's quite enough for the next month.'

'Well, I can't go.'

'Why not?'

'I've got a family. I mean, think of my children. What will you tell my boys when their dad doesn't come home one night.'

'Think of my rubber plant,' Hunter countered. 'Who will tend Rubbert.'

'Rubbert?'

'Rubbert Plant.'

'Mate, if it comes to it, I'll take care of him.'

'That's nice for Rubbert, but not much comfort for me.' Hunter stared out at the busy street. The taxis, buses, vans. 'So, I'm expendable, am I?'

Ahmed laid his fork down. 'What you are Hunter is local, a known face. I've never been there in my life and if they found out I worked where I worked, I bet DEATH might think that life was about over,'

'What if they found out what I do?'

'What do you do?' Ahmed asked.

'Well, my dad tells people I'm in recovery and leaves it at that. I just hope they think it's more collecting broken down vehicles or drug rehabilitation and not outstanding debts.'

'Mate, look. You don't need to tell me about going back somewhere you thought you'd left. I mean, I know the feeling, Ok?'

Though born in the Horn of Africa, Ahmed had grown up in southern Manchester, living on the same street throughout his youth, remaining at the family home during his university years before gaining a trainee position in television and making the big move to the capital. Ahmed had barely unpacked before television relocated to Salford and returned him to the north.

'Anyway,' said Ahmed, 'how's your Pyle thing?'

'There's been little change.'

'Are you following it online?'

'Don't ask silly questions.'

'Because there's a Twitter account called Pinpoint Pyle. Someone's superimposing head shots of him into crowd scenes.'

'Such as?'

Ahmed brought out his mobile to show Pyle in the vertigo inducing 1932 photograph, *Lunch atop a Skyscraper*. The writer repurposed as ironworker without shirt.

Also, Pyle as third warrior from the right in an action still from the recent superhero film, *Black Panther*.

The most recent tweet had involved Leonardo da Vinci's *The Last Supper*.

'And who is he in that?' Hunter asked.

'Some bloke from the next table asking them to keep the noise down. The accounts followers are only in the low hundreds, but it's a start.'

'This all sounds like something I would have zero interest in,' said Hunter.

'Well, in my line of work, I can't afford that luxury. But soon a lot of people will feel the same way you do, eyes and ears will turn elsewhere, which is why we need to move quick on this DEATH cult.'

'It's been less than 48 hours.'

'Exactly. You should've wrapped this up by now. The world wants to move on. If something big breaks in the meantime, these stories are dead. No one will care about them. Some people will still feast, but they'll be nothing more than side dishes to a larger meal.'

Hunter sat in thought, watching a double decker idle at a stop across Oxford Road, the banner of which was forcing the oversized countenance of some national rag's resident Opinion

Sphincter upon the world: jowl heavy; eyes barely discernible; constipated leer framed under a crescent of singed pubic hair.

'Was Pyle ever on Twitter?' Hunter asked, thinking again of his fruitless search online.

'Nope. Not a single social media profile. Just like you.'

'Can't be all bad, then.'

'Look, Hunter, I need this. If I get my producer a story like this DEATH cult, he'll let me work on something of my own.'

'Like what?'

Ahmed stood. 'Something investigative. Something real. Not just death or pets or celebrities.'

'I thought you were a big fan of celebrities?' Hunter joked.

'Only,' said Ahmed, placing their empty trays in a nearby bin, 'if they play for United.'

13

Hunter checked his watch. He still had an hour before his unexpected dental appointment. Not enough time to make returning to his office or apartment worthwhile, and so he walked the streets, glancing at the shops, the shoppers, and a TV news channel in a window reporting: PLAINVIEW MAN STATES OBVIOUS.

On Mount Street behind Central Library, Hunter noticed a young woman reading on a bench. His first thought being what she was reading – he recognised neither title nor author. His second thought was how. She was maybe two metres from a busy intersection: cars racing past; buses chugging by; people, so many people. Hunter could never read around distraction, he needed quiet.

The young woman turned her page, crossing left leg over right as she did so and in a flash, Hunter was reminded of his recent dream. Not so much of Vicky Park, but of himself as the chimney sweep, pursued by the giant canine and gazing into the toy shop window, spying Thornton Pyle, book in hand. Yet what, if anything, did this mean?

Possibly that he should relax his mind before bedtime or not indulge in late cheese or… and then it came to him. The sticker in Pyle's hotel room from Bhatt's Tomes, the shop only a short walk away on New New Mount Street.

Hunter had long shopped at Bhatt's Tomes, home of books old and new, second-hand magazines and periodicals. He would talk with Mr Bhatt about novels, sport, and the weather. Yet today there was no sign of the proprietor, only his daughter. Her father had told Hunter she was a university student, though this afternoon, leaning on the shop counter, the only thing she studied was her phone.

Hunter strolled the aisles, one eye on the customers, the other on the time and his impending appointment. Occasionally a cover would distract him, and he would pause, pluck the book from a shelf and read the writer bio. It was during one of these moments a voice came from behind him. 'What're you doing in here?'

Hunter turned to see the sizeable figure of Joe from The Three Jolly Bargemen. It took a moment for Hunter to process the enquiry. What was he doing? He was waiting for the daughter to leave and be replaced by her father, that's what he was doing. Hunter had a subject he would prefer to speak about only with Mr Bhatt. 'Just browsing,' was all he told Joe.

Hunter glanced at the counter and saw the young woman still scrolling. He would have to be patient. He turned to Joe. 'Are you in here a lot?'

'On my dinner hour, I am. I work in town.' Joe Dimly was employed in an Ancoats warehouse. 'I come in here for the football annuals, started collecting them the other year.' Joe brandished a pristine example for Hunter to see, *Shoot! 1988.* 'Football was better in the eighties,' he added.

It was for Hunter. Everton had won trophies in the eighties.

'Before this bloody VAR came in,' Joe went on. 'All this technology's ruined the game.'

Hunter had no wish to engage in this kind of debate and directed the conversation elsewhere. He pulled out his mobile to find the saved photograph of Thornton Pyle, then tilted the device Joe's way.

'Do you recognise him at all?'

'Of course,' Joe said, 'it's Gary Lineker.'

Hunter took his eyes from the screen to find Joe Dimly staring at the oversized book held tight in his hands.

'Not on the cover of *Shoot! 1988*. On my phone.'

Joe squinted into the mobile's screen. 'Not really, no. Is this the dog snatcher?'

'Something like that.'

Hunter watched Joe take his annual to the counter and pay. He saw the young woman put her phone away and smile, ring up the sale on the till, then offer Joe a bag which he declined. She went back to her phone and Joe Dimly nodded to Hunter as he exited, *Shoot! 1988* wedged under an arm.

Hunter once more checked his watch. He had less than thirty minutes before his meeting with Richard Shrub. The daughter would have to do.

'Is your dad about?' Hunter asked at the counter.

The young woman did not look up. She was tall and maybe twenty, dark hair tied back from her light brown face.

'No, sorry. He won't be in all day. Is there anything I can help you with?'

Hunter fidgeted, unsure where to put his hands. 'I was hoping to speak to Mr Bhatt.'

Her eyes left her screen to focus on Hunter. 'This is Bhatt's Tomes and I'm a Bhatt. Anjum Bhatt. *A* Bhatt. Anything you want to ask my dad about you can ask me.'

Hunter pondered how he should move forward. He decided on slowly. 'I'm looking for someone who was in here last week.'

'A customer?'

'Yeah, he bought something, and…' Slow then progressed to convoluted. '…and I found it and want to return it and wonder if he's been back in. He's a friend.'

'A friend?'

Hunter nodded.

'But you don't know how to contact him?'

'Well, he's a very private man. A bit of a recluse, you might say.'

'Oh, really? He's a recluse but he comes into our shop. Wait until I tell my dad about this. So, your "friend".' The word friend was now accompanied by air quotes.

'He's a writer, actually.'

'A writer? Your "friend" a "reclusive" "writer" comes in here?'

Hunter nodded again. Words appeared to be failing him.

'Is he famous?'

'It's…' Hunter wondered how much to say, then thought to hell with it, '…it's Thornton Pyle.'

'Thornton Pyle?' said Anjum Bhatt, her eyebrows raised. 'Thornton Pyle? *The* Thornton Pyle.'

'Yeah.'

'Never heard of him.' Her eyebrows returned to their previous unimpressed state, her dark eyes to her phone screen.

'Well, anyway,' Hunter started, 'he was in here sometime in the last week.'

'And did he buy anything?'

'As I said, yeah.'

'Good, because we get quite enough time wasters in here.' Her gaze rose to meet Hunter's and then fell away again. 'What did he buy?'

'It was…'

'Was what?'

'Was of a… special interest.'

Anjum Bhatt looked up, head inclined. 'Like arts and crafts? Hobbies, that sort of thing?'

'Well, it's sort of a hobby, I suppose.'

'So, your "friend", the "reclusive" "writer", has a "special" "interest"?' Her slender fingers were getting quite the workout.

'That's not for me to say.'

'Oh, it's a "secret" "special" "interest"?'

'Well…'

'We do have an espionage section. Though, for obvious reasons, it lacks signage.'

'I wouldn't say espionage is the right word.'

'Oh, I see. Could you be a bit more…' she paused, '…explicit?'

Hunter shifted, unable to meet the young woman's large eyes. 'I'd much rather speak to your dad about this.'

'Oh,' Anjum Bhatt replied, 'that is certainly explicit.'

In the dentist's third-floor reception on Peter Street, Hunter assumed the identity of Christ Abel Pankhurst to fill out the new patient form, then took a seat in the waiting area. He was not at the dental surgery to have a tooth drilled or pulled yet something about the situation gave him the fear. The white coats. The sterile ambience. The stacks of lifestyle magazines. This building had once housed a bar and Hunter wondered if there was a bottle of spirit around, some lost remnant from those days which might calm him.

An assistant appeared, declined to repeat Hunter's chosen pseudonym and led him through to the consulting room where a man waited. A tall, sullen man Hunter recognised as the third party from Delamere Forest's photograph.

'I believe you've met my fiancé,' the man said when his assistant had left the room. A surgical gloved hand was extended in Hunter's direction. 'I'm Richard Shrub. But please, call me Rich.'

Whether through nerves or curiosity, Hunter bypassed the pleasantries and the hand. 'Have you been following me?'

The man's plastic covered appendage wavered, then was raised in a show of contriteness. 'I'm sorry about that. If I'm honest, undercover operations are not a world I usually operate in. I normally stick to mouths. Please, take a seat. You can sit into the big chair if you like.'

Hunter reclined into the dentist's chair while Richard Shrub removed his plastic gloves and went to the sink.

'Dela has told me quite a bit about you,' he said, lathering his hands. 'Did you really see a peregrine falcon at a tram stop?'

'No, no, not at a tram stop. It wasn't trying to buy a ticket or anything. It was just on a nearby wall, perching. The tram stop was incidental.'

Shrub was now drying himself with a paper towel. 'But you're sure it was a peregrine?'

'Almost certain. It was too big to be a pigeon and too small for a child in fancy dress.'

The dentist sat down at his desk with Tupperware he had produced from a drawer.

'You don't mind if I eat while we talk, do you?' Shrub said lifting his coffee cup. 'Only this is my lunch hour. I told my assistant you're a rush job.'

Hunter still felt nervous. Perhaps it was the thought of being rebuked for not taking good enough care of his teeth or simply because he had seen *Marathon Man* once too often. 'Is that a Swinton Lions mug?' he asked, to take his mind off such things.

'Yes.' The dentist turned his cup to show the team crest. 'My dad bought it for me.'

'I'm more of a Salford Reds man,' said Hunter. 'Not been for years, though.'

Shrub nodded and swallowed. 'Me neither. We used to watch them a lot when I was younger. They'd left Swinton by then. We saw them all over the place. Bury, Whitefield, Leigh.'

'Why'd you stop going?'

'Time, if I'm honest. I met Dela and we usually have plans on Sunday afternoons.'

'Plans that don't involve chasing a rugby league team around Greater Manchester?'

Shrub gazed into his mug. 'Something like that.'

Hunter was calmer now. The sporting interlude had allowed him to relax while also putting Shrub at ease before Hunter got to the point. 'Why am I here?'

Unruffled by this abruptness, the dentist put his cup down and lifted a sandwich. Diagonally cut and not a salad leaf out of place. 'Because of my namesake, I suppose. How close are you to finding him?'

Hunter gave the man details. Posters, phone calls. A distinctly fictional account of their alleyway encounter.

'You saw him?' asked Shrub. 'How did he look?'

Hunter wanted to say pensive for no more reason than he enjoyed the shape of the word as it left his mouth. Shrub digested the information while eating his sandwich. Hunter then enquired of the sausage dog's backstory.

The dentist reached for his Lions mug. 'We had been at Dela's sister's house for tea. Dinner, I mean. We were there to meet her new boyfriend. He's a doctor, and Dela couldn't stop fawning over him all evening. 'Doctor this, Doctor that'. When we were back home, I'd had a drink or two and felt the need to point out that technically I'm entitled to use the title doctor, too. Well, my fiancé found this highly amusing and for the next week all I heard around the apartment was 'Doctor, Doctor, Doctor.' Then she seemed to stop, and I thought that was the end of it until I arrive home one day to be introduced to a dachshund, Doctor Dickie Shrub.' He paused for another swig of coffee. 'Technically, we're not allowed pets, but that didn't stop Dela. After two days the concierge came to see us.'

Hunter lay back, notebook and biro in hand, taking down relevant details. 'And you told him what?'

'Me, nothing. But Dela said fifty pounds and that seemed to take care of it.'

Hunter wrote *concierge?* and then crossed the word out. This was not a case of dognapping no matter the calls he received to insist it was. The little swine was at large.

'It is an unusual name for a dog,' Hunter stated.

Rich Shrub took a moment to ponder his sandwich. 'Dela suffers with an excess of... personality.'

'You don't find it a bit much?'

'Much, Mr Hunter? It grates on every conceivable level, that's how I find it. For years I've had to listen to 'Dick this, Dick that.' All through school, all through college, then university, dentist school. Now we go for a nice walk in the park and all I hear is, 'Doctor Dickie Shrub, Doctor Dickie Shrub'.'

'How long's this been going on?'

'Three months, six days.'

'That's a lot of walks in the park.'

'It's a lot of everything. 'Oh, Doctor Dickie Shrub, it's bath time again'. 'Oh, Doctor Dickie Shrub, don't do that to mother's leg'. 'Oh, Doctor Dickie Shrub, have you left another brusque statement on the bedroom carpet?'.'

Hunter's pen stopped. 'Brusque statement?'

'Turd, Mr Hunter. Dela can't bring herself to say turd.'

Hunter tapped the biro on the page and wondered how complicit this man might be in the case. How much calculated inattention may have been involved, the correct door or two left ajar, a trail of the dachshund's favourite biscuits leading away to freedom.

'If I'm honest, I actually happen to like the little sod,' the dentist offered, perhaps sensing Hunter's suspicions. 'I'd just like him more if he had a normal dog's name.'

'Like, Rex?'

'Or Rufus.

'Ruggles?'

'Any of those, really.'

They were drifting from anything which might be called a topic. Not that Hunter minded, he would bill the man for this time, but he was still curious as to why he was here. 'What exactly do you want from me, Mr Shrub?'

It was now time for the dentist to be nervous. 'Dela has hired you to find him. However, I would prefer…' he stopped and looked away.

Hunter waited for more which did not come, prompting him to ask the difficult question. 'You would prefer, I didn't?'

This would be a new one for Hunter. His entire business was based around finding things. To be hired to do the complete opposite rather defeated the purpose of his enterprise. Of course, there had been times when he had failed to find things despite his searching. Yet the idea of failing to even search and being rewarded for that would need to be thought on, though only after he had negotiated a fee.

'I'm not saying that…' Shrub insisted and seemed about to continue, only he did not.

'What are you saying, then?'

'I'm not a monster, Mr Hunter.' Rich Shrub stood and began to clear away his mug and Tupperware. 'All I'm saying is, if you find him don't call Dela. Call me first. There's been peace around the apartment while he's been missing and, if possible, I'd like to enjoy that a little longer.'

On the face of it, this appeared a simple enough request,

though Hunter felt the need to scratch away at that surface. 'What will happen if I do call you?'

'Nothing bad, Mr Hunter. Not all dentists are former Nazi war criminals. I've friends he could stay with rather than being in our cramped flat. Friends with a house and a garden. Friends who aren't violating their rental agreement.'

'And my fee?' Hunter asked.

'I don't know,' said Shrub. 'What would you consider a fare rate for not doing a job you're already being paid to do?'

Hunter ignored any slight and considered this premise. 'Half?'

'A third.'

Hunter tried to work out the middle ground between a half and a third, then decided a third would suit him fine.

'Perfect,' said the dentist. 'Dela intends to contact you today or tomorrow for an update.'

'And I'm to tell her what?' Hunter started to rise from the big chair.

'Anything that'll soothe her, that'll take her mind off unpleasant thoughts.' Shrub opened a drawer and took out a fresh pair of surgical gloves. 'Tell her the investigation is in hand,' he said slipping them on. 'That you're confident all will be well. Just, not quite yet.'

14

Hunter checked his messages and found nothing new. He did not return to the office or his apartment but took a bus out to the Height and the row of businesses on Bolton Road where The Red Herring lay sandwiched between a barber shop and laundrette. Hunter stepped inside the fishmongers and joined a queue.

The walls were lined with white tile and chalkboard pricing, its counters offered glistening produce behind glass. Hunter waited amid the seafood stink. He was less troubled about talking to Pat MacGuffin than he was of bumping into his father or Mrs Horn that was. He was working, and relative strangers he could deal with. The line moved forward a step.

Bullshit Pat MacGuffin was easy to recognise. The man's face may have been paler, his hair lighter, his bulk hidden under long white coat and dark apron of vertical stripes, but there he was, laughing with customers, moving swiftly among assorted fish, punctuating the air with the occasional bellow to some off-stage underling.

Hunter knew the man's face but not the man behind that face. The man behind the bullshit. He had heard of the supposed MI5 summer and much more. A possible spell in the SAS. The consultancy role on a James Bond film set. MacGuffin had been a figure of fun, infamous for tall tales. Falsehood appeared his nature.

The queue inched forward, and Hunter closed in on Pat MacGuffin.

What drove a person to lie so outlandishly? And what then drove them to run with it? At what point should a person step back and admit the lie? Yet what are they admitting when they do step back? To the world and to themselves? How easy did that first untruth slip from the tongue? They were, after all, just words, and words have only the meaning we ascribe them and often a second meaning, and sometimes a third. If meaning was not the point, were these words thrown out only to speak. To fill some perceived void. Spoken simply to be heard.

Hunter was now eye to eye with the fishmonger, who showed no discomfort at his presence.

'You're John's lad, aren't you?' asked MacGuffin.

Hunter nodded. Pat was around ten years younger than his father.

'Connor called me about you this morning. Said you'd done him a favour.'

'That was quick. It was only this morning I spoke to him.'

'Doesn't forget his friends, our Connor.'

'He said you worked with his old man?'

Was there a flicker at the edge of Pat's expression, a tightening of waxen flesh?

'When we were young, yes.'

Hunter may have asked which clandestine service the pair were employed by yet thought better of it. He wanted information from this man, not to antagonise him.

'So, what can I get you?' MacGuffin asked. 'It's on the house.'

'Well, I do like a nice prawn.'

'You've come to the right place then. We only have nice prawns here and all kinds. North Atlantics, Tigers, some big Kings.'

'I'll have some of each, if that's alright.'

'Certainly, sir.'

Hunter watched as the man picked and packed his prawns, talking as he did so.

'John's here most weeks. He's trying to up his omega-3s. A wise move at any age really.'

'Yeah, my dad mentioned he'd been in.' Hunter lowered his voice a fraction. 'He also told me you'd been talking about the library.'

Pat's hand jerked and a pallid King fell.

'They're slippery buggers, these are. I tell you what, I've got some more in the back, if you'd like to step through.' MacGuffin turned to the doorway behind him. 'Vince! Vince! Take over the counter while I deal with this gentleman.'

Vince appeared, a gangly monotone presence, and Pat led Hunter into the back of the shop and kept going out to the yard. They had been in the fresh air only a moment when the fishmonger was lighting up a cigarette with shaking hands.

'What did your dad tell you?'

Hunter was pleased to be out from the fishy stench, if only for it to be replaced by Pat's nicotine. 'Just that you'd heard things.'

MacGuffin inhaled, his fingers no steadier. The man did not look, to Hunter's eyes, like a former employee of the security services. MFI seemed more his realm.

Pat exhaled and his eyes closed. 'The library is open late on Thursdays. I like to go in after I've shut up here for the day. Or I did do.' The eyes opened and fixed on Hunter. 'I won't be going in tonight.'

'Why not?'

Pat took a long drag. 'DEATH.'

'They meet on Thursdays?'

MacGuffin nodded and the riddle was complete. Hunter had no desire to attend such a meeting but attend he would. Hunter looked at his watch. There were several hours to kill before 19:30. He would visit his parents, listen to their tales, store his prawns in their fridge, maybe even take a shot or two of liquid courage from his father's cabinet beforehand. Hunter had the information, though questions remained. 'What exactly was it you heard?'

The fishmonger's eyes darted around them, and he moved close. 'They mentioned poison.'

'Poison?'

'The first week, anyway. The next week there was talk of a gun.'

'A gun?'

Things were beginning to sound serious. Did Hunter really want to go there alone and unprepared? He did not consider himself a man of action, he was a lover not a fighter. Though his single status and current lack of carnal interplay might also negate the former. Yet how much should he believe this man?

What were his words worth? How much truth was there in someone for whom fiction had come so easily?

Hunter had a tangential thought. 'At the library, you haven't taken out anything by Thornton Pyle, have you?' He did not believe there was a connection, though thought it best to check.

Pat shook his head. 'Don't know the name. Biographies, histories, that's what I read.' He met Hunter's gaze and held it for a beat longer than necessary. 'These days, I'm strictly into non-fiction.' An unspoken transmission suggested topics he did not wish to speak of and for both their sakes Hunter did not ask.

Back out on Bolton Road, Hunter sent Ahmed Said Ali a text informing him the cult meeting was tonight and that with reluctance he would attend. The mobile was back in his pocket, and Hunter a step or two towards Viscount Drive and his parents when the device sprang to life.

He answered without even reviewing the caller, expecting an excited Ahmed. 'That was quick,' said Hunter.

'He's here,' said a voice hushed and female.

'Who's where?'

Was this the call Hunter had been told to expect from Delamere Forest? Was Doctor Dickie Shrub home and safe?

'Lark Hill Place,' the voice hissed. 'Your writer. Hurry.'

15

A taxi dropped Hunter off at the Museum and Art Gallery where he found Vicky Park not down in 19th century gloom but outside the redbrick entrance, her Victorian garb hidden under a waterproof anorak.

'You took your time,' she said as they went inside.

'Where is he?'

'He *was* down in Lark Hill Place.'

Hunter glanced at her lower half, hoping for heavy boots or a glimpse of red stocking. 'In the toyshop?' he asked.

'No,' Vicky Park replied, confusion in her tone, 'The Blue Lion, but now he's over there.'

Hunter followed her finger through the air to a bulky gent in the near distance, the rear of whom proved inconclusive for identification purposes. Hunter moved at an angle, allowing the face to come into view, and there he was. Thornton Pyle. "*Out there*" as Zora Liu had said. "*Loose*".

This missing man, the focal point for rabid online speculation, and much of Hunter's week, hiding in plain sight, and queuing at a museum café.

Had Hunter not been searching for the man, had he not saved a recent picture of the author on his phone, he may never have recognised Pyle. The writer was not exactly a famous face, not in the larger sense of celebrity. Not that of a popstar from an album or music video, neither the footballer gesticulating on a TV screen, nor film actress performing thirty feet high in a cinema. Pyle's novels were his face. If you knew him, you would know him. If you did not, you would not. Yet even with the reminder in Hunter's hand there was something different, something new. This man stood in line for sustenance had a moustache.

'Are you sure it's him?' Hunter asked Vicky.

'Definitely.'

'But what about the moustache?'

'What about it?'

'Did he have it last time you saw him?'

'No, but men grow moustaches. I've seen it happen.'

Vicky Park returned to a simpler time down at the Blue Lion tavern while Hunter edged closer to the queue. On his phone he went online and brought up different pictures of the novelist, yet none showed him with facial hair. Hunter held the device up aligning the screen with the man beyond; even with the addition of upper lip camouflage, this was Thornton Pyle.

He was taller than Hunter, also heavier, and aged somewhere around the mid-fifties. His shirt was light blue, his trousers red cord, a tweed waistcoat strained around his paunch.

Pyle conversed with a grey-haired lady behind the counter and Hunter, pretending to inspect a scale model in a cabinet, tried to pick out their words above the café ambience. Cutlery on plates. Late afternoon chatter. A child's wanton slurping. It was no good, he could hear nothing over that. Hunter stalked over and joined his second line in recent hours.

He was right behind the author, within distance of a citizen's arrest. Hunter noted the man's strong aftershave and hair suspiciously dark for his age. Thornton Pyle was waiting for coffee to brew and deciding on a bun.

'You have so many,' Pyle enunciated, 'I find it difficult to choose. What do you call this one?'

'An iced finger,' the grey lady replied.

'How quaint, I must say. And this?'

'Cinnamon vortex.'

'Cinnamon vortex? Really? I was at Cambridge with a girl called Cinnamon Vortex. Of course, she's probably a woman now. Would it be rude, I wonder, to have both?'

'Only if you leave without paying.'

Hunter glanced at his watch. It was already after five. The clock was ticking on his library appointment with DEATH. He could feel his impatience swell.

'I suffer from a sweet tooth,' Pyle went on. 'It is the lone flaw upon my character. A sweet tooth and, possibly, indecision. Yet as Joyce would say…'

Something deep in Hunter stirred, though not so deep as to stop it blurting from his mouth in short order. 'Is that Joyce from the non-artisanal chain bakery?'

'No.' Pyle did not even turn. 'As Joyce would say…'

'We don't take fifty-pound notes,' Hunter offered. This was highly unprofessional, but he could not seem to stop. 'That's what Joyce from the non-artisanal chain bakery would say.'

'I said, no!' The ire was clear in Pyle's voice. 'Where was I? Yes. As Joyce was wont to say…'

'The proletariat have nothing to lose but their chains?'

'As Joyce would say…'

'Do you want a sausage roll with that?'

Thornton Pyle spun to face Hunter and glared. A twitch around the man's mouth allowed his moustache to dance.

'Actually,' Hunter continued, 'that last one's not true. Joyce from the non-artisanal chain bakery would never say anything like that. It conflicts with her views on rampant capitalism.'

'Joyce!' Pyle announced with exaggeration and contempt, 'James!' Spittle was collecting on his lips.

Hunter paused, amused at the man's agitation. 'Well, that might be her surname, I dunno much about her beyond the apron and her keen interest in revolutionary thought.'

Pyle's eyes narrowed as he stared at Hunter. 'Who are you?'

'MacEwan,' Hunter replied. 'Coll MacEwan, and you're, aren't you…' he paused, '… aren't you off the news?'

The writer stiffened, attention flicking from Hunter to the grey lady, who gestured at the buns, hoping for a decision sometime before Armageddon or at the very least the ending of her shift.

'The news?' Pyle asked. 'What do you mean, the news?'

'Yeah,' Hunter said, 'you're off the news, aren't you?'

'No. No, no, no.'

'Well, yeah, I agree it's hardly news anymore so much as speculation and opinion. But that's beside the point. You're off the news.'

'No. I'm afraid you have the wrong person.' The man was rattled.

Hunter should not have been goading the object of a case but part of him was enjoying it far too much. 'Yeah, you're that newsreader, aren't you?'

'What?'

'That bloke who does the late news.'

A young woman and small boy joined the line behind them.

'What?' Pyle appeared thrown by Hunter's change of emphasis.

'Yeah.'

'No.' The novelist took a moment to compose himself. 'My name is… is… Stephen Pole. I'm a visiting lecturer. I specialise in…' And there, Pyle/Pole's brain seemed to freeze, puzzlement crinkling his brow. 'I specialise in?' he asked of no one.

'You specialise in?' Hunter also queried.

'I specialise in?'

'You specialise in?'

Pyle/Pole sniffed the air before repeating his enquiry, 'I specialise in?'

'You specialise in what?' said Hunter.

No answer came, only more snuffling from the writer as he turned his head, left and right and left once more. Hunter hoped the man was not about to have a seizure.

Pyle/Pole sniffed again, the action this time accompanied by a different question. 'Why can I smell fish?'

This prompted the grey lady to engage her own nostrils. 'I can smell fish an' all.'

The woman with the child to Hunter's rear also sniffed and confirmed the odours presence. Hunter himself tested the air and there it was, a seafood aroma. What was happening here? Were they all having a group hallucination? The result of a leak from the café counter chiller? Some rogue gaseous element seeping from a faulty connection into their olfactory byways.

An odd sensation began in Hunter's arm, an involuntary movement, a spasm he could not account for, and he wondered where all this might lead. Accident and Emergency was the current favourite.

Hunter followed the movement down his arm, to his hand, to the plastic bag he held and the small boy behind him poking the bag with his tiny index digit.

'F-I-ish,' the boy said, a syllable for each poke as he pressed into Hunter the memory of his prawns.

Neither Pyle/Pole, nor the grey lady, nor the child's mother were paying him any attention, only Hunter who, finger at his lips, attempted to quiet the boy. This did not work.

'F-I-ish,' the boy repeated. Then, 'Mummy? Mummy?'

'Not now, Albert.'

'But Mummy, he's got F-I-ish.'

They all stopped. The mother looked at her son, then at Hunter, then down to the plastic bag.

Hunter had already begun to protest. 'I haven't.'

'F-I-ish,' said the boy once more, his finger accosting the bag anew.

'I haven't. They're Prawns. Some nice, big Kings.'

'Something smells fishy to me,' said the grey lady.

'This man has fish,' Pyle/Pole put in loudly, addressing the entire café. 'This man has fish.'

'I haven't got fish.'

'It does say fish on the bag,' offered the young mother.

Hunter lifted his bag to read: *The Red Herring. Fresh fish and Seafood.* 'That's just the bag. Inside I've got prawns, look.'

Hunter held the bag out and the woman took a step back, pulling child Albert away with her.

'It is definitely fish that I smell,' said Pyle/Pole.

'They're prawns,' Hunter insisted. 'They're good prawns.'

Hunter brought the bag up to his face and sniffed inside. From the prawns he caught a fresh smell of salt and the ocean and in his mind's eye saw the crustaceans in their natural habitat, doing whatever the weird little alien beasts actually did. The whiff from the bag itself, however, was really something else.

A security guard appeared, two-way radio cradled in a colossal hand; his rugby player build mismatched with the hairless baby face atop it. 'Anything the matter, Iris?' he asked the grey lady.

Iris opened her mouth, but it was Pyle/Pole who spoke, an accusatory finger aimed at Hunter. 'This man has fish.'

The guard gave Hunter the once over while Pyle/Pole went on. 'This is quite beyond the pale, I must say. A man on a simple gallery visit should not have to deal with… with...'

'Prawns?' enquired Hunter.

'No,' said the writer, 'with…'

'The proletariat?'

'With being accosted in public,' Pyle/Pole almost spat the words.

The guard stepped in between the two men and turned to Hunter. 'Could I take your name please, sir?'

Hunter went quiet, the easy sport he had been making of the novelist had gone. He was always nervous speaking with authority, no matter how little he had done wrong, no matter even the level of the authority. Guilt would overcome him, as if all of life's missteps, each and every charge, were soon to be read aloud. He had similar feelings in the company of priests and doctor's receptionists.

His name, what was his name? Nerves had banished the alias he had just used from his memory, and he stared from Iris to Pyle/Pole, to the mother, to child Albert until inspiration hit in the youngster's ruddy cheeks. 'Finbert,' Hunter announced. 'Finbert Alley.'

The writer interjected over the guard's epauleted shoulder. 'You said you were MacEwan.'

'I have many names,' Hunter fired at Pyle/Pole, confidence briefly restored.

'Look,' said the guard. 'Mr Whatever, visitors aren't allowed to bring food onto the premises.'

'I'm not gonna eat them, they're raw.'

'We have signs, sir. They clearly state, "no food other than that purchased on the premises".'

'Especially no fish,' added Pyle/Pole, safe behind security.

'But they're prawns,' Hunter snapped back.

'That's not really the point, is it sir?' the guard explained. 'I'm afraid you're gonna have to leave.'

16

Hunter had been ejected from so few places in his life. Never one to push the boundaries of common decency, for him rule breaking seemed to require far more effort than he was willing to expend. The sole occasion Hunter had been made to leave a public house was down to the slightest of errors.

Sat at a table of an establishment in town, rather than the Height – had this happened on the Height, Hunter would never have heard the last of it from his father – a late teens Hunter had been with Claude, not at that time a postman. They were about to move on in their evening, and as Hunter had been doing more talking than drinking, an entire pint of Guinness stood before him. Not a man to waste anything, and with a gentle pressure from Claude, Hunter felt compelled to down the whole lot.

Soon after which the entire pint of Guinness had felt equally compelled to return to the outer world and settle on the pub's already garish carpet. Hunter was left staring toward an inky wet abyss. There were things present in that silky pool he would rather not speak of, and he imagined it a void to some dread parallel existence. One in which he might fall into and never find his way out. Out. The landlord had come over, and out was precisely where he wanted them.

But had it been a simple miscalculation or something worse? Something inside him, some terrible force? The old inner devil. He who had impelled Hunter to decline his father's choice of football team, and recently to goad Thornton Pyle rather than watch quietly from a distance.

Hunter was out on the Salford grass, among students milling under a sun which had chased off the earlier rain. He had his prawns in one hand and his mobile in the other, still geared-up from the recent drama he could barely find Zora Liu's number.

Eventually he made the call and before the editor had a chance to speak, the words, much like the popular stout, were forcing their way out of Hunter, 'I've found him.'

There was a pause on the line. Then, 'Who is this?'

'It's Hunter,' he replied. 'I've found him.'

'Pyle? You've found Pyle? Finally, some good news.'

Hunter brought Zora up to date on the last hour minus those acts he now deemed unprofessional.

'A museum?' she bellowed. 'He's in a museum?'

'Well, it's not just a museum. There's a gallery, as well.'

'He's in a museum? The office is in uproar and you're telling me this guy is out on excursions? My unpaid intern is a mess. She's been fighting so many fires on social media this week she has the digital equivalent of smoke inhalation. That poor girl has had to go home with stress, and I can't blame her, you know. To deal with all the bad attention this has brought us, we just don't pay her enough. Or, in fact, at all.'

Hunter watched as the door he had been ushered through opened again. He braced himself expecting the writer to exit, only to see the young mother instead, leading child Albert in the direction of the bus stop.

'Does he know who you are?' Zora asked.

'Pyle? No, just thinks I'm a local oddball.'

'Fuck, this is exciting. I'm going to need a cigarette. Give me a minute.'

Hunter heard Zora Liu stand and could picture the scene. A repeat of that he had witnessed in her office. The journey toward the cactus, the illicit vice removed from the plant pot. He heard a window latch click and a blast of street horns followed by prolonged exhaling.

'That's better,' she said. 'What's he doing now.'

'I dunno, I can't see him.'

'What? Why not?'

'He's in a building and I'm waiting outside.'

'Why aren't you in the building?'

'I'm keeping a safe distance.'

'Why aren't you in the building?'

'I had to leave for reasons best not gone into right now. But I did speak to him.'

'You spoke to him?' What did he say?'

Hunter caught the distant siren of a fire engine but could not tell whether it was from nearby Salford or the far-off capital.

'Not much really,' he told Zora. 'He claimed to be someone else.'

'But you're sure it's him?'

'Oh, it's Pyle, alright. Though, he now has a moustache.'

'A what?'

'A moustache.'

'Thornton Pyle does not have a moustache.'

'When did you last see him?'

'Friday. What's that, six days? Can you grow a moustache in six days?'

'I dunno, I've never tried.'

'Stay on him, anyway. I'll have my intern call Estella.'

'I thought she'd gone home.'

'Fuck, I'll find someone to do it. Stay on him.'

Hunter placed himself under the shade of a tree with an unobstructed view of the museum entrance. Anyone leaving would struggle to pick him out and his prawns would not degrade unlike in direct sunlight. They were good prawns and Hunter wished them to remain that way.

He was aware of a pulsing in his body, his systems preparing for the thrill of a chase. Hunter so rarely got to enjoy the activity of tailing a suspect yet was always prepared. His jacket was light and, more importantly, reversible. He had his sunglasses with him and kept a cap folded in an inside pocket for just this eventuality.

The jacket went from navy blue to beige. He put on his shades and took out the green cap with basketball motif that would obscure his almost black hair. And just like that Hunter was transformed. He was now a hard-to-define figure lurking in leafy shadows. Even his mother would not recognise him. Most likely she would report him to the police.

An engine sounded close by, and a taxi came around the corner to stop at the bottom of the steps. This unexpected arrival brought a knot of discomfort to Hunter's stomach. He had failed to factor private hire vehicles into his pursuit plans. The museum door opened, and Pyle strode out of the building and into the idling hatchback, and before Hunter could move the car had pulled away, taking Pyle with it, and leaving Hunter in the shade with his prawns.

Later that evening, sometime around nine, Hunter was back in The Three Jolly Bargemen, Joe Dimly loitering at his elbow and Vicky Park stood behind the bar. After losing Thornton Pyle, Hunter had returned to The Snooze Inn for a conversation with the receptionist as unilluminating as his previous one, wasting ten minutes discovering nothing beyond the fact Pyle had still not returned.

'How were your prawns?' asked Vicky Park.

Hunter raised himself from his half-empty glass. 'They were lovely.'

Hunter had left The Snooze Inn and gone home to the apartment on Little Peter Street, fried some of the big Kings with a little garlic and chorizo, then froze the rest. He had been sat eating and listening to his upstairs neighbours perform their hourly setting off of the fire alarm when a text message came through on his phone. A rogue request regarding some equally rogue package Hunter had not in fact ordered. He deleted the message and was putting the device down when he noted the time on its screen. Almost half-past eight.

Several flashes hit home as he chewed the crustaceans. He had missed his appointment with DEATH. All his work on the cult case was for nought and he would have to explain to Ahmed Said Ali why he had not shown up at the Height library as promised. He had also failed to call Zora Liu to update the editor on his Pyle status, an exchange he did not relish. Hunter finished eating, put his plate in the sink, left the flat and his mobile and made for the Bargemen.

'I've never seen anyone chucked out of a place for possessing seafood before,' the barmaid told him.

Joe Dimly cleared his throat. 'Charged with intent to stir fry?'

'That's very good. I'm impressed.'

'Why thank you, Miss Vicky. Where did this all happen, then?'

'Joe,' she said, leaning on the bar, 'you shouldn't ask questions you can't handle the answers to.'

'Aww come on, Vicky. Don't be like that.'

'Listen, Joe. If I told you that I'd just spent the day in 1897, what would you say?'

Joe stared at the barmaid, then at Hunter. He sensed some joke but was not certain. 'I'd say,' he said in ponderous thought, 'what was the weather like?'

'Dismal, Joe. Bloody dismal.'

Joe Dimly took his pint and went over to the fruit machine. Hunter finished off his drink then ordered a second.

'So, this detective lark,' Vicky began, 'is it like you see in the films?'

'The old noirs?'

She nodded. 'My mum used to love them.'

'Yeah,' said Hunter. 'Philip Marlowe, Sam Spade. Their workload was a bit racier, but I do see myself in a similar mould.'

'Oh right.' Vicky Park reached for a fresh glass. 'Except a bit less Humphrey Bogart and a bit more Mark E Smith?'

Hunter shrugged. 'You play the cards you're dealt.'

'But do you enjoy what you do?' she asked. 'Whatever that actually is.'

Enjoy may have been a touch strong, but Hunter did like his work. 'It's good being my own boss,' he told her. 'Making my own rules. The thing is there's a lot of paperwork. Invoices, records, tax. You never saw Bogey filling out all that shite.'

Hunter's only other job had been in his late teens and early twenties, in a warehouse where he discovered that regimented manual labour did not really suit his outlook on life.

Hunter turned the barmaid's enquiry back on herself. 'Which do you prefer, here or Lark Hill?'

'Oh here,' she replied, working the pump, 'by a mile.'

'Why?'

'For a start, the outfit's less restrictive. And you rarely get school kids on a day trip, which is a relief.'

'Kids are worse than this lot?'

'Definitely. They're all so bloody precocious nowadays. Not to mention unimpressed with everything 1897 has to offer. Don't bother trying to explain old money to this generation. They don't even know what new money is, they're all crypto this and Bitcoin that.' Her eyes did not leave the glass as the liquid rose. 'My dad had no time for precociousness. He wouldn't allow it in the house. Had a different name for it an' all. To him it was called being a little shit. Quite what he'd think of my two, I dunno.'

'You've got kids?'

'Don't sound so surprised. It's other people's kids I'm not so keen on.'

'How old are they?'

'Four and two. My mam has them tonight. They should be with my ex, but he got called back into work.'

They had begun to stray into the personal and Hunter wondered if she was subtly letting him in on her relationship status or simply filling time as she filled his glass.

'What does he do, your ex?'

'He's heavily involved in the sustainable wood industry, which before you ask isn't a euphemism for porn. So instead, my mam is probably filling them full of E-numbers and YouTube videos, which is unfortunate as I was hoping to keep them in a state of enforced ludditism until it began to affect their social standing. Still, it gives me a break after a day dealing with thirty bored Shirley Temples while trapped in a corset.' Vicky passed Hunter his fresh pint. 'At least with this lot in here, all they want is a drink.'

'That it?'

'That and for someone to occasionally acknowledge their existence. Which does tend to lead to another drink.'

'No trouble, then?'

'No. They're a good crowd. And if any stepped out of line, I'd just refuse to serve them. That'd restore order quick enough. If all else fails, there's always karate.'

Hunter took a mouthful of ale and swallowed. 'You know karate?' He imagined her belted in white robes, poised in some martial stance.

'Not me,' she said. 'The Alsatian.'

'The Alsatian knows karate?'

'No. The Alsatian *is* Karate. And don't look at me, I didn't name the poor sod.'

A woman approached and ordered. She was early-fifties, raven-haired, and grinned at Hunter as the barmaid worked.

'Aren't you gonna introduce me, Vicky?' Her eyes did not stray from Hunter as she spoke.

'I'm Vicky, you're Margaret, and this,' a small bottle and glass was handed over, 'is three pound ten.'

The woman smiled and paid, then winked at Hunter and left. Hunter inhaled almost half his pint, then asked, 'Do any in here know how you spend your days?'

'No and I'd prefer to keep it that way.'

'But what if you were late for your shift one night and didn't have time to change?'

'You mean, what if I turned up here in full 19th century costume?'

Hunter nodded, his dream of the previous evening flickering through his mind. The barmaid crossing her red-stockinged legs, the shine of her heavy boots as they kicked.

Vicky Park scanned her customers. Those sat at tables, those propping up the bar, those loitering by the karaoke machine. 'I don't think half this lot would even notice.'

Hunter lifted what was left of his drink. 'And the other half?'

The barmaid lowered her voice to a whisper. 'They'd find it far too erotic.'

17

Friday morning on New Mount Street and Hunter was at his desk early, laptop open and admiring his bank balance. From Connor O'Connor there appeared a generous "consultation fee and further retainer". Hunter had already been paid similarly titled if not quite so grand amounts by P&P publishing and Delamere Forest, and more was to come from Rich Shrub, yet now he had to earn a little of this money with some difficult phone calls.

He called Zora Liu from his landline and in what might be termed luck, she was not yet at her office, allowing Hunter to leave a message with reception. Not being clear on how much he should share with anyone he did not know, Hunter spoke vaguely.

'Tell Zora, her Hunter has lost his quarry. Her Hunter,' he repeated, 'has lost,' he paused for added drama and to hear a distant keyboard clack, 'his quarry.'

Next up was a mobile call to Ahmed Said Ali, whose voice was one of anticipation until Hunter explained the situation.

'You didn't go?' Anticipation had stepped back in favour of exasperation.

'Circumstances conspired to waylay me.'

'Don't give me pretty words, I want substance.'

Hunter considered forgetfulness an ethereal excuse unlikely to improve the researcher's mood, and so said nothing. He could hear a busy workplace on Ahmed's end, but no longer Ahmed. Had he left to bang his head against some nearby partition or perform a silent scream in the stationary cupboard? In time, he returned.

'This means we've got to wait a week for the next meeting?'

'Unless we get a break in the meantime.'

'For fuck's sake, Hunter.'

'I'm sorry, Ahmed, I am. It's just I had movement on my Pyle thing.'

Ahmed's tone appeared to soften. 'What movement?'

'Actual Pyle movement. I saw the man.'

'You saw the man?'

'I spoke to the man.'

'You spoke to the man?'

'Yeah.'

'What's he still doing up here?'

'That's unclear,' said Hunter beginning to relax having successfully diverted the conversation. 'Now, don't screw me over on this, Ahmed.'

'What do you mean?'

'Well, this is just between me and you, Ok? I don't want this getting out. Not on television, not on social media. I don't want to scare him off.' Hunter may already have scared him off. 'One last thing, though.'

'What?'

'Can you grow a moustache in six days?'

Ahmed went quiet again, thrown by this tangent. 'Do you mean me personally or anyone?'

'Anyone?'

'Why, Hunter, what do you need a moustache for?'

'Nothing, really.'

With booted feet resting on the corner of his desk, Hunter was rewarding himself with a low-sugar ginger biscuit when the landline rang. A blast of complaints from Zora Liu was his first fear and he was tempted to wait out the infernal trilling. Yet in this new era of taking responsibility, of admitting mistakes, of growing into a more rounded human being, this era Hunter intended not to last beyond midday, he lifted the receiver.

'The Pot of Beer. Hunter, speaking.'

'I saw one of your posters,' came the abrupt reply. 'They didn't mention his name.'

It took Hunter a moment to recognise the voice and recall his conversation with the dentist Shrub, the warning that his fiancé would call. Hunter put down his ginger biscuit.

'Well, Ms Forest, I felt it best to include only the basics.'

The omission had been a classic move on his part. Withhold a key piece of information to test the veracity of those who contacted him. Also, not to give the impression the plea was just some student prank – *missing dog with ridiculous name, call this premium rate number now!*

'But why?' she asked.

'Because there are people out there who don't act with the

best intentions,' he told her. 'They see a situation like this and see an opportunity for chicanery. I've already had one phone call asking if there's a reward.'

That the caller had less enquired of a reward than demanded one was best not relayed to a fretting owner.

'Do you think I should offer a reward?' she asked.

'Not yet.'

'But might it help?'

Hunter sighed, removed his feet from his desk and sat upright. 'It might and might not. You must trust me on this, I'm a professional. And I do actually have some good news for you.'

'Really?'

'Yeah. Another call, but this time about a sighting. He's been spotted in the Northern Quarter.'

'Oh, thank God, he's alive.'

'Alive and well. According to this caller.' The sighting, of course, was Hunter on his arse in an alleyway.

'That's such a relief. Do you think you'll find him soon?'

'Ms Forest.'

'Call me Dela, I've told you.'

'Well, Dela, I don't like to put unrealistic time frames on anything. I don't make promises I can't keep. The world of investigation is a tricky one. You can never know what's around the corner, what the next knock at the door will bring.'

'It's odd, of course, that you should mention doors Mr Hunter. It's just,' she paused, and Hunter heard sniffles, 'I keep waking in the night, thinking I can hear him scratching at ours.'

'I think that's perfectly understandable, given the circumstances.'

'That Doctor Dickie Shrub might be trying to get back in?'

'Yeah, or it's the ghost of a 19th century mill worker.'

'A what?'

'The ghost of a 19th century mill worker,' Hunter repeated.

'But...' Dela Forest's sniffles had gone, 'a ghost? Why would I have a ghost?' Her tone was now somewhere in the region of perplexity.

'Dela, how much do you know about the area you live in?'

'I know what it said on the website. Ancoats Urban Village. Up and coming. Regeneration, that sort of business.'

Ancoats Urban Village. Hunter almost laughed. He sat back, lodged the landline handset at his neck, put his feet back on the desk and picked up the half-eaten ginger crunch. 'The thing is, Dela, there are some folk who when describing Ancoats and its environs like to use the term "cradle of industrialisation". But not me.'

'Why not?'

'Because it's far too many syllables. Ancoats had a reputation. It was cramped, plumbing was scarce. The Industrial Revolution chewed workers up and spat them out. Life in that part of town was not a happy one. They were underpaid. They were overworked. This is all classic back from the dead justification.'

'And so, you think...'

'What do I think, Dela? I think I'd be more surprised if the place wasn't haunted, that's what I think.'

'But *my* building...'

'*Your* building is a good couple of hundred years old. It stands to reason a structure lasts for long enough, it'll see a person or two clock out inside of it. And not in a whistle-blown, end of shift scenario either.'

There was silence from Ms Forest.

'Did you know, Dela,' Hunter spoke into the void, 'that half of all deaths happen inside buildings.'

'Do they?' Her voice had returned and brought with it the sounds of panic.

'Yeah.'

'And the other half?'

'Erm, outside, I believe.'

'But…'

'In those days, you had no health and safety regulations. No hi-viz vests, no chunky goggles. Industrial accidents were rife. Some of those machines were death traps. Your spinning jennys, your rogue looms, the odd runaway throstle. The worst, though, was the spinning mule.'

'The spinning mule?'

'Yeah. After a while it would get irate and start biting. The whole thing was cruel, really.'

'But the estate agents…'

'You live in a converted mill, Dela. It might look brand new now, but history isn't so easily wiped away. Laminate flooring and fitted kitchens are all very well, but are you confident the developers shelled out to have that place properly exorcised first?'

Hunter stuffed the rest of his biscuit in his mouth, feeling the warming tingle of his ginger snack and a job well done. This surely would take his client's mind off her missing dachshund.

18

Morning ticked over into afternoon and Hunter prepared to wind down for the weekend. He had made no plans. No evening beers with Claude. No visits to see his parents – he had been on the Height quite enough for one week. Hunter would try to relax, tend to chores around the apartment, wait for notifications from the Everton match and generally endure the downtime revelry of his upstairs neighbours. He might even finally tackle Samuel Beckett's *The Complete Dramatic Works*.

But why hold out for the weekend to read Beckett, Hunter thought. The book was right there on his desk, and his afternoon devoid of activity. *Waiting for Godot* was waiting for him. A decision was made. Hunter would fill himself a generous glass of Irish cream, grab a handful of ginger biscuits and settle in for a few hours reading.

It took five seconds and a whimsical rap on cheap wood for this intention to be erased as Hunter looked up to find Estella de Fenestrate framed in his open doorway. With her wool olive greatcoat, polished boots, and ushanka fur hat, the redhead's outfit was one Hunter might term eastern front chic. *Godot* would have to wait.

'I'm awfully sorry to drop in unannounced,' she said. 'I was going to call. But then, you see, I didn't. Those two hours on the train go by so much quicker than you expect.'

Hunter offered her a seat, then noticed how untidy his office was. He moved the almost week-old free paper to a place under the desk more commonly known as the floor. Beckett was left where he lay.

'Did you speak to Zora?' Hunter asked.

'Yes. Or rather, no. I heard the voicemail her reception left for me and thought I might be of some help. The quicker we can bring this to a resolution the better for all. Plus, there are a few people I need to speak to professionally and I have a few friends up here, so thought why not. Oh, and I brought you this.' She reached into a canvas tote and laid a hefty paperback in front of him. 'It's a proof of Thorn's latest.'

At the Rising of the Cock, was the title, and Hunter gave the novel a quick glance then mentally consigned it to the nearest registered charity.

Estella noticed the tome already on Hunter's desk. 'Oh, you're a Beckett man.'

'Actually,' Hunter waved his hand in what, if later questioned, he would classify a literary gesture, 'I prefer his earlier stuff. Are you booked into anywhere?'

'A boutique place near the station.'

'Not The Snooze Inn, then?'

'The Hotel Mamucio. I gather you spoke to Thorn?'

How much of their encounter had filtered through Zora, her receptionist and into Estella's voicemail he could not be sure, so Hunter found himself recounting his progress of the last three days as he stood and made for the filing cabinet. There was Pyle's flight from Media City as told by Ahmed Said Ali. The writer's abandoned room at The Snooze Inn. His sudden reappearance at the Salford Museum and Art Gallery.

The agent sat thinking this over as Hunter poured them both a budget Irish Cream.

'And you're sure it was Thorn?' Estella asked.

'Yeah. He had a moustache, but it was him, alright.' Hunter handed her a full tumbler and returned to his desk.

'He had a moustache? I've never seen Thorn with facial hair of any kind. I didn't have him down as the type.' Estella sipped her liqueur in thought. 'What was it like?'

Hunter threw back a mouthful. 'Too big for a Hitler, too small for a Dali.'

'And was it real?'

'Difficult to say.'

'But you can say it was him?'

'If it wasn't Pyle, then he has a moustachioed doppelganger called Stephen.'

'Stephen?'

'Stephen Pole. That's what he said his name was. He also said he had a sweet tooth?'

'You see, now that does sound like Thorn.' Estella took another sip. 'I wonder, might he be suffering some form of amnesia?'

It would be a very convenient form, Hunter thought. One which struck just prior to appearing on television to beg forgiveness, one which made him forget his name, his life. Also, the act of shaving his upper lip.

'Does he have a history of this sort of thing?' Hunter asked.

'Pretending to be other people? Hardly. Thorn adores being recognised. I don't believe he's ever felt uncomfortable with fame. He likes to be reminded he's special, you see.'

'And is he special?'

Estella smiled and took a further sip. 'That is a conversation for another time. I should really get back to my hotel and unpack. Perhaps, we could meet later and discuss this in detail? What is there for a girl to do in Manchester on a Friday night?'

'Are you looking to be entertained?'

'Hopefully.'

Hunter reclaimed the free paper from the floor and scanned listings only just in date.

'What are your feelings towards musical theatre?' he enquired.

'Somewhat in the neutral range.'

At the Opera House that evening was *H.M.S Pinochet*, the high-kicking tale of a shopkeeper's daughter who dreams of one day peddling arms to Latin American dictatorships. It's accompanying Big Number, 'I'm Gonna Sell, Sell, Sell 'til They Send Me to Hell' was enjoying its sixty-sixth week in the charts.

Estella shook her head. 'I'm afraid not. My father, you see, was involved in trying to have it banned. He'll probably have a crony or two outside with an angry placard and If word got back to him that I had seen it…'

Hunter was relieved. Musicals were not his idea of Friday evening entertainment, though he did enjoy *Spamalot*.

'How about a band? he asked, moving to the gig section. 'Portuguese Leather Goods are on at the Ritz.'

Estella's face bore a look of objection unimproved by such choices of Gas Carcass Yes playing Academy 3 or I Don't Want Chicken at the Night & Day.

'What does this city have to offer in a culinary sense?' she asked, placing her now empty tumbler on his desk.

That evening Hunter and Estella ate at Le Clochard et Dauphin, a French restaurant on New New Mount Street where candlelight was the only illumination, slow jazz drifted up to a high ceiling, and staff melted cheese in a manner both time consuming and deeply perverse.

The pair had met outside Estella's hotel; Hunter having gone home to change into an outfit of meticulously prepared indifference. Light shirt and dark jeans, his trusty boots remaining over fresh socks. Estella wore a floral print dress under fitted leather jacket, fire engine red lipstick setting off her flame hair.

Hunter knew the restaurant's maître d', Michel, having been hired by the man for a case. Wrenched from the signage, the Dauphin had been taken in the night and held for ransom by a rogue nationalist group. Their demands being the removal of French language classes from the school curriculum, the return of Calais to British control, and the immediate exile of all cheeses not of UK origin. After seven days on the case, Hunter suggested to Michel the money he was being paid might be better spent on a replacement sign, and the very next week a new Dauphin was installed above the doorway.

Hunter also knew Michel was not actually Michel and most certainly not French, but actually from Droylsden and named Michael. His language skills gleaned from GCSE textbooks; his Gallic sensibility honed on a steady diet of Jean-Luc Godard films.

Estella ordered the crépinette de veau et foie gras, Hunter the filet basquaise. Wine and food were served, and conversation soon turned to Thornton Pyle.

'How well do you know him?' Hunter asked.

'Thorn? I was assistant to his former agent, Tomkin Soup, and when Tomkin had his accident, Thorn knew and trusted me, so the role was mine.'

'Accident?'

A waiter was pouring an expensive white as Estella replied. 'Yes, he was struck by lightning while playing golf.'

'And he died?'

The waiter's hand stopped, Estella took a taste and nodded to both men.

'Hang on,' said Hunter. 'Didn't Pyle's editor die the same way?'

'Leslie Organ? Not at all. They were under very different circumstances.'

Hunter was confused and drained his wine. 'No, Zora definitely said he was hit by lightning playing golf.'

'Yes, I suppose that's true. And it was the same course, but their deaths were very different. They were two years apart. Tomkin was about to tee off on the seventh and Leslie was berating his caddy somewhere along the back nine. Very different, you see.'

Hunter refilled his own glass, while Estella returned to Pyle and her food.

'Anyway, Thorn and I already had our working relationship, so it seemed for the best. And it was, until Zora Liu stormed into town.'

'You two don't get along, do you?'

Estella put down her fork and took up her wine with a smile. 'You really are very perceptive. No, we don't get along at all. Zora is... Zora's the new appointee wishing to prove her worth. I respect her, I do. She has a good reputation in New York circles. But this is London.'

Hunter was not enough of a pedant to flag up the obvious and Estella continued.

'She has fresh ideas and while they may work for some writers, Thorn and his career will not benefit from a freshening up, from being brought into the new century.'

'And why's that?'

The agent cradled the glass in her hand. 'Because she was right about one thing.'

'Which is?'

'Which is Thorn is an idiot.'

Hunter sat back, appraising the woman before him, her features framed by copper-gold hair. This was a turn he had not expected.

'Tomkin knew he was an idiot,' she continued. 'The first day I met Thorn, Tomkin said to me beforehand, 'Estella, just smile and agree with him, and don't ask anything too far-reaching'. You know Tomkin was Thorn's uncle?'

Hunter nodded.

'Beyond that connection, Tomkin would likely not have taken

him on. Have you read Thorn's work?'

Hunter brought his wine to his lips. 'I've read him up to a point.'

'And which point is that?'

Hunter took a mouthful and swallowed. 'Somewhere around the second paragraph.'

Estella laughed. It was unrestrained and raucous and out of sync with the rest of her character. 'Tomkin felt much the same way, yet Thorn was family.'

'But he's won awards?'

'He has won awards, he's a bestseller many times over. Yet one person's award-winning bestseller is the next person's overrated crap. Thorn, in his way, is a very good writer. But his way is not for everyone.'

'Is it for you?'

Estella smiled. 'Between you, me and this exquisite wine, no.'

'But you represent him?'

'I represent him accordingly.'

'And what does that mean?'

'It means,' she paused, head inclined in the diffuse light. 'It means I respect the choices of others. I may not adore his work, you see, yet others do. And so, I represent him as any professional would. But most especially, I do it with care. With sensitive editing. With an eye on the road ahead of us. And, most importantly, with safe, anodyne interviews we can control.' Estella stopped. 'You're looking at me like you don't approve?'

Hunter parted his lips to speak but nothing came out.

'Are you so fussy in your choice of client?'

Hunter remained quiet and focused on his glass.

'You see, Thorn can craft beautiful sentences and paragraphs,' Estella went on, 'How much there is beneath that is another matter, but the main item to remember about Thornton Pyle is nowadays his books are years in the making. He fleshes them out and pares them back. He toils over each and every word. He works very hard. But he does it in a room, on his own. I would not have let him near that radio programme. Producing well-balanced thoughts on demand is not Thorn's strength. Drop him in a studio with the day's hot topic and he's no more rational a statement to make than whosoever sweeps up afterwards.'

Hunter sat listening as Estella refilled her wine, then gestured at a passing waiter for another bottle.

'Why are we always so surprised to learn a person reasonably talented at one pursuit might be entirely useless at another?' she asked of no one in particular. 'The idea a body of flesh and blood might be held together by nothing more than contradictions is one few seem inclined to grasp. Thorn's weakness is that of humanity in general. He believes he's special and we elevate certain people through a need to believe that one of us, at least, is special.'

'That we're better than the animals.'

'That someone on this earth knows what they are doing.

'That someone's in charge.'

'It's why so many need a God.'

'The benevolent and all-knowing father figure.'

'The steady hand on the tiller.'

'Firm but fair.'

'Experienced at the wheel.'

'Leading us to salvation.'

'Conspiracies, you see, are the same belief flipped.'

'The evil geniuses manipulating our every move.'

'Their nefarious schemes.'

'The Illumi-naughty.'

'When in reality we all are trapped somewhere in the middle'

'Life is mainly middle.'

'Herded not to Heaven or Hell.'

'But led like cattle.'

'Driven by an idiot without a destination.'

'An idiot without a licence.'

'An idiot without even a cap.'

'His only qualification the genitals he oozed out of.'

'An idiot who looks like an idiot.'

'An idiot who sounds like an idiot.'

'A charlatan in fancy dress pocketing your fare.'

'I wouldn't trust this lot with a pencil.'

'And yet here we are.'

'Once more under spiv rule.'

'What a time to be alive.'

'Who then is the true idiot?'

'Truth matters not; only what people will believe.'

'Football transfer gossip was the original fake news.'

'We're post-truth now.'

'Truth requires an investment from people.'

'We're post-competence.'

'Competence requires an investment *in* people.'

'Technology is our new truth, our new God.'

'And on the seventh day he sported leisurewear and surfed the web.'

'Also, our new Devil.'

'What I like most about the internet is the off button.'

'Technology our new driver.'

'It would drive us over a cliff if it didn't need rebooting quite so often.'

'Stop the world I want to go to the ladies.'

'LOL.'

'BRB. AFK.'

Hunter stared out through the window onto New New Mount Street, watching Friday night crowds pass businesses closed for the evening. Mixed groups in no real hurry, the occasional lone figure moving at speed. He saw the bookshop, Bhatt's Tomes, and could have sworn that was Mr Bhatt himself locking the shutters. For a moment, Hunter thought of rushing out to question him, then remembered the wine and the woman who would soon be returning from the lavatory. There would be time to visit there again at some point.

A waiter brought more wine and their desserts, two Breathless soufflés, before Michel the maître d' approached. The tall stocky man pausing to check the vicinity before reverting to Michael d'Droylsden.

'How do you think your lot'll do this weekend?' he asked Hunter.

'Everton? Anything better than a defeat and I'll be happy. What about City?'

'Anything less than a win…' Michael stopped as Estella came back and switched to Michel, signing off with, 'bon appétit, madam.'

Hunter waited for Estella to take up her glass, then asked, 'Does Pyle know he's an idiot?'

Her smile was bright again, her lipstick reapplied. 'Of course not. Thorn, you see, has been indulged his entire life. To expect him to have arrived at an epiphany which would shake his foundations to the core, which would eradicate his entire belief system, I'm not sure there's enough therapy in the world to cover that.' Estella took a mouthful of wine and tilted her head. 'Do you know you're an idiot?'

It was Hunter's turn to grin. 'I've long known I'm an idiot.'

'Really?'

He sat forward, elbows on the table, dessert spoon in hand. 'The thing is, for ages I thought it was just me. I'd look at all these successful people, the qualified people, the well-respected people, their job titles, their suits. I'd see them and think they had something I lacked. Something inside them. Some special power. I believed they were making sensible decisions, having sensible thoughts. But outside of that job title, underneath the nice clothes and bank balance, what did they have? What were their ideas, their motivations, their beliefs? What did they think about? How did they spend their time? How did they spend all that money?'

Hunter sank the spoon into his souffle.

'I kept my eyes open, I observed, I listened. To the clients I worked for, to the people I came across in my work. And my conclusion was that what they really had inside them was the same thing I had. An idiot. A different type of idiot, granted, one with different interests and pastimes, things society thought worthier, and of greater tradition and greater profit, but still an idiot. Did it hold them back? No, they pressed on regardless. So, that's what I did. I pressed on.' Hunter reached for his glass. 'It's freeing when you accept it.'

Estella had watched him throughout his monologue, wine in hand, appraising him with her red smile. 'When did you first realise?'

Hunter's life contained many instances of idiocy. There was the way he would eat a pie, flipping the savoury treat upside down and making a careful incision around the edge of the base before lifting away the flap of pastry, allowing him to peer inside and assess the patient's chances of survival before proceeding to soak up any excess fluid with a chip. It was a practice that (a) annoyed his father and (b) Hunter would continue with well into his thirties, mainly because of (a).

Then there was his teenage habit of barking the word "bridge" in full James Brown holler each taxi ride across the River Irwell into central Manchester. The type of behaviour many would have put down to simple youthful exuberance or, more specifically, alcohol.

But the first time Hunter truly realised he was an idiot was after leaving college. He had taken a job in a warehouse on the Salford side of the ring road and was yet to be issued any uniform. Hunter had been on his own in the canteen, eating sandwiches made by his mother, minding his own business and wearing a retro Northern Ireland football shirt in green, the number 7 worn by George Best printed in white on the reverse.

Hunter was aged nineteen or twenty, and self-involved as people of that age usually are. His family had Irish roots, though history other than ancient never held much interest for Hunter. His grandmother had come to England in the forties, meeting and marrying a local man. Hunter's father had been born back over on the Emerald Isle, by accident or design he did not know.

In a picture album, Hunter had seen his father sat on a rock at the Giants Causeway but never enquired about it, could not say how old his dad had been then. Was it the face of a young man? He could not tell; the photo was out of focus. It was the face of his father and that was about all Hunter was sure of. He could not judge by scale either, measuring his father against the surrounding rocks for an approximation of age. The picturesque area was so named for a reason. In summary, Hunter knew little of these Irish roots, had no wish to dig further, yet adopted them anyway.

And so, Hunter was on his own in the canteen when a man sat down at his table and began to converse. A man with an accent like his grandmother. The man asked Hunter where he was from. Hunter's answer, in an accent of pure Salford, was the Height. He made reference to his grandma and the man asked where she was from. Hunter stated the city, but when asked whereabouts in said city could not answer with any real accuracy. The man asked if Hunter had been over to Ireland. His answer here was no.

This stranger had shown more interest in Hunter's grandmother in five minutes than Hunter ever had. Though the man did not chide him, it was a chastening experience for Hunter. The man did not say Hunter was an idiot, he did not have to. Hunter felt like one. He would, if being completely honest, admit the main reason he wore the shirt was, purely and simply, to be a contrary prick.

'Are you an idiot?' Hunter asked Estella.

'Of course,' she smiled, 'we all are idiots.'

Hunter raised his almost empty glass. 'To idiots.'

*

In search of a final drink, the pair found themselves on the streets of Ancoats Urban Village. Their evening had been a pleasant one and Hunter, stomach full of expensive wine and high-priced steak, wondered where it might end. The mixing of business and pleasure so rarely came up for him.

They were on Gun Street when Estella's mobile went off, and Hunter watched as she scanned the screen only to ignore it. Was this call from a significant other, perhaps? Or an other hoping to become significant? They had not spoken of anything so personal. Neither had mentioned a partner of any type, Hunter certainly was single. The call was not his business but did remind him of a detail he had forgotten to share.

'At the studio,' he began, 'right before Pyle was due to go on, he was on his phone.'

'Really?' Estella turned as they walked. 'With whom?'

'No one knows. But after that he was gone.'

'Running from or towards, I wonder.'

'Towards? Does he know anyone up here?'

'I would have thought not but beyond our agent-client relationship, who can say.'

They walked and passed couples similar to them, tentative first-daters unsure of the future, maintaining polite distances. Hunter felt a stab of cold at his neck and a question.

'Doesn't it grate,' he asked, 'representing someone like Pyle?'

'Not really. You see, Thorn's very much a type I'm familiar with. We have a number of Thorns in the family, and I've represented them for more than forty years. He reminds me of my father, actually. Outwardly successful, respectable, yet beholden to certain ideals, lacking in fresh thinking, convinced of how the world should be. My mother is much the same. Both too concerned with how others perceive them. Cliches to the point of parody. Were they not my parents, I would have little to do with them.'

On the pavements of Cotton Street, the pair passed new bars and eateries, the nearby Hallé St Peters and the Cartwright & Co. warehouse. A group of raucous youths ran around them, bright shirts and brighter dresses flashing by, and Estella and Hunter turned inward allowing the group to pass, ending up face to face and no more than an inch apart. Hunter could smell her perfume, feel warm wine breath. Her green eyes pierced into his. There was a moment when that inch might have dissolved and their lips locked, only for a dread eruption from Engels Passage to rent the night air.

They heard a shriek – the first blow struck, perhaps, in some long-simmering struggle – and then laughter followed by a scampering upon cobbles. From the shadowed passage, emerged a dachshund. The sausage dog stopped, recognised Hunter and growled in a tone lower than its belly.

'Do you two know each other?' Estella asked.

'We've met once before.'

Hunter had no wish to end up on his backside again, especially in front of Estella de Fenestrate. He moved into position as if tending a five-a-side goal: crouched, arms spread wide, palms open toward the incoming. Doctor Dickie Shrub pawed the stones, growled once more and then charged, aiming for a space to Hunter's right.

Hunter shifted to intercept him, confident he now had the hound, but the dachshunds action was mere feint and when his pursuer was fully committed the dog adjusted his tiny limbs and darted the opposite way, leaving Hunter flapping at a breeze and before you could say the free development of each is the condition for the free development of all, the canny canine was off and away up Karl Marx Alley.

Thirty minutes later Hunter was back home on Little Peter Street and tied to his own bed. Astride him, a naked Estella de Fenestrate dispensed rude proclamations in bellowed RP.

While they undressed, she had made remarks which gave Hunter pause. They concerned the thickness of his boots, the coarseness of his hands. With regards his hands, Hunter did not consider them all that coarse. There was likely a spectrum for such matters, from carpenters and brick layers at one end across to television palm models at the other. It gave Hunter no pleasure that he was somewhere toward the latter. As for his footwear, the leather was thick and worn yet that was rather the point. They communicated a history of toil to which they had never been subjected. They had character. Over two hundred pounds worth.

Estella had tied Hunter's left hand to the bedpost with his belt and then searched around for another to secure his right. Hunter, though, possessed only a single belt – he could, after all, wear only one pair of slacks at a time – so he was left to watch her pale form glide out of the bedroom to find a suitable stand in. She soon returned with the power cord from his kettle.

Estella's flame hair was tied back, her manicured fingers digging into his chest muscles. 'You coarse little monster,' she shouted between heavy moans and the enthusiastic clapping of flesh.

The subtext of this outburst may have registered with Hunter had he not become distracted. His mind was not full of the cherry red nipples which danced before his eyes, nor even whether he had remembered to water Rubbert Plant. No, his mind was fixed upon his upstairs neighbours.

The tables had been turned. It was now he making noise beyond midnight – more accurately, of course, it was his guest. Hunter wondered how much they could hear and if he might receive a passive aggressive note over the next few days. Some carefully composed missive almost apologetic in its accusatory tone.

Estella's nails dug deeper into his chest; her moaning punctuated with three powerfully loosed words. 'Common labouring-boy.'

Hunter almost laughed. He had not worked in a manual sense since the early 2000s. His father would find this hilarious, not that he discussed this kind of thing with his father. Not that, in moments such as this, he should even be thinking of his father.

A sudden pain cleared Hunter's thoughts, a pain of burning cheek and ringing ear. He had not registered any movement, but had Estella just slapped him? Could she hear his inner monologue? Was he talking out loud?

The slap yanked Hunter back into the moment, and he wondered how far this might go. Another slap? Worse than a slap? Estella's fingernails dug back in above his heart and Hunter's pulse raced. Might events require a safe word? In the early going, they had failed to establish one. In that case would the phrase 'safe word' itself suffice? As in the first use of a bicycle chain, factory set to all zeros.

'You little wretch,' Estella growled, the look in her eyes intense enough to raise a panic in Hunter.

Who was this fiery banshee writhing upon his crotch, and what foul intentions did she harbour? Might she do him serious harm? Hunter had no wish for his life to terminate in a bawdy headline. This, all things considered, was an unfortunate note on which to ejaculate.

19

Hunter was tending a pan of sausages when his mobile rang. It was around one in the afternoon and almost time for his second meal of the day. In good spirits he answered without thinking and was surprised to hear the voice of Zora Liu.

'Where the hell are you?' she demanded.

'How did you get this number?' was Hunter's reply.

'You called me from it two days ago, remember?'

That had been a mistake. In all the excitement of cornering Thornton Pyle he had forgotten to restrict his caller ID.

'I did try your office,' Zora continued, 'but, you know, you weren't there, Mr Hunter.'

'I'm never there on Saturdays. I'm here.'

'Which is where?'

'Home, obviously. My home, specifically.'

'Don't specifically me, have you spoken to Estella this morning?'

Define 'this morning', he thought. Technically the time she

had Hunter tied to his own bed had been this morning. Though he had slept since then, so the activity also came under the heading of 'last night'. Hunter had woken around nine to find Estella gone and himself untied. Also, the kettle power cord thankfully undamaged from its unorthodox usage.

'Her reception told my reception she was heading north.'

'I did see something of her yesterday.'

'And what did she have to say Mr Hunter?'

On Zora's end of the line, he could hear birdsong mixed with passing vehicles. She would be getting the spit and sizzle of Hunter's dinner to be.

'We're outside business hours, Zora. You don't have to call me Mr Hunter.'

'What then?'

'Plain Hunter will do. Though I suggest you'd be better off dispensing with names altogether, as a time-saving initiative.'

'And why would I want to do that?'

'Because you have the time it takes for these sausages to cook.'

'What happens then?'

'Well, I put them on the barmcakes I've lovingly prepared to receive them and sit down in precious silence and eat the whole lot.'

This brought quiet from Zora Liu, leaving Hunter with engine hum and nature tweeting until the editor returned with a question. 'You're putting sausages on a cake?'

'It's not actually a cake, that's just the name. It's a bread thing.'

'A bread thing?'

'Yeah.'

'Oh, you mean like a roll.'

'I think roll is underselling it.'

'A bun, then.'

'No, bun sounds more like a cake.'

'Is it a cake, or isn't it?' Zora snapped.

'I'd say bap.'

'What?'

'A muffin.'

'Wait, a muffin is definitely a cake.'

'A barm.'

'Barm?'

'Yeah.'

'Ok, so if I go into a store and ask for a barm, they'll know what I'm talking about?'

'In London?' said Hunter, turning his sausages with a spatula and meticulous care. 'They won't have a clue. Stick to roll. Are you a big bread fan?'

'Sure, I like bread, why?'

'Because you've just wasted thirty seconds on the subject and brought the time I put this phone down and my feet up that much closer.'

'You can't take the day off.'

'No, you're right, I can't.' Hunter laid his spatula on the countertop. 'I'm taking the whole weekend off.'

'What?'

'It's all there on my website. Hours of business, Monday to Friday in nice clean font.'

'I haven't seen your website. Estella took care of all that. I don't internet anymore, you know this.'

'Me neither, really. I've never seen the fuss about the internet.

My tolerance is low when it comes to people droning on about their lives, their views on every little thing, their nuggets of wisdom no deeper than an eye bath.'

'I'm beginning to know the feeling,' said Zora.

'So, what is it that got you hooked?'

Hunter heard the rustling of paper and plastic, the scratching and firing of a flame, then sounds of inhalation.

'Narrative,' Zora exhaled. 'I love narrative, and the internet is all narrative, you know.' She took another drag of nicotine. 'It's comedy. It's tragedy. It's five-line flash fiction trying to sell me a designer fanny pack. It's someone I exchanged a half dozen words with two decades ago at a Brooklyn middle school live streaming their latest worst day ever as another tear laden epiphany from a crosstown Manhattan bus. Narrative. I can't get enough of the stuff. I gobble it like candy. It's why I got into publishing. Anyway, stop trying to distract me, you can't take the weekend off, you're on a case.'

'It's accepted industry practice, nowadays.'

'When did this happen?'

Spatula once more in hand, Hunter rolled his sausages. There were four in the pan. Three he would surgically cut and lie flat on the barmcakes. The other he would enjoy straight off a fork.

'Zora, when was the last time you hired someone like me?'

'Someone like you? That would be never.'

'Well, things have changed since never.'

'So, you're going to do what exactly?'

'With my weekend? Everything or nothing, I've not really decided yet. Maybe, a bit of both.'

'This is stupid.'

'That it is.'

'Well, at least you agree.'

'No, I mean it's STUPID, the Sanctified Trade Union of Private Investigators and Detectives.'

'The what now?'

'The Sanctified Trade Union of Private Investigators and Detectives.'

'STUPID?'

'Yeah.'

'You're with STUPID?'

'I am with STUPID and proud to be.'

Laughter filled Hunter's ears, laughter that turned to coughing. 'That's ridiculous. STUPID? Do they hand out buttons, print T-shirts?'

'Yeah, but no one wears them anymore.'

'No shit, Sherlock.'

'They're not exactly subtle and this business relies on subtlety.'

Zora inhaled. 'I can't believe this.'

'Why not? The right to withhold our labour on weekends is one of the 1978 Spade Marlowe accords.'

'Spade Marlowe accords?' she exhaled.

'Also known as the Bogeys.'

'This really is stupid.'

'Not at all. It's a group of like-minded souls standing together under one umbrella. Organised. Stronger as a whole. Judged by the acronym alone, I grant you, there are some negative connotations, but look beyond that and their basic principles are sound.'

'Oh, really.'

'Yeah, as well as the power to define our work week, they

offer pension advice, discounted life insurance and legal support, access to therapy, plus the odd cut price deal on a trench coat.'

'What?'

'The trench coats are decent quality as well, if a little impractical for our line of work.'

'Wait.'

'They're even less subtle than the T-shirts.'

'You're in therapy?'

'Not me personally. Not yet anyway. But we're a progressive lot and we have to be. A high number of us turn out to have troubled souls. A suspiciously high number, in fact. The question for many of us being, does the work attract these unfortunates or create them?'

'And which is it?'

'No one's sure. Studies are ongoing.'

'Are you a troubled soul, Hunter?'

'Only when I don't get my weekends off.'

The phone in his hand shook and dinged.

'What was that?' asked Zora.

'Give me a second.' Hunter checked the devices screen. 'Ok, I'm back.'

'What was it?'

'An important notification.'

'To say what?'

'Everton 1 Arsenal 0.'

Zora took another longer drag.

'How are you planning to spend your weekend,' Hunter asked, 'apart from eating into my leisure hours?'

'So far, I've read three newspapers, cover to cover including the ads. And I've just spent a half hour trying to order a sandwich maker over the telephone.'

'Why?'

'Because there was an ad, and I wanted a sandwich.'

'And how do you feel now?'

'Kind of like I'm over the concept of a sandwich, you know. I'm out in the garden, bored and stressed.'

'And you decided to call me? How flattering. Is there no one else?'

'Everyone I want to speak to is on New York time and so probably still in bed.'

'Don't you have friends?'

'Of course, I have friends, but if I called them at what, 8am their time, simply because I was bored, guess what, they would not be friends much longer.'

'What about family?'

'There's my mom, but if I call her this early and it isn't an emergency, she may never pick up when it is.'

'Your authors? Call one of them.'

'You want me to call FYI Crisp just to shoot the shit? The man's almost eighty. He'll be awake but he'll be writing. I doubt he'll appreciate the interruption.'

'Whereas I do?'

'He'll be working. Whereas you're supposed to be working.'

'And so, here we are.'

'Here we are.'

Hunter had not planned on being quite so sociable over the weekend, beyond muttering loudly at his upstairs neighbours' shenanigans. He fumbled for additional small talk. 'Is it a nice garden, at least?'

'It is. The hedges are high, so I'm not overlooked, there's a pond, a good size tree. I'm currently watching a squirrel rustling some birds nuts.'

'The natural worlds many varied wonders. I thought the capital was supposed to be boredom proof?'

Zora made a noise he did not take to be positive. 'It's no New York.'

'I'm sure there's plenty to do if you look.'

'That may be, but I can't just forget the situation for the weekend. This Pyle thing is a real itch I can't scratch. I am trying to relax, I'm taking deep breaths, I'm letting my jaw rest open. Just hanging loose, you know. Not that I'd do it in company. It isn't a real good look.'

'Are you doing it now?'

'Kind of, but it makes talking difficult. Plus, I think the squirrel is judging me.'

'Zora, stub out your cigarette, get up and go to a museum, a gallery. It's what Pyle's doing. There's that Bacon retrospective at the Tate.'

'Bacon is not to my taste.'

'How about an exhibition of Bob Dylan needlework?'

'A what now?'

'Bob Dylan needlework.'

'I knew he painted, but…'

'It's a display of his most caustic lyrics. The works he used to needle people with.'

'Not actual needlework, then.'

'No, actually actual needlework. Someone has sewn them all onto LP-sized canvasses alongside an embroidered Bob from throughout the years. I went the other day.'

Zora coughed. 'Why would somebody do that?'

'Which? Go and see them or sew the things in the first place?'
She coughed again. 'Both.'

'Well,' said Hunter, contemplating his life choices, 'It's something to do, isn't it. I bought one. A smaller version, 7-inch sleeve size and framed.'

On Hunter's souvenir was sewn a tousle-haired figure in dark glasses, who might conceivably have been anyone, at what appeared to be an upright piano. A harmonica was positioned at the figure's mouth by a holder which resembled more some post-accident system for nibbling on a chocolate bourbon.

'What does yours say?' asked Zora Liu.

And you, you just believe anythin' you hear,
Some kinda all you really agree with you can cheer.

Hunter sang this over the phone, adopting a nasal croon, accentuating the rhyme ending each line.

'And that's your best Dylan impression, is it?'

'That's Bob, on his day off, frying sausages.'

'What's the song?'

'Some unreleased mid-sixties rarity. I've got it up in my office.' A sizzling came to Hunter out of the pan, his meat was almost done. It was time to slice and let them cool a little on the barmcakes, melting the margarine, then burying the whole thing in ketchup. 'We should probably cut to the chase, Zora, what is it you want from me?'

'A little competence would be nice.'

'Competence? Let's not be naïve now.'

'Naïve? Who's being naïve.'

'Zora,' Hunter stuck his fork in the fourth sausage, 'never

mind post-truth, we're beyond that. The world we live in now is post-competence.'

'I haven't the time for your esoteric excuses.'

'Yes, you have Zora. You've all weekend.' He heard her inhale and pressed on. 'We're told everything is supposed to be that much easier and quicker these days. That much more reliable. And so, we're all surprised when things fail. When systems don't work as they should. I, however, I expect failure. I'm braced for it. What surprises me is the smooth, problem-free transaction.'

Monologue over, Hunter took a premature bite of sausage. 'Fuck!'

'What is it?' Zora asked.

'It doesn't matter,' he articulated around a singed tongue. 'My advice to you, Zora, is adjust your expectations accordingly.'

'Oh, Hunter, my expectations have never been lower.'

'I did apologise for Thursday.'

'Yes, but how did you lose him?'

'I made a slight miscalculation. On Monday I'll pick up where I left off.'

'But he could be anywhere by Monday.'

'He could've been anywhere two days ago, but he wasn't. He was still up here. Why, Zora? Why stay? He's had since Monday to get far away from all this, but he's still around. I don't think he's going anywhere.'

'You don't think?'

'No. I don't think.'

'This is unacceptable, Hunter.'

'And yet.'

'And yet.'

There was a pause. Hunter heard more distant animal sounds and capital traffic, but not the editor. He wondered if she had left him in favour of the squirrel, until she returned with a heavy sigh.

'So, what happens next?'

'Well, Zora, I'm gonna end this phone call. I'm gonna sit down with my sausage butties and no distractions, and I'm gonna enjoy each mouthful; I'm gonna still my mind and banish all thought of Thornton Pyle. And I'm gonna to try to do all that while hoping Arsenal don't equalise.'

20

By Sunday morning the events of late Friday had acquired for Hunter an aspect of the unreal. The mid-coital slap. Doctor Dickie Shrub's fleeting appearance. The menu price of a filet basquaise.

He had not heard from Estella, though her silence might not purely be down to embarrassment. She had mentioned people she had to speak with, friends she wished to see. Yet their evening together was dissolving in Hunter's mind. He could not retain certain details. What time events took place. How they got from one part of town to another. Other details, such as Estella's pale buttocks as she moved around his apartment, or the vigour in her breasts while he lay bound to the bed, would be etched in his mind for years to come. So too the menu price of a filet basquaise.

Hunter had not gone out at all on Saturday, and while he saw no problem with this, he knew there were those who believed this a waste, some moral dereliction in not contributing to the nation's economy, an immense failure to grasp capitalism's greasy baton and sprint with it toward penury. And so, just before noon, Hunter ventured forth.

A little earlier, he had sat down next to his rubber plant with the intention of reading, taking advantage of his upstairs neighbours seemingly unconscious state, only to find he had nothing he felt like reading – Beckett's *The Complete Dramatic Works* waited back at his office on New Mount Street. He decided to head for New New Mount Street and Bhatt's Tomes.

While searching for a new book, Hunter would ask Mr Bhatt the questions he had intended to ask on Thursday. He would make his enquiries in a clandestine friendly manner, talking with the proprietor of literature and sport so that no one, not even Hunter himself, could imagine he was working.

When Hunter arrived the counter was unoccupied, the shop quiet as silent customers scanned shelves. He moved along spines hoping to find a purchase, only for a man in a hat two aisles away to draw his attention.

This was not your average October headgear for Manchester. Munich, possibly. A beer hall, certainly. There was a feather in the band and Hunter identified it as a Tyrolean hat. He wondered if this man was a member of some visiting oompah gang until the man turned, stopping Hunter in his tracks.

Could that be Pyle? As the man was busy in the adult section, he could not see Hunter pull out his phone and scroll to the saved photo of the missing writer. Hunter lifted the device, matching the picture to the behatted man. It *was* Pyle, though minus the moustache.

Hunter felt his pulse quicken but forced himself to move slowly, stepping back behind a tall shelf, removing the cap he never left home without from his jacket pocket and slipping it onto his head. He peered out again. Pyle had not strayed far, and Hunter took a deep, calming breath. He was not as set as he would have preferred but the job threw these surprises at you.

As the author moved along the aisle, Hunter did likewise in the opposite direction. As Pyle shifted right, he shifted left. When Pyle stopped, he stopped. The pair involved in a dance only one of them was aware of. Thornton Pyle seemed carefree, certain his continental headgear was camouflage enough.

'Can I help you?' The voice behind Hunter gave him a fright and he turned to see Anjum Bhatt.

For a moment Hunter went blank, he was unprepared to explain himself, so reached for the standard excuse of shop loiterers everywhere.

'I'm just browsing,' he told her.

'Browsing,' she repeated. 'I like to keep an eye on the browsers. We get the same faces in almost daily, picking up the same books, reading a chapter or two before leaving. This kind of activity does not contribute to the unit rental.'

Hunter watched her eyes flick to the shelf before him. The corners of her mouth rose. 'Are you browsing for anything in particular?' she asked.

'Yeah,' Hunter replied about to reach for the nearest book, 'I was looking for the…' He now stood where Pyle had been, right in the middle of the substantial vintage pornography section. 'I'm here for the…' Hunter dropped his hand and mentally clutched at the first thing that came to him. '…football annuals. That's it, I'm looking for the football annuals.'

'And yet you ended up here.' Anjum Bhatt gestured across the sprawling adult section.

'I got distracted,' he told her.

'That happens a lot. This area's a true mystery. My father's had men round to look into it, but it's like a reverse Bermuda Triangle. Once they're here we can't seem get rid of them. Within its borders they're powerless to leave. They forget their names, their families, their life's purpose. So the phenomenon persists.'

Hunter nodded merely for something to do. At a loss for what to say, he blurted out, 'I'm here with my friend.'

'Your "famous" "friend"?' Anjum Bhatt formed air quotes for each word in long slow movements. 'The "writer"?'

'Yeah, he's…' Hunter moved to point out the behatted man, 'he's just over…'

But Pyle was gone.

Out on New New Mount Street, Hunter scanned passing crowds for the writer, eventually sighting his distinctive felt hat on the pavement opposite. Hunter crossed and fell in a distance back. He could see the feather dancing in the breeze and bemused expressions from passers-by turning to look. Pyle did not move fast or check behind him, convincing Hunter the man was unaware of his presence.

From a stand Hunter picked up a free newspaper to add to his camouflage, the front-page headline reading: UNITED STRIKER ENJOYS DRINK AT LAST CHANCE SALOON. After a series of unhurried turns, they were on Whitworth Street West where, just before the Ritz, Pyle deviated into an alleyway.

Hunter sped up and then stopped to peek around the corner. Pyle was ambling along obliviously, and Hunter resumed his pursuit. At the end of the alley Hunter stopped again, putting half a head beyond the brick work onto the Rochdale Canal path. Pyle was strolling the narrow walkway with not a care in the world.

Hunter stepped forward and leant on the barrier, pretending to focus on the paper. There were no crossings for a good distance and any turn by the writer would only put him back on Whitworth Street. He could let Pyle open up a gap. He waited until the man was alongside apartment balconies then started after him.

At the next alleyway Hunter felt a jump in his heart rate as Pyle paused. Hunter also paused, wedging the folded newspaper into his jacket and stooping to check his boot laces. He glanced up and saw Pyle reach into a pocket and pull out a paper bag, then bring something from the bag up to his mouth. A second later he walked on.

A woman head to toe in black lycra jogged past Pyle and the writer turned to watch her. Hunter, cap down and head slightly bowed, had his mobile to his head and was nodding, throwing in the occasional quiet laugh, and pointless hand gesture. If his target recognised him, he did not show it in his pace. The woman passed Hunter, and on he and Pyle continued, approaching a line of narrowboats roped to the barrier.

At that moment the phone in Hunter's hand began to shake, ringtone blasting at his ear, intruding on the sedate waterway. Hunter checked the screen, saw MUM as the contact name, and flicked the device to silent, then looked ahead.

Pyle was standing maybe ten strides before him, fingers once more at his mouth. Whether or not Hunter's cover was blown, this man knew something was amiss. Hunter approached slowly, noticing Pyle was feasting on some form of pastry.

'Can I have one?' Hunter asked.

'No,' the author said, 'you may not. Do I know you?'

Hunter shrugged and put his mobile away. 'That's more a question for you to answer, really.'

Silence engulfed the pair which, before Hunter knew it, he was already breaking, loosing thoughts he felt sure he was only thinking. 'Where's the moustache?'

Pyle's cheek quivered in rogue spasm. 'I think you have me confused with someone else.'

Hunter stepped carefully, not wishing to tip his hand more than he already had. 'But aren't you Stephen Pole?'

Again, the twitch. 'No. My name is Stefan Ple. I'm an Austrian gentleman.'

'Austrian? You don't sound it. Ple, eh?'

The man nodded and took a further bite of pastry.

'Took you awhile to come up with that, did it?'

As Hunter stared at the author's upper lip, recognition crackled around Pyle's eyes, brought on by either Hunter's face, or his sarcasm.

'I remember you now. Yes. You're the fish man.'

'Let's get this right,' Hunter stated, 'They weren't fish, they were prawns.'

This distinction went unheard. 'Finlay something? Finbar?'

'Finbert.'

'Well, Fishy Finbert, are you following me?'

Hunter glanced around the canal area in thought. 'That would depend on where we're going.' The Bridgewater Hall was nearby, and Rain Bar across the water. 'Where are we going?' he asked.

'That is none of your business.'

'Wait a minute,' said Hunter. 'You're not Pole or Ple, are you?'

Something was taking hold in Hunter. An impatience he could not control.

'Who I am is none of your concern,' answered Pyle.

'No, I know who you are. You're that writer.'

A distant engine chugged and in Pyle's face there was a twitch within a twitch. His voice became a rasping whisper. 'I must say, you are very much mistaken.'

'I've read your work.'

The man went still, mouth hanging open, this being a turn he had likely not anticipated. 'Really?'

'Up to a point, yeah.'

'And what point is that?' Pyle asked.

'Usually the first mention of your name.'

The writer bristled, and Hunter felt the urge to continue poking him verbally. 'Piles, isn't it? Mr Piles?'

'Pyle. It's Pyle. P-Y-L-E.'

'Of course, Yeah. Pyle, singular of Piles.'

The distant chug was now a canal boat heading their way.

'Shouldn't you have been on the telly last week?' Hunter continued. 'That dinnertime show?'

'I do not *do* daytime television. I am a serious novelist. I will not explain myself to the masses. I will not talk away the magic of my work.'

'It wasn't your work you were supposed to talk about though, was it?'

Pyle ignored this. 'Fourteen books I have written.' He stepped toward Hunter, pressing a sticky finger into Hunter's chest. 'Four-teen. My body of work…'

'Your body of work?'

'My body of work...'

Hunter lightly moved Pyle's digit away. 'I've a question about your body of work.'

'Yes?'

'From your body of work, which of the fourteen would you consider the anus?'

'What?'

'Or is there more than one?'

Thornton Pyle's face was almost scarlet, his mouth quivered with rage. 'I must say…' he began, only for Hunter to interrupt.

'I'm not sure what all the fuss is about with writing.'

'What?'

'It's just making things up really, isn't it?'

'I really must say…'

'I mean it's a trade, I'll give you that.'

'Is this some type of joke?'

'But I would put you on par with a brick layer.'

'What?'

'I mean, you're not inventing the words, are you? They already exist. You're simply fitting them together, placing them in an arrangement, creating a greater whole. A whole that some might want, and others think is a pile of shite.'

'How dare you.'

'You're a brick layer with words.'

'This is preposterous.'

'Words. And nicer shoes.'

Pyle stared at Hunter. The canal boat was closer now, its engine loud.

'Who sent you?' the writer demanded.

'I dunno what you mean.'

'Who sent you?' Pyle was agitated. The pastry he clutched now forgotten and somewhat squished.

'Maybe…' Hunter felt the need to test a theory, the borrowed books from the Height library still nagged at him, '…maybe, it was the DEATH people.' He watched for Pyle's reaction and saw only confusion.

'I have never said anything remotely disparaging about deaf people. Sign language is really quite ingenious.'

'Not deaf, DEATH. D-E-A-T-H. Expiration? Final rest? The eternal sleep?'

Pyle's confusion grew and Hunter changed tack. 'Ok, it was the telly people, really.'

Pyle's confusion turned to horror. 'No.'

'The telly people, yeah. And my name isn't Finbert, it's Bingsley. That's right, Ken Bingsley, I'm a reporter for Speculation at Whenever.'

'No. No. What do they want, Bingsley? What do they want?'

Thornton Pyle's rejection of daytime television was a stance Hunter could understand. He had long stopped turning his own set on should he be home during the lighter hours. Bar the occasional sporting event, he had not watched morning or afternoon programming since a September Tuesday over twenty years ago.

Back then Hunter still worked the early shift at the Salford warehouse, and afterwards he would take the bus home to the Height. On this day, he dropped in to see his grandmother and found the old lady perturbed. She had mislaid a particularly cherished Daniel O'Donnell cassette.

Hunter made a quick search of her terraced house but with no success and so the two sat watching the news and then an Australian soap opera readying themselves for the afternoon detective series, pondering this missing tape with a ginger biscuit in one hand, and cup of tea in the other.

His gran had long told Hunter that when it came to tea, he made 'a lovely drop'. As a child he was proud of this supposed ability, had shown the old woman the cub scout badge he earned for just this sort of task. His grandmother had given him a smile and a twenty pence piece. Yet in his early teens Hunter became suspicious, as many in that difficult age range are wont to do. He was less trusting of the world and its ulterior motives. Was this easy flattery and monetary recompense simply a way for this old woman to avoid leaving her chair, walking to the kitchen and putting the kettle on?

With the age of twenty-two looming, Hunter had lain somewhere betwixt these viewpoints. If it was the former, and he did indeed possess such a skill, then Hunter had an extra line for his curriculum vitae. If it was the latter, well, he could only tip his cub scout cap to the wily old dear.

Ordinarily, Hunter did not even drink tea. He made it but did not drink it. Yet on this day, tired from a warehouse shift and subsequent fruitless quest, he wished to see what he might be missing. And so, the pair were sat, mugs and biscuits at the ready, waiting for *Murder She Wrote* to begin. Only *Murder She Wrote* did not begin.

Attention and the broadcast cut away to events in New York as the city became ash and blood on the screen before them. Hunter had not watched daytime television since. Or drunk tea.

As they witnessed the towers disintegrate, his grandmother had fallen quiet. Only after her death years later would Hunter realise how little he knew of this woman beyond her love of, in no particular order: Our Lord and Saviour, Jesus Christ; tea; and Daniel O'Donnell. Hunter's Irish roots remained undisturbed; knowledge of the family tree vague beyond the more obvious branches.

The Northern Ireland city his grandmother had left, and where his father was born, was one riven by tension, but Hunter never associated the place he saw on the news, a place of explosions and soldiers, murals and gunfire, with the one his gran would visit for a month each summer, to stay with siblings and catch up with friends. The link felt as unreal as the hellish pictures on the TV screen before them.

Hunter shifted his eyes to watch his grandmother. There was something in the way she cleared her throat, a discomfort Hunter could sense. She wished to speak. Hunter thought he knew what she wanted to say yet had no wish to pre-empt her words. They were her words, and Hunter felt he had no right to them. And so, he sat and gave the old woman time.

'Well,' she said when finally she turned, her soft white curls unmoving, her soft Irish brogue unsteady, 'how about another drop of your lovely tea.'

On the Rochdale canal, the approaching boat chugging past crafts moored and empty had almost reached Hunter and Pyle. This barge close enough now to make out its name, the David Essex, and notice the young family holidaying therein.

'Bingsley,' Pyle roared above the din, 'what do they want?'

'The telly people?' shouted Hunter. 'You know what they want.'

Pyle stood, pastry in hand, staring at Hunter but also through him. When the writer's focus shifted, Hunter followed his gaze, first to the moving boat and then the nearest static one, then to the barrier and lastly back to Hunter. The author held out the crushed pastry to Hunter and for no reason beyond politeness and a growing Sunday afternoon hunger, Hunter took it.

Thornton Pyle dusted the crumbs from his palms, took a step away and, in a movement Hunter could only applaud for a man the novelist's age, Pyle was over the barrier and onto the static craft. Without turning to look back or impart some witty rejoinder, he leapt.

Hunter did finally recover the Daniel O'Donnell cassette. For want of a bookmark, his grandmother had used it as a place saver in a copy of *The People's Friend*.

Pyle landed on the forward part of the family's barge where the mother seemed unsure what was happening. At the other end the father stood at the tiller with two children, a young girl waving and a boy of similar age with a finger so far up his nostril he might be scratching the hypothalamus. The man began to shout at Pyle, but Pyle ignored him, lifted his Tyrolean hat to the mother in a gesture of 'good day, madam. Do excuse me,' and with a second leap landed on the opposite bank.

The family could only stare while Pyle lifted an apologetic hand and said something Hunter could not hear over their engine. The barge carried on; the father's mouth opening and closing in fury or amazement lost to the noise of his craft. The writer turned to Hunter and shrugged, lifted his green felt hat once more, then started to walk away.

Hunter saw where he was headed, an alleyway from which he might soon disappear. Yet if Hunter could get around the buildings on his side quick enough, might he cut Pyle off on Trumpet Street? He would have to hurry, and hurry he did, racing to the nearest exit out onto Whitworth Street and barrelling down to the lights, rushing between shoppers, forced here and there onto the busy tarmac where bovine horns greeted his trespassing. The newspaper fell from his jacket and was forgotten.

A right onto Albion Street and Hunter was on the bridge, casting a glance down to the canal and the all too recent absurdity. He reached Trumpet Street in maybe a minute and a half but found not a soul on the cobbles. Thornton Pyle had once more slipped from his grasp.

21

A new week on New Mount Street found Hunter in creative form. He had printed a map of the area fanning out from the Trumpet Street canal exit and was marking hotels with a circle. Within a short walk, he had four. Expand that walk and the number doubled. What Hunter intended to do with this, he was not sure. He understood it was not just hotels Thornton Pyle could have disappeared into but anywhere. Pubs, restaurants, tattoo emporiums. Even Hunter's own block. He had found and lost the writer barely five minutes from his flat on Little Peter Street.

Some long-forgotten drum fill was tapped out on Hunter's door and the postman Claude stepped into the office. Satchel over a shoulder, glasses sliding down his nose, an arm outstretched with the usual stack of correspondence.

'How was your weekend?' Hunter asked, laying down his map to receive the letters.

'Not long enough, pal,' Claude answered without pause.

'They never are.'

'What about yours?'

When asked to account for his downtime Hunter may have felt shame at achieving so little had his idea of a good weekend not been precisely that. Two things stood out, of course. There had been unusual intercourse with an attractive woman, and Everton had held on for victory. Hunter did not disclose the former but did bring up the latter.

'Don't mention football to me,' the postman told him.

'Any football?'

'Any of it. All of it. I'm done. How goes the searching?' Claude asked to change the subject. 'Any luck with your dog and that writer?'

Hunter laid down the letters and picked up his map. He gave it one last glance then screwed it into a ball. 'Minimal,' he replied. 'Though I did find some stuff about this DEATH cult. You'll never guess where they meet.'

Behind his spectacles Claude's eyes narrowed. 'St. John's graveyard?'

Hunter shook his head.

'After hours at the Reaper & Sons funeral home?'

'Nope.'

The postman blew out his cheeks. 'I don't know, pal. Just tell me, I've got a round to finish off out there.'

'Come on, Claude. You can do this.'

'To be fair, pal, I've always wondered about the logic of telling someone, "you'll never guess", only to insist they do just that.'

'You really do lack a curiosity of spirit, don't you?' said Hunter, as he balanced the ball of paper on the back of his hand.

'It's not my lack that's the problem. It's other people's excess.'

'Fine, fine. It's the Height Library.'

'Really?'

'Yeah, they even promise refreshments.'

'A DEATH cult that puts on a spread? Now that I'd never have guessed.'

'Well, even maniacs like a biscuit.'

'And when does all this fun and games happen?'

'Thursdays.'

'Maybe I'll join up after all. I was only in there last week.'

'The library?' A flicker went on in Hunter's brain, causing the ball to tumble groundward. 'When last week?'

'It escapes me.' Claude clicked his fingers to jog his memory. 'Same day you told me about all this. When was that?'

'Wednesday?'

'That was it, I was returning some books for my mam.'

'And did you happen to take any out while you were there?'

'I did, aye. You're bloody good at this detective work, aren't you? I borrowed a couple of this fellas, actually.' Claude tapped Thornton Pyle's forthcoming novel which still lay on the desk.

'You twat,' said Hunter, recovering the balled-up map on the floor and launching it his friend's way.

'What've I done now?'

'I had that down as a possible lead.'

'And is there a link, do you reckon?'

'Not anymore, I don't.'

To look at this in a positive sense, it was an avenue of investigation ticked off. It was progress. One less lead to chase up. Yet Hunter still had so little to go on it felt like a blow. 'So, what did you think then?' he asked.

'To the books?' Claude picked up the paper projectile and flicked it deftly into Hunter's bin. 'Well, pal, they were supposed to be hilarious. It said so on the covers.'

'And were they?'

'To be fair, not by any definition of the word I'm familiar with.'

'This is his new one.' Hunter gestured at the proof.

Claude lifted the book. 'Fuck me that's heavy. I bet there's a lot of big words in there.'

'You can have it if you like.'

'Maybe I'll take you up on that…' Claude tested the tome's weight, hefting Pyle's latest offering through a practiced backhand, '…if I ever need to anaesthetise a rottweiler.'

Hunter flicked through his post. There was little of interest. More bills, more offers of credit, and yet another letter for Mr Elvis Love, this time from a company named Centaur Insurance, offering comprehensive packages for horse lovers covering both rider and animal. Hunter crossed out the address on the front, circled the one on the rear, wrote in clear capitals, RETURN TO CENTAUR, and passed the envelope back to Claude, who smiled and congratulated him on the witticism.

'What did happen with the football?' Hunter now felt safe to ask. 'I forgot about the United game.'

It had been the late kick-off on Saturday, United against the visiting Wolves.

Claude was by now drifting toward the exit. 'Well, our mutual friend scored.'

Hunter felt a glow of pride; had his advice had anything to do with it? The postman did not seem overly pleased, however. 'Surely that's good news,' said Hunter.

'It would be had it gone in the correct goal.'

'An own goal?'

Claude nodded. 'An own goal and another defeat.' He once more changed the subject. 'Did you watch the Everton game?'

'I saw the highlights.'

'Good result that, pal.' The game had finished 2-1.

'It nearly wasn't thanks to VAR.'

'To be fair, I hardly think you can blame VAR for your sides lack of midfield penetration.'

'I don't care. Their goal was never a penalty.'

Claude wavered in the doorway. 'I'm not so sure.'

'It was a dive.'

'It was a poor challenge.'

'It was a bloody dive.'

Claude shrugged. 'It was deep in that great big grey area in between. Which is what football is, to be fair. 90 minutes of mostly grey areas on one big green area.'

'It's 98 minutes if United are losing,' Hunter offered. 'Technology is ruining the game.'

Claude shook his head. 'No, no. Technology isn't the problem.'

'Course it is.'

'No, pal. It doesn't implement itself.'

'I know what it can do to itself.'

'Technology isn't to blame,' Claude said and checked his watch. 'Some computer is not giving Arsenal a penalty. The problem is this technology is in the hands of a human being. It's just another referee in an office somewhere, surrounded by screens and too much information. Slow motion, fast forward. Seventeen angles of the same vague incident. But that human is still the one making the final decision. All technology has done is give them more ways to make the same bad decisions they've always done.'

Hunter would not be swayed. 'It was never a penalty.'

'Have you read the FA laws recently, pal?'

'Has anyone?'

'To be fair, it's all about interpretation.'

'That's a very big word for a Monday morning.'

'It's all how an individual sees an incident.'

Hunter checked his own timepiece and contemplated an Irish Cream. 'Are you saying all this to wind me up?'

A smiling Claude readjusted his satchel and glasses. 'Only partly.'

Hunter could still hear Claude's footsteps on the stairs when he noticed the Thornton Pyle proof remained on his desk. He pushed the tome away with an index finger while his other hand brought toward him Samuel Beckett's *The Complete Dramatic Works*. Hunter had barely opened the cover and found his place at the opening of *Waiting for Godot* when his landline began to ring.

'The birthplace of the Industrial Revolution, Hunter here.'

'I've still got your dog,' came the echoing reply.

Hunter recognised the caller, put down the Beckett and rested his boots on a free corner of his desk. 'And I hope you both had a lovely weekend together. Get up to anything nice? A brisk walk, perhaps? A gambol in the fields? Half an hour's boisterousness with a nice big stick?'

'Very funny. It's two grand I want now.'

'Double?' asked Hunter. 'That's a bit much, don't you think?'

'Not at all. Each time you mess me around it's gonna go up. Consider yourself warned.'

'Hang on, hang on. I'm messing you around? If anything, I'm the passive party in this equation. You're the one who's kidnapped my dog. Dognapped, I should say. You're trying to extort money from me. All I've done is pick up the phone twice, and neither time with any real enthusiasm.'

'Look, I didn't ring for your life story. Do you want your dog back or not?'

Hunter took a moment to breathe and ponder the Irish Cream in his filing cabinet. 'Ok, I want him back.'

'Right well let's get the fuck on with it then, shall we?'

'Is he on the line?'

'He's on the line,' the man said. 'Talk to him and get it over with.'

Hunter cleared his throat. 'Are you alright?' he asked slowly and clearly.

There was a click and a hiss in his ear before he heard, 'woof, woof,' followed by a further click.

Hunter sat with this a moment, then asked, 'is that two barks for yes or two barks for no?'

Click, hiss, 'woof, woof,' click.

This did not clear up the situation but Hunter moved on regardless. 'Are you still there, mate?' he asked the man.

'Yes, are you happy now.'

'Happy is probably a bit strong, but I'm willing to proceed.'

'Good. Two grand. In a jiffy bag. The bin near Debenhams. Got it?'

'I've got it. Now...' Hunter began, '...if you could just confirm his name for me.'

'What?'

'Just confirm his name for me. It's right there on the collar.'

'Collar?'

'Yeah. I mean, I'm willing to pay up and I do feel relieved after speaking to him, but the thing is I need you to confirm his name for me. It's just box ticking, really, for my insurance. To be sure I'm getting the correct dog back. I know I'm getting the correct dog back, and even if it's not the correct dog, he does sound like the sort of canine I could really get along with, but these companies have paperwork and whatnot that needs to be filled in correctly. There are official hoops I've got to jump through for any claim. You understand that don't you? It's bureaucracy. Pure bloody bureaucracy. Hello? Hel-lo?'

The phone was back in its cradle and *The Complete Dramatic Works* in Hunter's hands, though he wondered if this might be a fool's errand, if a quiet moment to sit and read would ever again present itself. Hunter debated this inwardly for twenty minutes and could have gone for longer had his landline not rung once more.

'The birthplace of Dean Martin,' he said, 'Hunter here.'

'It's Shrub.' Hunter required only these two words to realise the man was not in a pleasant mood. Hunter, full of good cheer from his recent japery, searched for a topic to lift the conversation.

'I hope you had a good weekend, Mr Shrub. How did Swinton get on?'

'Excuse me?'

'The Lions, the rugby?'

'They don't play over the winter anymore. It's a summer game now.'

Hunter was thrown. 'When did this happen?'

'When I was eight.'

'And you're how old now?' The man did not speak, and so Hunter felt compelled to. 'I must be out of the loop.'

'Evidently.'

'Did you get up to anything nice, Mr Shrub?'

'Me and Dela, Dela and I, went out for dinner. I mean, lunch.'

'And did Dela and you have a nice dinner lunch?'

'Yes. It was… it was… fine.'

The man's mood, if anything, seemed worse.

'Well,' said Hunter, 'I'm glad you called. Because I've good news for you. And also, some bad news.'

With no deliberation the dentist asked for the bad news first, adding, 'Dela asked me to call you. She has a lot on her mind and it's all getting too much for her.'

'Ok. Well, the good and bad news is actually only the one item and it's good for Dela and bad for you.' Shrub muttered a low expletive, but Hunter went on. 'Doctor Dickie Shrub was seen around Ancoats on Friday evening. He's back over your side of the ring road. Doctor Dickie is on his own turf.'

'Can you not call him that?'

Still in playful mood, Hunter felt tempted to repeat the dog's full name simply to irk Rich Shrub, though weighed this momentary high against the man's obvious Monday morning dejection. 'What would you like me to call him then?'

'How about 'the dachshund'?'

'Ok. *The dachshund* has returned to home ground.' As this felt like some coded missive to be swapped on a Moscow park bench, Hunter felt the urge to repeat it. '*The dachshund* has returned to home ground.'

Shrub sighed. 'That is certainly news, but not really why I called.'

Hunter was confused. 'Oh, why did you call?'

'Because I'd like to know why you told Dela our apartment was haunted.'

'Ah,' said Hunter.

'This is what has become too much for her. I'm a busy man. I don't have the time to be making calls like this. I've a whole reception of teeth to attend to.'

'Now, Mr Shrub, let's remain calm. I don't believe I stated anything definitively. I merely…' Hunter sensed movement in his doorway and glanced up to see Estella de Fenestrate in her olive greatcoat. He scanned the office in the hope it was presentable, then gestured for her to take a seat and continued his call. 'I merely floated a theory, Mr Shrub. Speculation, that's all. To take her mind off *the dachshund*. This was what you hired me for wasn't it?'

'Speculation or not, Dela has hired a medium.'

'Really?' Hunter lifted his eyebrows for Estella's benefit. The agent across his desk looked good, even if she was wearing considerably more clothes than the last time Hunter had seen her. 'To do what?' he asked Shrub.

'To do whatever the fuck it is fucking mediums fucking do,' the dentist replied. 'A fucking séance, probably.'

Hunter feared for the man's next patient. But only briefly.

'A séance?' He sat forward. 'I've never been to a séance. Can I come?'

'Why?'

'Well, it's something to do, isn't it?'

Rich Shrub gave him the details and rang off, leaving Hunter alone with Estella for the first time since Friday night or, more precisely, Saturday morning.

'Good weekend?' he asked.

'Yes.'

Hunter waited for her to elaborate. Instead, she stated, 'that was an odd phone call.'

Hunter smiled. 'Half this business is odd phone calls.'

'And the other half?'

'The waiting in between.'

'But you're going to a séance, how exciting.'

'I'd invite you along though I'm not sure it's a plus one type of occasion.'

Hunter went to the filing cabinet and poured each of them an Irish Cream. As he did so he updated her on their Pyle problem and his canalside contretemps.

Liqueur in hand, Estella sat sipping in thought. 'And he admitted who he was?'

Hunter nodded. 'Never took responsibility for the moustache, though.'

She smiled. 'How did you manage it?'

'I flattered his ego a little.' Hunter swilled the silky liquid in his glass. 'And then, I trod all over it.'

Estella's smile grew, her lipstick a more sedate shade than the bright Friday night red. 'Have you informed Zora?'

'Not yet.'

'I can do that for you.'

Her handbag buzzed and she pulled out her phone.

'Feel free to take it,' said Hunter.

'No, no, it can wait.'

She put the device back in her bag and something in her face communicated to Hunter the phrase "spurned former lover". He had made that face often himself, also been on the other end of the line a time or two. Their Friday evening had still not been mentioned. Did she feel embarrassed by the situation, even guilty? Was there someone back in the capital she had betrayed? Hunter wondered if their tryst might ever be spoken of before she returned there. Or even repeated. Would she once more tie him to his own bed? He could think of worse places to be shackled to.

Estella had picked up a stray poster off his desk. 'Is this our little friend?'

'*The dachshund*, yes.'

'Poor little fellow. A friend of mine has one just like it. She's up here working at a gallery in Liverpool. That's where I spent the weekend, you see, at her place on the Wirral. She's a cousin of a P&P higher up. I thought I would do some investigating while I was there, root out any industry gossip I may have missed, but there wasn't much to share beyond prosecco.' She turned a wrist to inspect her watch. 'Anyway, must get on. Calls to make.'

'To Zora?'

'Amongst others. Ciao.'

22

Hunter's Monday morning had already been eventful, and dinnertime brought him not an hour's break but a text from Ahmed Said Ali. A meeting was hastily arranged and half an hour later they met in Piccadilly Gardens, joining the queue outside Instant Shawarma.

'Did you watch the United game?' Hunter asked, zipping his jacket closed. The open expanse of the Gardens left them vulnerable to a chilly breeze and Hunter regretted his deficiency of layers. Last week's unexpected warmth was no more than a memory. Hooded tops and jumpers would be an everyday item until the resurrection side of Easter.

'Don't talk to me about football,' Ahmed told him. 'I'm here on business.'

'The business of eating a kebab?'

'Should we ever get served.'

The line they were in had yet to move.

'If people are queueing round the block,' said Hunter, 'that must be a good sign.'

'Of what? That their service is painfully slow? I told you we should've gone down the road.'

'To Shawarma Chameleon?' asked Hunter. 'I've heard stories about what goes into their kebabs. It's not what you'd expect.'

A single man entered the premises and the line took a half-step forward.

'So,' Hunter began, 'what's this business of yours?'

Ahmed lowered his voice. 'Did you hear about that body on the Height?'

'What body?' Hunter replied in a hushed tone.

'You didn't hear?'

Hunter shrugged. It kept his joints limber in the cold.

'Don't you look at the news?' Ahmed continued. 'Don't you keep up with events?'

'What, obsess over humanity's infernal spiral? I don't see the point. Anything I need to know about, people will tell me. And anything I don't need to know about, people will tell me that an' all.'

Ahmed paused to consider if this contained a slight directed at himself, then pressed on. 'Whatever, mate, they found a body.'

'On the Height?'

'Yes.'

'Dead?'

'Of course, dead. You can find a live body anywhere you look.'

'I thought you were bored of all this shite?'

'I am,' replied Ahmed. 'Would I like to work on something else? Course I would. Something worthwhile, something positive.'

'Not United, then?'

'Piss off. I don't decide what we put out there. I just run around attending to the whims of my producer. As such, have a guess what was on that dead body?'

Hunter could have guessed but would likely have been wrong, meaning he would probably have to hazard further suppositions, dragging the suspense out even longer. He recalled Claude's earlier words and instead reverted to his shrugging.

'A card.'

Hunter paused a moment. 'Are we talking birthday or get well soon?'

Ahmed checked for eavesdroppers before speaking. 'One of your D-E-A-T-H cards.'

Each letter of the cults name was accompanied by a jabbed finger in Hunter's upper arm, and he went still as his mind raced. He had not taken the death part of the cult seriously and that may have been a mistake. Might this loss of life have been averted if he had made his Thursday evening appointment? Was there blood on Hunter's hands?

They took another step towards sustenance and Hunter watched his own breath leave his body then disappear in the frigid air. 'What do you want me to do?' he asked.

'Speak to the police. See if you can get more out of them than I did. All they gave me was the party line.'

'I'm not on good terms with my local constabulary. They consider me an amateur meddler.'

The pair were finally across the threshold of Instant Shawarma.

'Better an amateur meddler,' said Ahmed, 'than a member of the national broadcast media.'

'PC Lesley Trade speaking, how may I help?'

Hunter was back on New Mount Street, at his desk, feet up and boots off. A sizeable kebab lay in his stomach while half a dozen butterflies danced above it. Hunter's issues with authority were bringing on his nerves.

He had nothing to fear. He would keep his sentences short and to the point. He took a calming breath. 'I'm ringing about this body on the Height.'

'I see,' said the policewoman, and Hunter heard a familiar rustle in the background, a notebook opening. 'And you have information regarding this body, do you sir?'

'Not yet, that's rather why I'm ringing.'

There came a silence. No words, no breathing. Not even a rustle.

'Are you... *press*?' she asked eventually. The overemphasis on her final word was not a positive one.

'Not at all.'

'Right, well, as I've told the... *press*, the body of a ninety-three-year-old man was found dead in his home in the early hours of Sunday morning.'

Hunter himself was making notes: *93; Sunday morning; home.*

'And was there anything suspicious about it?'

'Suspicious, sir?'

'Yeah, you know, foul play an' all that.' Hunter recalled his conversation with Pat MacGuffin, the things the man had overheard. 'Poison,' Hunter suggested now, 'gunshot.'

'A poison gunshot?' PC Trade asked. 'That's a bit much, don't you think, sir? This is Salford, not a Le Carré novel.'

'Poi-son *comma* gun-shot.' Hunter enunciated. 'And to be clear, it would be more seventies era James Bond than Le Carré.'

The policewoman coughed. 'I have nothing further to tell you.'

Hunter took a moment to consider this cough. Was it a real cough or a subtle message to him, some signifier that her words did not contain the full truth? Maybe they were in a Le Carré novel.

'Nothing suspicious?' Hunter enquired. 'You're sure about that?'

'Sir, do I need to repeat the bit about him being ninety-three?'

'But you can't tell me how he died?'

'An autopsy will be performed in due course.'

'Right. But did he have anything strange on him?'

'Strange?' she asked.

'Yeah.' Hunter's biro hovered over the lined page as he awaited her answer.

'You mean like a funny hat?'

'No, I mean in his pockets.'

'A funny hat in his pockets?'

'No, a DEATH card.'

There was quiet once more. Hunter's patience had given out and he had shared more than he should. PC Trade coughed again, then Hunter heard a strange click on the line. Was he being recorded? Should he end the call now?

'Who is this?' she asked.

'I forget.'

'Do I know you?'

'No,' he told her. 'But I get that a lot.'

'Could I have your name please, sir?'

'My name?'

'Yes, you do have a name I take it.'

'Erm…' Hunter was flustered, his usually sharp mental reflexes blunted by proximity to the forces of control. 'Erm.'

'Is that first name or family, sir?'

'Neither. I'm Del.' From some forgotten corner inspiration had emerged. 'Del Shelaghaney.'

'Well, Mr Shelaghaney.'

'Please,' said Hunter, 'call me Del.'

'Well, Del, as I told you earlier, I've nothing further to tell you. But thank you for your call. I'm putting the phone down now.'

'Wait,' Hunter almost bellowed. 'Wait. Can I just ask one more thing?'

PC Lesley Trade sighed. 'Fine, go on then.'

'Thank you.' Hunter readied his final question and his biro. 'This funny hat the man had with him, could you describe it for me please?'

'Well?' said Ahmed Said Ali over the phone.

After speaking with the police Hunter had taken ten minutes to decompress, attempting to still his mind and heart rate. In the interests of professionalism, he abstained from a glass of Irish Cream though did allow himself a low-sugar ginger crunch. He then rang his contact to report the findings.

'Well,' began Hunter, 'the most I could get out of them was the fact this body of yours may or may not have been wearing a funny hat.'

Ahmed quietly processed this dramatic turn of events. 'What sort of funny hat?'

'That, like much else, is so far unclear.'

'And that's it? You didn't get anything new?'

'The funny hat is new.' There was an audible cry of exasperation in Hunter's ear, which he tried to drown out with his own voice. 'You do know the guy was ninety-three, don't you?'

'So?'

'Well at the risk of repeating myself, the guy was ninety-three. Why would this DEATH cult kill a man who was ninety-three?'

'Why would anyone kill anyone?' said Ahmed. 'Maybe this guy was about to expose them, maybe he had secrets.'

'To what,' Hunter asked, reaching for another ginger biscuit, 'long life?'

It was late afternoon, the sky outside darkening, the lights of the apartment across from Hunter's office on but nobody yet home. He had left his last piece of business, phoning the offices of P&P, to the end of the day. A receptionist patched him through to Zora Liu, and while holding muzak played, he prepared himself for the now familiar tones of New York disappointment.

'Mr Hunter, how nice to hear from you. Well-rested from your weekend off, I hope?'

'Did Estella call you?' he asked. If she had done, Hunter would not have to relive once more finding and losing Thornton Pyle for a second time.

'Estella is not really the calling type,' Zora told him. 'Unless she wants something, you won't hear from her. You have news for me?'

Hunter said yes.

'And is this news best received by a cactus and an open window?'

Again, Hunter answered in the affirmative.

He heard her chair scrape on the wooden floor. 'Give me thirty seconds.'

Even accounting for the low threshold of expectations that was your average Monday, Hunter did not regard this a good start to the week. Were he in a more positive mood he might count the narrowing down of leads as helpful: the aged corpse appeared a dead end; the borrower of Thornton Pyle's Height library haul had only brought him back to himself. On the other hand, Hunter did have a séance to look forward to. Yet if a future date with the past dead is the most notable event on your social calendar, how might one judge one's own existence?

In need of cheer and a pint, Hunter dropped in at The Bargemen to see if Vicky Park was working. She was not. He stayed for a lone drink, nodded to Joe Dimly, then headed home.

23

Tuesday was not merely cold but also wet, and rather than take the tram across the city Hunter decided to wait it out. Yet after ten minutes of early morning hoovering from above, his mind was swayed in a different direction. Hunter put on a hooded top, laced up his boots, added a waterproof coat to the ensemble and ventured forth.

Following his Sunday wrangle with Thornton Pyle, Hunter had taken to walking the canal tow paths on his way to and from New Mount Street. Experience told him the likelihood his quarry would reappear was slim, though as with the map the day before he had to feel as if he was doing something.

Hunter went to stand where the writer had made his dramatic escape two days previous, the exit onto Trumpet Street lying beyond not just the canal but now also a curtain of rain, the downpour poking holes in the water's surface. He put the memory behind him and moved on his way.

As Hunter passed under Oxford Street his views switched

from fashionable waterfront homes to brickwork back ends. Perspectives not conceived with public eyes or award nominations in mind. The city behind the city. Flat and functional, like the rear of a film set.

There were chimneys and large warehouse windows, old style lampposts and gates which led nowhere. Graffiti was sprayed over all in every colour imaginable. Tags and cartoons, slogans and scores. UNITED 5 CITY 0 was just about visible in fading red upon aged brick. A little further along and in recent light blue was UNITED 1 CITY 6. Then, in tall, green ragged capitals, TIMES ARE A-CHANGIN', with the later addition in smaller, neater script underneath, BE SURE TO PUT YOUR CLOCKS BACK.

Beyond Princess Street, Hunter came out briefly in the Gay Village then submerged again at the train station. Across the ring road, and he was in Ancoats leaving the canal and his hopes of running into Pyle behind. He canvassed the regenerated streets on his way to the office for sign of Doctor Dickie Shrub, swapping one futile task for another. On New Mount Street, Hunter found Connor O'Connor once more waiting for him under stairwell and hood.

Upstairs, with the door locked and his head uncovered, the bearded footballer spelled out his woes.

'What it is mate is, I think I might go back to the NFTs. I'm not sure this karma business is for me.'

Hunter was hanging up his waterproof coat and, on passing the filing cabinet, debated a morning Irish Cream. 'Why?' he asked, 'what happened?'

'You haven't heard?'

Hunter sat down without liqueur. 'Not the details.' He did not watch United highlights.

'Well, I do my best never to go in our penalty area if I can help it,' O'Connor began. 'Usually, I'm on the halfway line ready to attack.' As he talked the striker aimed his thumb at a smudge on his pristine trainers. 'As far as I'm concerned, the nearer I am to the opposition goal, the better my chance to score.'

'But?'

O'Connor's head shot up to give Hunter a hard stare, and Hunter, realising his faux pas, raised his hands in apology.

'What happened mate was, it's late in the game and they have a corner and somehow I end up defending. Maybe it was subconscious. Maybe I was thinking about this karma business and thought I'd help out at the back. Anyhow, I'm near the penalty spot and the corner comes in and I take my eye off it to watch their number 49, he's lurking on the edge, waiting, like I'd be doing. Anyhow, next thing I know I feel like someone's just slapped me on the backside and half a second later their fans are going crazy. I turn around and our keeper is flat on the grass and the ball's in our net. We kick off and straightaway the ref blows for full time.'

Hunter decided an Irish Cream was definitely in order and went to pour himself a tumbler full, offering one to O'Connor which was declined.

'I don't think you can judge the effects of karma on a few days,' Hunter said, on returning to his desk. 'This is a sizeable change in outlook. A long-term deal. Think of it like an injury. You have the corrective surgery, but you're not playing the next game, are you? This sort of business requires time and commitment.'

'Commitment isn't a problem, mate. It's time I don't think

I've got much of.' O'Connor's attention returned to his trainers. 'What it is is, we were training yesterday and the way the gaffer was talking, the formation he had us in, I think this Wednesday I'll be on the bench. I should be there now at the facility, but I rang in and told him I wasn't feeling well.'

Hunter sat back, considering the benefits a low-sugar ginger biscuit might provide his client.

'It's not been a good few days,' said the footballer, now scratching his beard, 'and it isn't just the training. Sunday morning, I woke up to find my bum cheek bruised and a picture of me all over the internet.'

Hunter paused. 'A picture of your bum cheek?'

'No, mate, worse. A picture of me after the game. In a restaurant. Smiling.'

Hunter put down his glass and opened his laptop to go online. He found the photograph easily enough, it being the first result to appear when searching the footballer's name.

He recognised the headline, UNITED STRIKER ENJOYS DRINK AT LAST CHANCE SALOON, and underneath was a portrait shot of O'Connor, glass of wine in hand, sat opposite an attractive blonde woman. An open-mouthed grin was on the footballer's face, and one buttock rested off his chair.

'I told you, didn't I. Every twat's a paparazzo, these days. Some arsehole at a nearby table must've took it and put it on Twitter and next thing you know it's everywhere. I was getting messages about it before I'd even ordered dessert.'

Hunter reached for his liqueur. 'This is unfortunate. And worse than that is things aren't gonna get any better.'

'What do you mean?'

'Everything is news nowadays, anything that'll get a click,

especially if, like this, the public is doing half the media's work for them. And do you know what's coming next?' Hunter put his feet on his desk. 'A 36-hour news channel.'

O'Connor stared, his face part horror, part mathematical confusion. 'How's that gonna work?'

Hunter shrugged and watched his client attempt to process this dire information.

'So, just because we don't win, I'm not allowed to smile, ever? Not even in the presence of a beautiful woman and a nineteen-pound mushroom?'

'This,' Hunter said swirling his glass, 'is the world we've created.'

The young man opposite him stood and made ready to leave, covering his head so only the bearded lower half was visible.

Hunter, though, had one last question. 'Before you go, just out of curiosity, was it the same bum cheek?'

With little on his agenda and several units of alcohol in his system, Hunter called his mother. He had not spoken to her in almost a week, had ignored her call on Sunday while tailing Pyle, and thought he might also catch up on any DEATH related gossip. She did not answer, and he did not leave a message but thirty seconds later she rang him back.

'Mum, how are you?'

'I've just had the fright of my life, that's how I am.'

'It was just your mobile, mum,' said Hunter, already considering a refill of his tumbler. 'I did advise against having *The Omen* theme as your ringtone.'

'It wasn't that.'

'What then?' Hunter's intrigue sensor kicked in. 'What's happened?'

'The Williamsons were round doing the windows.'

'The twins?' Hunter relaxed.

'Of course, the twins, why do you keep asking that?'

'Mum, what's so terrifying about having your windows cleaned?'

'Well, they wear matching overalls, don't they. Matchings caps, an' all. Dirty Old Town Twindow Cleaning printed on them. *No twindow too big, no twindow too small.*'

'Never mind the twindows,' said Hunter, 'how big are these caps?'

'Behave, will you. Their motto is on their business cards. Anyway, you wave to one as he goes up a ladder at the front then when you go into the kitchen you see the same vision go up a ladder at the back. It's not half confusing, I tell you. It's like that film.'

'*The Matrix*?' Hunter guessed.

'The one where all those fellas look the same.'

'*The Matrix*?'

'The one where all is not as it seems.'

'Mum, *The Matrix*.'

'*Boys from Brazil*, that's the one. I never could look at Gregory Peck the same way after that.'

Hunter headed for the filing cabinet. 'How's dad?'

'He's still having problems with the water people.'

'Has he managed to speak to anyone yet?' Hunter asked unscrewing the bottle; it was running dangerously low.

'Not yet,' Mrs Hunter said. 'The thing about the water people, son, is they're so difficult to get hold of. Anyway, what's all this about you being in The Red Herring?'

Hunter stopped. 'How do you know about that?'

'Claude's mum saw you. Is that where you get your fish from?'

Hunter brought the Irish Cream back to his desk and also two ginger crunches. 'They were prawns, but I wasn't there to shop.'

'Did you not think to call in on us?'

'Mum, it was work and I didn't really have the time. Plus, you might not've been in.'

'You could have rung to see.'

Hunter swigged straight from the supermarket brand bottle. 'Fair enough, I'm a terrible son. Feel free to share that with Mrs Horn.'

'Mrs Euphonium.'

'Fine, Mrs Euphonium. Anyhow, mum, on a hopefully unrelated note, do you know anything about this body they found over the weekend?'

'What are you suggesting?'

In his mind Hunter was headbutting the blank plaster wall. 'That Mrs Horn…'

'Mrs Euphonium.'

'That Mrs Euphonium might have a dark secret.'

'Nonsense. I've known her forty-odd years. Margaret wouldn't hurt a fly.'

'I wonder if her two dead husbands would agree.'

'Stop that. They both died of natural causes, as you well know.'

'And what about number three, how's he doing?'

'Jack? Ailing.'

Hunter checked the time on his watch and returned the

conversation to his original enquiry, the ninety-three-year-old corpse.

'Oh, that was poor Mr Roberts,' said Mrs Hunter, 'off Wickerman Close.'

'Do I know Mr Roberts?'

'Not any longer I should think.'

'What happened to him?' Hunter enquired.

'His daughter found him. It was his heart.'

'Not Mrs Horn, then?'

'Behave yourself.'

Hunter ate half a ginger biscuit then asked, 'did you know him at all?'

'Mr Roberts? Only in passing. He was quiet, kept himself to himself. What is it with you and the dead all of a sudden?'

'Well, mum, I'm off to a séance this afternoon, and I thought I'd get myself in the mood.'

'A séance? That'll be nice for you.'

'Really? I didn't think you believed in all that stuff.'

'I don't think I do, but then I don't really think about it all that much. I've seen ghosts in films and on telly, but never in the house. I'm not really sure what I'm supposed to be looking for.'

Hunter took a moment to think. 'Chills up the spine, maybe. Unexplained cold spots in normally warm rooms.'

'Sounds more like a reason to buy a draft excluder, if you ask me. But a séance, that might be fun. I never get invited to anything like that.'

'Well, mum, on the off chance these things are real, is there anyone you'd like me to say hello to while I'm there?'

Mrs Hunter went quiet a moment. 'Not really, no.'

24

Once more in the Ancoats area, Hunter trod his usual circuit – Cotton Street and Gun Street, Karl Marx Alley and Engels Passage – with no end in sight for his canine quest. At the former mill turned residential block where Delamere Forest and Richard Shrub lived, Hunter buzzed apartment 49 on the intercom and rode the elevator up to their floor. The door opened and before Hunter could take a step inside, an unknown woman loomed out at him. She was squat, grey haired and aged somewhere deep in the retirement zone.

The woman's lips did not move yet a voice addressed Hunter, 'I'm so glad you could make it,' and Ms Forest appeared. 'This is Madame Bickerstaff.'

Madame Bickerstaff allowed Hunter over the threshold and into an open plan main room only to circle him, moving in occasionally with a narrow-eyed stare.

'Child,' she stated, her inspection complete, 'you have about you an aura.'

Hunter had not been called "child" for nearly forty years. The "aura", he blamed on his aftershave.

'Let us have a sniff,' the older woman lunged toward him nostrils first. 'Heavens, such a stink. By what name does the foul beast go?'

'Artifice.'

'Sounds about right.'

'Bickerstaff?' Hunter asked, the name sounded familiar. 'Do you have that place across from the indoor market? Above the vape shop?'

He would notice the sign often – *Futures, Pasts Told Presently by Madame Bickerstaff* – it was weather-beaten and out of sync among the pristine modernity.

'Yes, child. Since the year nineteen hundred and seventy-five have I occupied that space. Not that I was above the vape shop then, mind. Over slow time have I seen that unit barter in many transitory curios: Scientology, video rentals, hessian. All of which I have tried, yet none could I quite get along with.'

Hunter enquired how she felt about the vape shop.

'Much the same.'

The medium began to set up the dining table, clearing away teacups and saucers to a breakfast counter, and Delamere Forest switched the conversation to her missing dachshund.

'Richard told me there was a sighting of Doctor Dickie Shrub over the weekend.'

Hunter noticed his secret client hanging back in the kitchen area, still in his dentist whites. The two men were introduced as if they were strangers, and Hunter caught a whiff of something surgical as they shook hands. Shrub put a little extra force into this greeting, while Hunter tickled the dentists palm with a rogue middle finger.

'The Doctor looked well,' Hunter told Ms Forest. 'Sprightly even. I'm quietly confident you'll have him home soon.' He turned to Madame Bickerstaff; she had in her hand a candle as round as her head. 'You can't get in touch with dogs as well, can you?'

The old woman placed the candle in the tables centre. 'Only dead ones, child.'

Hunter took a moment to inspect the Forest/Shrub abode. It was minimally furnished and tastefully decorated. Few prints, fewer plants, and was that a set of Pyles on the bookshelf? The apartment's shell had retained much of its former life – exposed brickwork, metal joists, floor to ceiling beams. Hunter wondered how many twelve-year-olds had lost a finger on this very spot to some spinning mule?

Out on the balcony, Hunter was greeted by an unimpeded view of a similar balcony across the street. He was about ten feet away from a man dressed as a U-boat commander and smoking a pipe. Hunter went back inside.

The medium had finished arranging the table and was speaking to Dela Forest. 'Now, you say you heard noises at a door?'

'Yes, it was the bathroom door in the main bedroom.' Ms Forest led them through a corridor to the haunted site, and the quartet assembled in silent expectation. For five minutes they stood, staring at the ominous oaken rectangle and heard not a sound. Madame Bickerstaff opened the door, and slowly they entered.

In the tiled room was a walk-in shower, an abundance of

beauty products, and a tub little bigger than an eye bath. Hunter listened for anything out of the ordinary, picking up naught but the hum of a neighbour's extractor fan.

The medium's nose began to wrinkle. 'There is an odour, is there not?

Beyond the dentist's sterile funk Hunter smelled nothing, but then maybe he lacked the imagination for this type of endeavour. If Hunter had experienced strange noises and smells so close to a lavatory, his first call would be to a plumber.

Unmolested by angry wraiths they returned to the living space. The lights were turned off, the blinds drawn, the U-boat commander shut out. Sat around the table, the ill-matched foursome joined hands.

'Nooooooooow,' Madame Bickerstaff spread this single syllable over at least three seconds, 'we must first reach my Molly.'

'Molly?' asked Dela.

'My guide, dear, in the spirit realm. My link to the other side. You say the soul we wish to banish is one of the unhappy, the unfulfilled, the unwashed?'

'Yes, I've been reading about them, how they used to live, the conditions, the squalor. It's horrifying, and yet oddly compelling.'

The medium nodded. 'It is one thing to have their plight atop your bookshelf. Quite another for them to be revolting in your en suite. My Molly shall be a useful bridge in this matter. She too knew unfulfillment.'

Hunter had so far remained a quiet observer, but this piqued his interest. 'In what way?' he asked.

The old woman turned to him. 'Molly Mavis was a song and

dance girl from many, many years ago.'

'I used to perform,' Dela offered.

'Yes, dear, I suspected you had a touch of the theatricals, but of Molly Mavis you will not have heard. Her star did not shine bright for long. Though she did perform at the 1965 Royal Variety Performance.'

'Oh my God,' said Dela, 'did she meet the Queen?'

'She would have, dear, had they not removed her from the presentation line. While our beloved Lizzie was busy with Peter Sellers, a man came along and deemed poor Molly too twitchy to meet a reigning monarch.'

'Too twitchy?'

'My Molly had embraced the swinging sixties, whereas the London Palladium had not.'

'Would it be rude to ask how she died?' Hunter asked.

Madame Bickerstaff's gaze narrowed in on him. 'You are a direct one, child.'

'Life's too short to be otherwise,' Rich Shrub put in, glancing at his watch. They were his first words since Hunter had arrived and the medium gave him a stare as if to issue a curse, then returned to Hunter.

'If know you must, she travelled to America to rebuild her career, to seek fortune and fame.' The old woman's eyelids began to close. 'Alas, her first week in New York and on the very cusp of stardom, she was involved in a most terrible accident on Broadway.'

'Was she knocked down?' Dela Forest enquired. 'I was almost knocked down on Broadway while on holiday. Those taxi drivers are a menace.'

'No, dear, no,' said the medium, eyes open again. 'Hers was

not a road accident. It was opening night, the zenith of all she had worked for. A noted playhouse sold out, an audience full of the great and good for a production that would run for a decade. My Molly was excited though not without nerves and seeking to calm herself, she took a little something. Perhaps, a little too much something. On the final number before intermission, the poor girl got carried away and tapped herself clean into the band pit.'

'Oh my God,' said Dela. 'That sounds awful.'

'By all accounts, dear, yes. On her way down she took out half the brass section.'

Madame Bickerstaff had barely finished her last syllable when her head snapped left, and she began to whisper into thin air. 'I am sorry Molly. I know it's no laughing matter, Molly. Let's not do anything drastic, hmm?'

It was now Hunter's turn to appraise her, and he watched as the medium returned her attention back to those gathered.

'She is very sensitive, my Molly. Every day people wish to speak to the dead and yet no one ever asks to speak to her. It does nothing for her moods.' The old woman's head snapped away once more. 'What? Oh, Molly. No. No, Molly. No. This really isn't the time, Molly. Please, Molly. Fine, Molly. Fine. I shall at least enquire.' Her head centred again. 'This is highly irregular, and I do apologise, but if none of you should mind, and at no extra charge, my Molly would like to sing for us?'

With no one brave enough to turn down a disgruntled spirit's song, Madame Bickerstaff looked to the left and began swaying. Dela Forest stared into empty space and smiled. 'She has such a beautiful voice.'

This was a surprise to Hunter as, in a failure of the renovation's soundproofing, all he could make out was the nearby ring road. He took in the faces of those around him. The medium, lost in the moment. Dela Forest, head inclined and beaming. Rich Shrub, glaring at Hunter with an expression half in disbelief, and half on the time.

Hunter felt strangely neutral. Did he believe? In an echo of the television of his nineties youth, did he *want* to believe? He raised his eyebrows, an act the dentist greeted with heavily rolled peepers. No more than half a second later, a teacup fragmented on bare brick wall.

'Molly!' Madame Bickerstaff roared, ripped from her reverie. 'That was a perfectly good cup.'

Hunter studied the scene: the breakfast bar where the cup had been placed; the red brick now stained brown; bone china pieces scattered on an empty dog bed. All their hands were still joined on the table. If it was a trick, he could not see how the old woman had pulled it off.

'I do apologise,' said the medium. 'Molly can be quite temperamental if things are not just so.' Her silvery dome flicked left. 'What is it, Molly?' Her eyes turned to Hunter. She began to nod and not to him. 'Yes, Molly, yes. I quite understand.'

Her head straightened, and she cleared her throat to address Hunter, then extended a nicotine-yellow finger his way. 'I'm afraid *you* must go.'

'Why me?' he asked, more than a little put out. A museum café last week. A séance this. Where would Hunter be ejected from next?

'My Molly cares not for your Artifice.' The mediums attention switched to Rich Shrub. 'You also must leave.'

'What?' the dentist protested.

'There is something about you my Molly does not like.'

'But I'm not wearing any aftershave.'

'That,' Madame Bickerstaff told him, 'might well be the problem.'

25

Banished to Ancoats streets with an odd client, Hunter felt ill at ease. If he hoped Rich Shrub would return to his practice, then the man showed no sign of hurrying off to inflict mouth-based discomfort on anyone. At least Shrub had put his long coat back on over his dental attire, for Hunter would not wish to be seen strolling the cobbles with a man dressed in surgical whites. This did not feel like a pint in a pub moment and to ditch him was perhaps rude so, not without reservations, Hunter invited Shrub back to New Mount Street.

How curious that less than a week ago this man had been following Hunter, leaving strange notes with postal workers, and fearful of being seen at this office, yet was now making himself comfortable in the only other chair.

'Do you really think we're haunted, Mr Hunter?' Rich Shrub asked, both coats now removed and folded over the seatback, shirt sleeves rolled up to his elbows.

Hunter was at the filing cabinet breaking the seal on a fresh bottle of supermarket brand Irish cream.

'Well, I'm no expert, but I don't think it's a clear-cut yes or no question. I mean, outside of Hollywood and your excitable TV shows, is there really even a way to measure these things, all this so-called paranormal activity? I think it's less about what a person finds in a situation and more what they bring with them. Openness, pre-conceived ideas, good old-fashioned gullibility. One person's proof of demonic presence is another's reason to buy a draft excluder.'

'Yes, but how do you explain the teacup?'

Hunter could not, it was quite the conundrum. Bar the local phenomena that was Metrolink time, he had never before witnessed the unexplainable. His current theory was some tiny spring-loaded device attached when the medium had cleared the table. Hunter shrugged and passed his visitor a tumbler of silky, cheap liqueur.

The man took a mouthful, then asked, 'is this new?'

Beyond the bottle still in Hunter's hands there was little in the office which could be described that way, and he turned from pouring himself a glass to find Shrub admiring the Pyle proof which had been on his desk since Friday.

'Yeah. I don't think it's out yet.'

'I find it weird, all this about him being missing,' stated the dentist.

Hunter did not wish to discuss his ongoing case and was silent. Shrub did not pursue the topic, concentrating instead on the book in his hand.

'*At the Rising of the Cock*,' he read aloud. 'What's it about?'

'Not a clue.' Hunter had not even cracked the paperback's ample spine. 'I've never really got along with him.'

'If I'm honest, he's probably my favourite writer,' said Shrub, leafing through the opening pages. 'I love all his novels.'

Hunter remembered the set of Pyles back in the dentist's apartment. 'Even *Adolf and the Bulge*?' he asked.

'Especially *Adolf and the Bulge.* I found it very moving.'

Hunter held back from asking in what direction. 'Well, you can add that to your bookshelf if you like. I won't be reading it. And you'll save me a trip to the charity shop.'

'Thank you, that would be great.' Shrub took another mouthful of booze. 'I might even get him to sign it. If he comes back, that is.'

Hunter was halfway to his desk but stopped. "Comes back" seemed a bizarre choice of words. Where did this man believe Pyle had gone? Was their conversation about to veer into alien territory? The dentist did not on the face of it appear the alternative belief type but then so few people actually wore tin foil hats these days.

'"Comes back"?' Hunter asked Shrub.

'Although, what he'll think about me having a free copy is another matter. I'll still buy the hardback when it's out. I do like a nice hardback.'

'Fuck hardbacks,' said Hunter, 'what do you mean "if he comes back"?'

The dentist froze, mouth open, confused either by the question or Hunter's coarse outburst. Hunter took a step toward his guest, who finally answered. 'Well, he came into my surgery.'

'What?'

'Yes, that's what I meant about it being weird for him to be missing. All this talk about him having disappeared and then there he is.'

'What?'

'In my big chair.'

'Forget your big chair, start at the beginning.'

Shrub took a slug of liqueur. 'Well, he had molar pain. I took a look and it needed to come out, so out it came. I told him to call back in if he had any more trouble. He said he was staying nearby.'

Hunter drained his Irish Cream and returned to the filing cabinet for a refill. 'And when was all this?'

'Yesterday afternoon. He was in my reception at the same time I was on the phone to you. He was in a lot of pain and wanted an emergency appointment. I was going to pass, but then recognised the name and managed to squeeze him in on my break. It's funny really. My favourite writer, one minute nowhere to be found, the next I'm rooting about in his mouth.'

'Did he say much?' asked Hunter, back behind his desk.

'You mean other than, 'aahh'?' the dentist grinned,

Hunter glared at Shrub and the man's smile disappeared.

'Sorry, industry joke. No, he didn't speak much, and I didn't press him. It isn't professional, really. You want the patient to be at ease. You don't want to give them flashes of Laurence Olivier waving a sharp implement around. If I'm honest, I'd hoped to talk with him when we were finished, to tell him how much I enjoy his work, but the woman who met him afterwards didn't seem in a good mood.'

'Woman?' Hunter leaned forward. 'What woman?'

Shrub took another mouthful from his glass. 'She was out in reception. Ready to spirit him away. I understand, of course. He must be a busy man. The pressure he must be under at the moment. He must have a lot on his mind.'

'Never mind his mind,' said Hunter. 'This woman, what was she like?'

The dentist paused to collect the memory. 'Tall. Attractive. Well-spoken. She was a redhead.'

Rich Shrub left New Mount Street under the weight of a heavy paperback and the hope his apartment was now free from spectres of a bygone underclass. Hunter's interest in the séance had lessened and he sat with another glass of Irish cream, a stack of ginger biscuits and too many questions.

How many tall, attractive, well-spoken redheads were there in this city? And how many of them might take an interest in Thornton Pyle's dental care? If this was Estella de Fenestrate, someone who had not found the time to call Zora Liu with news of Hunter and the authors canalside encounter, could the thought of telling Hunter she had now located Pyle just as easily have slipped her mind?

It was possible. Estella had hired him, though it was P&P who were footing the bill. He was an outside contractor employed to complete a task and that task seemed complete. To whom would the act of informing him his labour was no longer required fall? Zora? Estella? The unpaid intern?

Estella was in Shrub's surgery with Pyle over twenty-four hours ago, yet when Hunter had called Zora late yesterday, she had heard nothing. Did the wheels of publishing turn so slow? Surely, he pondered, someone should have contacted him by now. Surely incompetence was not as widespread as all that. Which left Hunter with the dread thought that no one beyond

Pyle, Estella, Rich Shrub and now himself knew the writer had been found. He sat back, dipped his biscuit in the liqueur, and tried to piece together the previous day's dinnertime.

Hunter had been speaking with Shrub on the phone while Thornton Pyle was in the dentist's reception wanting an appointment. At the same time, Estella had arrived at Hunter's office and soon after had received a call she did not take. Was this Pyle with news of some impending extraction? Had Estella gone straight to him after leaving Hunter? Had Pyle been having surgery while he and Ahmed Said Ali queued for a kebab? Hunter finished his biscuit and reached for another.

What did he really know of Estella de Fenestrate? They had spent an evening together; he had seen her naked and they had indulged in a round of kinky sex. But beyond that…

Hunter knew Zora Liu's opinion of her. Maybe he should ring the editor and see if she was now aware of the good news. Glass in hand, feet on his desk, landline pressed to an ear, he called P&P.

The editor was busy in a meeting and Hunter trod carefully with the unpaid intern.

Was this meeting regarding Thornton Pyle? No, it was not.

Had Estella de Fenestrate been in contact? No, she had not.

Did the unpaid intern know if the missing writer had been located? The unpaid intern was not unpaid to speculate on such matters.

Hunter left a message for Zora to phone him if there were any developments and rang off. He put down his drink, grabbed his jacket and some ginger biscuits and left the office, strolling down Ludgate to Old Mount Street and the Angel Meadow park.

It did not escape his notice that an hour or so ago he was in a finely appointed home ready to commune with the dead, only to now find himself seated on damp grass covering the former burial ground for thousands of the city's industrial poor. In an area Friedrich Engels once termed 'Hell upon Earth', Hunter was deep in his own infernal abyss.

Had he been duped? Hunter did not like the idea of being used as an instrument in another's power game. A pawn to be teased, directed, and sacrificed on a board he could not see. And to admit this was the case would be to admit how easily he could be manipulated. How easily his head was turned by money, velvet tones, and a pretty face. Was his father correct? Was Hunter really nothing more than a hired lackey to those with more money than sense?

Of course, Hunter was an idiot; this he admitted, this he embraced. But Hunter believed he was his own idiot, not someone else's. In the face of mounting evidence, how much truth remained in that belief? All Hunter could say for sure was he was in a bind. The next step, if indeed there even was one, felt beyond him.

And so, Hunter searched for distraction in the world before him, and for a ginger crunch from his coat pocket. Anything to take his mind off this predicament. Hunter munched and watched the handful of people around the park on a chilly October afternoon.

There was the aged tour group led around by a flat-capped man stopping to point at walls L.S. Lowry may have sat upon while making preliminary sketches. A lycra-clad blonde jogging on the spot, cordless white earbud at each pierced lughole. There was the handful of millennials tight rope walking a height of three feet between skeletal poplars and a park bench philosopher sharing his nuggets with the squirrels. Then there was the woman pushing a cart and emptying the bins, her yellow Hi-Viz vest bearing the words MUNICIPAL WASTE.

Hunter, cross legged upon the grass and half-chewed biscuit in his mouth, gasped as if drenched in ice water as inspiration flooded his brain cells, then immediately began to choke.

Bin, he thought, as he tried to cough ginger mush from the wrong passageways. *Waste*.

The people in the park were now watching him. The aged tour group, the lycra blonde, the acrobatic millennials. Hunter did not care for the way in which the lady with the cart brandished her brush and decided on a quick exit. He stood, brushed the accumulated nature from his jeans and headed back to the office at a spluttering trot.

On New Mount Street, coughing now abated, he was through the heavy doors with ease and up the stairs two at a time. Barely thirty seconds had elapsed between Hunter's stifled eureka moment and returning to his desk, to delve his hands deep in his own rubbish.

As Hunter only emptied his wastebin when the contents had spread to the surrounding floor, he easily found the map he had launched at Claude a day ago. Hunter unfolded the paper ball on his desk, pressed out creases with a fist, and stared at the printed area.

Rich Shrub had told him Pyle was staying near his dental surgery on Peter Street, which occupied a short stretch centrally on Hunter's map. Depending on one's definition of near, two of the hotels he had circled were on Peter Street itself and several more in easy distance. The two on Peter Street stood out as they just so happened to be of the higher star, higher priced variety.

Hunter had thought it odd an author of Thornton Pyle's stature would have been staying at The Snooze Inn. The man did not seem the budget type. These two offerings felt much more his style. Yet what was Hunter to do with this information? He might pass his evening in these hotel's restaurants or bar areas, spending his ill-gotten gains while on the lookout for Pyle. But Pyle would surely recognise him, and the game be given away.

There was the question of whether to ring Estella and if so, what to say. Perhaps call under the pretence of a drink or subtle hint at further coupling, then drop in the news Pyle had been spotted visiting a dentist.

No, that would not do. Hunter did not wish to tip off Estella that he might be on to her, if indeed there was anything to be on to. He would not ring Estella, at least not yet. A plan was forming. One which would require preparation, patience, and a clear head.

26

It took until the next morning for Hunter to be ready. Phone in hand, he allowed himself a few steadying breaths before proceeding. Estella answered on the third ring.

'Good morning,' she said. 'Are you my alarm call today?'

'Where are you?' Hunter asked.

'I'm at the hotel, why?' The question had startled the agent, as was his intention.

'The Mamucio?' Hunter could see the building from where he stood, in a disused doorway on a wet side street. It was raining when he left his flat thirty minutes ago but had stopped. Estella was not given the chance to answer, when Hunter fired off a further enquiry. 'How is it?'

'Expensive,' she said, relaxing, 'but so very worth it.'

Hunter looked at the hotel and wondered which of the windows was hers. 'We've had a development,' he dropped in casually and waited for her response.

Estella de Fenestrate was careful as she spoke. 'What sort of development?'

'A possible sighting.'

'Of Thorn?' Her utterance dripped with concern, either for the writer's safety or whatever scheme the pair were caught up in.

'You were expecting Lord Lucan riding Shergar down Deansgate?'

The laughter in Hunter's ear sounded false as commuters passed in front of him, left to right on their way to work having arrived at nearby Piccadilly Station. Eight hours from now they would pass going the opposite way and Hunter hoped not to still be by this dirty door when they did.

'Pyle was spotted Monday afternoon,' he told Estella, 'On Peter Street.'

Her laughter ceased. 'Doing what?'

'My tip-off wasn't sure, he disappeared again. But looking at where this was, I've narrowed it down to three possibilities.'

'Which are?'

Hunter cleared his throat. 'A hair salon, a dental surgery, or the army recruitment office.'

If he had expected a reaction to the middle suggestion, he was disappointed.

'I see,' came the calm response. 'And what do you propose to do about this?'

'Well, I thought I might canvas the hotels around that way. Sit in their bar areas. Soak up some 4- or 5-star ambience. Slowly chew an overpriced snack.'

'And you intend to do this now?'

'No,' replied Hunter, 'I've only just had my breakfast. Plus, there's been a different sighting. Our canine friend. A jogger saw him round Ancoats, and that was less than an hour ago so I'm heading there first before the trail goes cold.'

'Riiiiiiiight.' Estella drew the lone syllable out while she thought.

'I shouldn't be longer than a couple of hours, though,' Hunter told her. 'I could give you a call when I'm done, maybe we could stake these places out... to-geth-er?'

Hunter filled the last three syllables with notes of carnal implication and Estella answered positively. Arrangements were made, and their call ended. Hunter flicked his phone into silent mode and fixed his attention on the hotel's sole entrance, waiting for the familiar flame hair to appear.

As tempted as Hunter had been to make the call last night, he also knew the evening dark would not have helped his pursuit; following a woman in such circumstances was liable to find him the wrong side of a jail cell. He also wanted time to phone the two hotels, enquiring at reception if they had guests by the name of Thornton Pyle, Stephen Pole or Stefan Ple. He had made three separate calls to each, changing his voice and throwing in a few fresh aliases: Burgess Anthony; Wilson H Anthony; and Dave.

Hunter had then rooted through the cardboard box in his office, choosing clothes with care, assembling outfits which would not stand out and could be easily interchanged. His first was a bucket hat in subdued blue and his trusty reversible jacket, currently in its beige format. The plain grey T-shirt underneath bore no slogans and no brand. His jacket could switch to navy in seconds and the inside pocket contained his cap. He was prepared for a long pursuit.

Yet Hunter knew he could only prepare so much. Estella de Fenestrate might simply have phoned Pyle, ordering him to stay in his room or check out and move elsewhere. Hunter, however, had gambled she did not quite trust this man to take care of such an everyday action. That, as in Hunter's bedroom only half a week past but which now felt like an eternity, she would feel compelled to take charge.

No more than ten minutes had elapsed before Hunter was proven correct. Estella appeared in the Mamucio's arched doorway, pulling her thick green coat around her and exchanging words with a liveried doorman. She checked her phone and set off.

Hunter remained on the opposite side of the road, passing behind bus shelters and hurrying beyond a parked double decker. He was slightly ahead of Estella and watched her pass a supermarket and a coffee shop while he waited for the lights to change. As she made the left turn onto Portland Street, Hunter was still waiting to go. Before the traffic had fully stopped, he darted across the street, joining Estella on the lefthand pavement, and scanning rears of heads looking for hers. He found her with ease.

As he trailed the agent, Hunter once more attempted to piece the situation together. At what point did she know Pyle's whereabouts? Had the writer contacted her when in need of dental care? Or did she find out beforehand? Did she know over the weekend? Did she know while Hunter and her were together on Friday evening?

Or, and this was the theory Hunter was leaning towards, had she known from the beginning? Was Estella on the other end of Pyle's phone conversation at the studio prior to his disappearance? What conspiracy had the two been involved in? And where did Hunter fit?

The Bob Dylan quote from his office wall came back to him now:

And you, you just believe anythin' you hear,
Some kinda all you really agree with you can cheer.

Why had he put his faith in Estella de Fenestrate? Because of the way she looked and spoke? Because of her status and education? Or because their ideas had chimed with one another? But did they, really? Could Estella have simply been telling Hunter what he wanted to hear, what would enable her to twist him to her own needs? Had she been playing him like a cheap harmonica?

A bum note on Aytoun Street brought Hunter out of this reverie and he saw a tram gliding towards the intersection and sounding its horn. He did not wish to get stuck and lose Estella, but equally did not want to get too close and give himself away. It was a tricky calculation. He tried to balance the situation just right, yet his timing was off and together with a gaggle of office workers heading for their desks he ended up trapped while the tram passed. His luck was doubly out in that the tram was a double, and while the four carriages slowly trundled by Hunter began to sweat despite the coolness of the day.

With the Metrolink gone Hunter sped over the road to search for Estella but could see no sign. No red hair, no green coat. Through a restaurant window, he checked breakfast diners, those seated at tables or stood at the bar. Still no Estella. But in his peripheral vision, he caught a flash of red and green and focused his attention. It was Estella and yet not Estella, she was too small. Was she about to enter some tiny doorway through which he could not follow?

Then his brain clicked into gear. She was not in the restaurant but in the window. In the glass. A reflection from across the street. She must have crossed as he waited on the tram. Hunter kept her in view and at the next set of lights, followed her over to the other side.

They were skirting the edges of Chinatown, every other shop a noodle joint. At a newsagent, Estella ducked inside while Hunter leaned against a wall two units away eyeing the sandwich board headline which blared: END IS AT HAND BELIEVER REFUSES TO DENY FUTURE CITY BREAK.

As Hunter stood, he watched pockets of fans with matching scarves in town for that evening's United game, a European group clash. They were out early to survey the city and show their colours, and Hunter thought about negotiating some form of trade. A scarf would add an extra layer to his disguises not to mention his level of warmth.

Yet the time this would take might cause him to lose Estella. And if he should bump into Claude, out on his postal round, Hunter would be further delayed and have much to explain. Instead, he settled on changing hats and turning his jacket inside out. He had gone from beige and pale blue to navy and green in but a moment.

Estella emerged from the newsagents with a pack of cigarettes. She paused a moment, removing one and lighting up before loosing a grey cloud into the air and moving on. Estella crossed the lights of Princess Street but remained on Portland.

She seemed in little hurry and was taking the least complicated route, sticking to main roads. Someone more experienced with the city might zig zag the backstreets or take the waterways, but not her. A right turn put the agent on Oxford Street where she seemed to be confirming Hunter's theory. Hotel one would be appearing soon.

Separately but together, they approached St. Peter's Square and its tram lines before which Estella crossed. Oxford Street was now Peter Street, and she was in front of the Highland hotel, and still smoking. Hunter had remained on the Central Library side of the road and was waiting for her to stub out the cigarette and make a move into the grand baroque edifice. Yet all she gave it was a brief glance as she passed. Not the Highland, then. Over Mount Street and in the distance, Hunter could see the building that housed Rich Shrub's dental surgery. Hotel two was only minutes away.

Beyond the building that had once been Discotheque Royale, Estella's flame hair was extinguished. She must have turned left. Hunter waited for a taxi to move off and then hurried across.

He peered around the corner and saw Estella finish her cigarette then walk into The Georgian. Hunter waited fifteen seconds then approached, but at the entrance, nerves stopped him in his tracks.

Modelled on a sandstone palazzo, the building that housed the hotel had long been a favourite of his father. A city landmark with ties to radical movements, a venue for notorious gigs, yet now reduced to 5-star status and so disowned by the old man. In an echo of Estella's parents' umbrage at her attending the wrong class of theatre production, if it became known Hunter frequented such places as this there was every chance his father, no matter the man's lax attitude to where he bought his fish, might label him some manner of Iscariot type figure. Enter, however, Hunter must.

He took a deep breath and sensed a hint of Estella de Fenestrate's recent cigarette. He could no longer see the smoke, but the nicotine stink was clear. Hunter readied himself, he could not know what awaited him inside, or how all this would play out. He counted to three then stepped forward.

With one foot across the threshold Hunter was struck neither by guilt nor a doorman's palm. Instead, standing hands on hips and barring further incursion was Estella de Fenestrate herself.

The agent stared at him. 'What *are* you doing?'

Hunter was thrown for only a second, then reversed the situation. 'Maybe I should ask what *you're* doing?'

He watched her face carefully. Her eyes did not a blink, nor even narrow.

'Did you follow me here?'

'Or,' Hunter mused, 'did you lead me?'

'Must you answer my questions with other questions?'

'Is this where Pyle's been hiding out?'

Her mouth fell open, her head inclined. Neither movement overwhelming evidence of guilt.

'What *are* you talking about, Hunter?'

'Don't play dumb, Estella. I know. *I know.*'

Was there a tightening in her expression? She was a confident woman, with no particular tell or nervous tic to give her away. The pair were in the reception area now and to anyone watching would appear a couple having some restrained difference of opinion.

'You're behaving very oddly,' she said.

Hunter smiled. 'Odd is as odd does. Tell me, is his tooth any better?'

'How do you…' she stopped. Her mask had slipped if only for a moment.

'I have my ways,' he told her. 'I might be an idiot, but I do have certain talents.'

The question of talents was a spurious one and Hunter was glad she did not require a full list. Yet idiot that he was, had Hunter not given Delamere Forest a tale of undead mill workers she would never have hired Madame Bickerstaff. Had Hunter not asked to be present at the séance, he would never have then been asked to leave and felt compelled by a politeness he did not in fact possess to invite Rich Shrub back to his office. And if Rich Shrub had never entered Hunter's office, *At the Rising of the Cock* would still be taking up valuable space on his desk.

Estella watched him, considering perhaps stepping outside for another cigarette. 'You should come up,' she said eventually.

They were in an elevator, and then a corridor where she opened room 49 with a key card. Inside waited Thornton Pyle.

The writer had been sat on the bed, his coat on, his bags packed. He stood when the door opened, gesticulating. 'What is this about, Estella? What is this panic?' Pyle wore no hat or moustache, and upon seeing Hunter he froze. 'Bingsley? What's he doing here?'

'Be quiet, Thorn. Let me think.' Estella paced over to the ample window and looked out on Peter Street below.

Pyle glared at Hunter, then followed her. 'You've brought *him* here?'

'Don't blame me for this mess.' She turned on the author, a long pale manicured digit poking him in the sternum. '*You're* the one who went to a bloody museum, *you're* the one who went to a bookshop and a fucking dentist.'

Pyle stumbled back. 'But my tooth. My tooth. It needed attention.'

'You should have asked me to get you something. You should have asked reception to get you something.'

'But I was in pain.'

'We're all in pain, Thorn. It's the human condition. I told you to bloody well stay put.'

'You still haven't answered me Estella, what's *he* doing here?'

Hunter, unsure of his part in all this and having adopted a casual pose by the closed bathroom door, was asking himself the same question. Events had moved faster than anticipated. He had thought through the following and observing sections of his morning, yet not the confronting. He had not planned on confronting anybody; it was not really his style. Hunter's intention was to gather evidence and present it to Zora Liu and P&P, at which point he would be done with the case and could get back to dogs, death cults and misfiring Premier League footballers.

Estella was once more staring out of the window. 'He's here, Thorn, because he knows.'

Pyle's head swivelled from his agent to Hunter and then back again. 'You told him? I must say, Estella, this is…'

Here Hunter felt the urge to step in. 'The thing is she didn't need to tell me. I worked it all out.'

The pair looked at him; Estella in amusement, Pyle in something approaching apoplexy. The author was stood between the desk and the bed and Hunter squeezed past him on his way to the minibar.

'Neither of you are what I'd call professional,' he said crouching to inspect the chilled goods. Hunter removed a chocolate bar and a tiny bottle of luxury Irish cream, took a mouthful of each, and swallowed. 'Feel free to invoice me for these,' he said to no one in particular.

Thornton Pyle had returned to sitting on the bed and was regarding his brogues.

Estella grinned at Hunter. 'And just what is it you think you've worked out?' she asked.

Hunter gave himself a shot of miniature liqueur, the higher alcohol content of which scorched his throat on its way down. 'A conspiracy.'

'It was her idea,' Pyle blurted.

'Stop panicking, Thorn. He's not the police. A conspiracy to do what?'

Hunter shrugged. 'Whatever it is conspiracies do.' He took a second bite of costly chocolate.

'If you even knew what you were trying to prove,' said Estella, 'you could prove nothing.'

'It was her idea.'

'Thorn!'

'I wanted to apologize.' Pyle's head was raised as he spoke directly to Hunter. 'Not that I wanted to do it on daytime television, yet I wished it over with. I want my life back. I enjoy my life.'

'But someone stopped you from apologising, didn't they?'

Hunter asked. 'Someone phoned you at the studio, while you were in make up?'

Pyle nodded, eager to confess all.

'This is nonsense, Thorn,' said Estella. 'You're a grown man.'

Pyle turned to his agent. 'You shouldn't have put me in this situation, Estella.'

'You put yourself in this situation. I don't control your mouth, and I wasn't the one who put you on the fucking radio.'

'But you allowed it to happen,' said Hunter.

She laughed. 'It is flattering you believe I have such power, Mr Hunter.'

'It was her idea.'

'Stop saying that, Thorn,' Estella snapped, then fixed her gaze on Hunter. 'A situation arose, and I managed it accordingly using the tools of modern life to our advantage, you see.'

Hunter thought he caught a slight emphasis on the word 'tool'.

'You mean, according to how best make the situation work for you?' he asked. 'For promotional purposes? For marketing his new book?'

'I told her I did not need this,' Pyle pleaded, 'did not want this. *At the Rising of the Cock* stands up perfectly well on its own.'

Hunter took another slug of booze. The bottle was nearly empty already. 'One thing I'm not clear on,' he began, 'is why you were at Larkhill Place?'

Pyle's head angled slightly. 'The Victorian street?'

Hunter nodded.

'That was research purposes for my next novel. The prequel

to *The Life and Grime of Frank Reactionary*. It's to be set in that era. I must say, it's more a novella, really. The working title is *Workhouse to the Alehouse – A Life in Two Swift Halves*.'

'And when's that out?'

'Likely, next year.'

'Any chance of a signed copy when's it's done?'

Pyle almost blushed. 'I think that could be arranged.'

'Great,' said Hunter. 'It's always handy to have spare bog roll round the flat.'

'What?' Pyle raged.

'Jesus Christ, Thorn.' bellowed Estella. 'You really are a fucking simpleton at times. Just ignore him.' She went to sit on the room's only chair. 'This will all be over soon and none of it will matter.'

'I think people will decide otherwise,' countered Hunter.

'Well, decide they can. And in a day and a half's time we shall all be home and getting on with the rest of our lives.'

Hunter stared at the redhead. 'What do you mean?'

'Oh, Mr Hunter, have we moved beyond your level of understanding?' When he did not answer, she continued. 'Thorn, you see, is finally going on television. Aren't you, Thorn?'

'Yes.' The writer was back inspecting his shoes. 'Despite my considerable misgivings, I shall appear.'

Hunter felt more than the buzz of expensive alcohol in his system. 'What?'

'Tomorrow afternoon,' said Estella. 'Thorn will make his plea for forgiveness. It's all been arranged. The public and the nation's media require Thorn to atone for his sins.'

'I shall appear,' said Pyle, 'appear and apologise. I shall be prodded and degraded for the benefit of the masses.'

'Oh, you don't have to apologise, Thorn. You can dance around the issue. Smother the message in sub clauses.'

'I don't so much mind apologising, Estella. It's not as if I'll actually mean it. I'll just be making things up.' The words were aimed at his agent, yet Pyle's attention was fixed on Hunter. 'It's what I do apparently.'

27

Hunter left The Georgian and was headed back to New Mount Street. His lower half took care of the motion required to carry him along while everything above the waist was focused on his next move. Hunter's stomach toyed with nerves as well as the chocolate and luxury liqueur, his heart beat faster than normal, his ears heard the dial tone from his mobile. He had called Ahmed Said Ali.

The dull buzzing fell in with the slap of boots on pavement; Hunter was moving swiftly. By the time he heard Ahmed's voice he was already at Albert Square and the town hall and was speaking over him.

'Listen, Ahmed,' Hunter began, 'I've found Pyle. What's all this about tomorrow?'

Yet the words of the television researcher had carried on behind this question. Hunter was speaking to a voicemail system. He swore, urged Ahmed to pick up if he was there, then left a message and rang off.

Now on Cross Street, Hunter had still not slowed. His next call was to Zora Liu. He relayed the pressing need of the situation to a P&P receptionist and was connected a moment later.

'What's the big fuss?' asked Zora.

'You might want to embrace the cactus,' Hunter replied, giving her thirty seconds to assume the position before he started to explain.

By the time he was finished, Hunter was beyond Market Street, approaching Exchange Square, and beginning to sweat. Zora was quiet bar the inhaling and exhaling of nicotine, and occasional interruptions of, 'Assholes. Fucking assholes.'

'What are you gonna do about this?' Hunter asked and the editor paused to think. When her eventual answer came it was not to his satisfaction.

'What is it you expect me to do?' she said.

Hunter stopped. He was on Balloon Street and sat down by the Robert Owen statue to let his body settle. 'I dunno,' he said. 'Something, at least.'

'Something? Ok, the first something that springs to mind is standing by this window and smoking until I run out of cigarettes. Then I'll probably send out for another pack.'

'Can't you tell someone?'

'You want me to tell someone? You want me to tell my boss? Because I have a boss, you know. Plural, in fact. You want me to walk in and tell my new bosses, that an author this company has a long history with may or may not have manufactured a controversy with the plan of boosting his, and by extension, their company's sales?' Here she inhaled. 'Is that what you want me to tell them? Because do you know what I'll likely be told?'

Hunter did not know.

'That moral arbitration is not a feature of my contract.'

Hunter lay back on the brick plinth, hearing the rumble and squeak of a passing tram. His vision now dominated by cloud, but for the face of a grey stone man comforting a kneeling child.

Zora exhaled and continued. 'Firstly, I'm new here. Secondly, I'm already not in their good books. The blame for this mess has been put squarely at my door and it's a door which doesn't even have my name on it yet. My word to them will not mean much, you know. Which brings me to point three. Your word,' she inhaled again, 'will mean,' here she exhaled, 'even fucking less.'

'Why?'

'Why, Mr Hunter? I don't know. How about because a week and a half ago no one had heard of you. You have no reputation, no standing, no contacts to vouch for you. You're a wildcard hired off the internet by one of the supposed guilty parties. My bosses would not see you as a credible source for information.'

'But...' was all Hunter could think to say.

'But, what?

'There must be something we can do.'

Zora coughed. 'Unofficially,' then coughed once more, 'I am open to suggestions. The thought of someone like Estella de Fenestrate putting one over on me my first weeks on the job is not a pleasant one.'

Hunter considered this as he lay flat out on the plinth. 'What about social media? Can't you out him on Twitter or something?'

'No. Can't you do it?'

'I don't have any accounts,' he told her.

'Neither do I.'

Hunter thought more on the idea. 'Can't you get your unpaid intern to do it?'

'No,' said Zora, 'absolutely not.'

'Why?'

'Because it's too much. It's unconscionable. It's really not the kind of thing we don't pay her for. Besides, she quit an hour ago. Turns out some of us will only do so much for so little. Or nothing at all, if you want to get especially pedantic.'

Hunter sat upright. Not through inspiration, but because acid had begun to seep into his pipes. 'I think you should do it, Zora.'

'That will not be happening.'

'Go on, Zora.'

'Fuck you, Hunter. I'm not going online. I don't want to. I mean, I do want to obviously, you know, that's the nature of addiction. But I can't. I shouldn't. If I go online, I'll get distracted by some drama that has nothing to do with me and before I know it, I'll be six months older.

'Look, if any of this conspiring Pyle business got out, how much difference do you think it would make? Don't answer because I'm going to tell you. None, that's how much. Sure, there'll be people out there who'll get pissed about it. They'll tweet at us, they'll call the office, they might even stand outside with a placard. But you know what? The people who want to buy his books, will still buy his books and the people who don't buy his books, still won't. This, essentially has been Thornton Pyle's whole career.'

Hunter gripped his mobile tightly. Had he not let his phone insurance lapse he might have launched the device at some nearby brickwork. 'So, him and Estella just get away with it?'

'You know, someone recently told me something which stuck in my mind. Do you want me to share this nugget with you?'

'Not really, no.'

'Well, Hunter, you're getting it anyway. We live in a post-competence world, adjust your expectations accordingly.'

Hunter had been back at his desk on New Mount Street several hours when he finally heard from Ahmed Said Ali.

'Where've you been?' Hunter enquired into his mobile, not entirely politely.

'At work, mate. Some of us have a proper job. I'm a busy man, Hunter. I've things to do. Like sorting out your Pyle problem.'

Hunter had a glass of supermarket Irish Cream in his hand; it was quite the comedown after his brush with the full-price version. 'You've heard then?'

'It's been difficult not to,' Ahmed told him. 'My producer hasn't stopped going on about it.'

'The shouty man's been shouting?'

'He's not happy.'

'Why?' Hunter moved the glass to his lips. 'He's getting his celebrity apology. What more does he want?'

'He's not a man who likes being messed around. You of all people should know that. He likes to get his own way. I mean, if someone's going to get stiffed, he prefers to be the one doing the stiffing. But your Pyle business, it's left him sore.'

'Tell him not to run the segment, then.'

'In a perfect world, Hunter, I would do, but he'd likely not listen and just get irked a subordinate was telling him how to do his job. Plus, it's content, isn't it. If we don't run this, someone else will and we'll still have to find a five-to-ten-minute piece to show. And seeing as you've given me nothing on this DEATH cult, mate, here we are.'

Hunter swilled the cheap booze in his glass. 'What if told you there was more to this than anyone thought?'

'Such as?'

'Such as conspiracy. A plot. Such as this whole thing was a ruse from the start.'

'If you told me all that,' said Ahmed, not even pausing to consider the idea, 'what I would say and then what my producer would echo in a louder, angrier southern voice would be, what do you have to go on? How incriminating is your evidence, how solid is your source? We can't just put this on national television with nothing to back it up.'

'I'm not going on national television,' said Hunter.

Ahmed stifled a laugh. 'Mate, no one is putting *you* on national television. But someone else will be and they'll require a bit of proof or the like should any lawyers come calling. Now what've you got?'

Hunter pondered this, lifting the liqueur to his lips once more. For evidence he had nothing more than a vague unrecorded conversation in a 5-star hotel room and as Zora had so recently pointed out, as a source he was not what many would call credible.

'Look, Hunter, I've got to go. I've stuff to do and I'm finishing early today. I'm taking my lads to the United game. But as for this Pyle business, as I've told them with the football, you can't win all the time. If you lose, you lose. You've just got to suck it up and hope tomorrow will be better.'

*

Wednesday evening in The Three Jolly Bargemen saw the match being shown on a large screen in the snug. Hunter was seated at the bar with a pint, preferring to watch Vicky Park serve a customer, while Joe Dimly loomed next to him.

'What's happening in the United game?' Joe asked.

United were already a goal down and, as predicted, Connor O'Connor had been relegated to the bench.

'It's on back there,' Hunter gestured.

'I know, but I can't watch. I get all nervous. Are we playing well?'

'Define "we",' replied Hunter.

'United,' said Joe.

'Define "well".'

Joe Dimly drifted away and Hunter glanced over at the screen which showed the score remained the same, but also Connor O'Connor, the camera having found him huddled in some colossal item of branded teamwear and sitting uncomfortably even on a cushioned side-line seat. The expression on his face was one Hunter could imagine on his own. Ridiculed. Cast aside. No longer able to influence events.

'Bad pint?' a voice asked behind him. Hunter turned and Vicky Park was leaning on the bar. 'You've barely touched it.'

'I'm not sure I'm in the mood,' he told her.

'Rough day at the office?'

'Rough day everywhere, really.'

'Who'd be a detective, eh?'

'Maybe, I shouldn't any longer.'

The barmaid's eyebrows rose. 'Oh right, are you thinking of

packing it in then, handing back your magnifying glass and deerstalker?'

Hunter had spent a week and a half on three cases, none of which had been solved to his satisfaction. 'Is there any work going here, behind the bar an' that?'

'Not at the moment.'

'How about on the door?'

Vicky Park gave him a hasty appraisal. 'I'm not sure you've the required aura for door work.'

'I've Artifice,' Hunter suggested.

'You've what?'

'Doesn't matter.' Hunter shifted the conversation to one he had been thinking on for a week or so. 'So, how many evenings do you do in here then?'

'Three or four.'

'And what do you do on the ones you have off?'

'Not a great deal, really.'

'I don't suppose,' Hunter started, 'you'd fancy going out for a drink sometime?'

The barmaid's face tightened.

'Not here,' he added. 'Anywhere you want, or I could surprise you.'

Her body tensed; her eyes searched for someone in need of serving. Hunter's stomach dropped. He was already at a low ebb, and this was not, were he approaching the situation with a critical mind, the best point to ask a woman he barely knew out on a date.

Vicky Park folded her arms and leant upon the bar. 'It's a lovely offer, but I'm afraid the answer's no.'

'Are you seeing someone?' Hunter asked.

'It's not that, it's just…'

'Just what?'

The barmaid chose her words carefully. 'I want to say, don't take this personally, but there's probably not a way for anyone not to take what I'm about to say personally.'

Hunter's stomach was now below street level.

'Which is what?'

'Which is, I'm a single mum with two kids and two jobs. And while I would like to meet someone and be in a relationship again, I don't want it to be with just anyone. I want the right one.'

'And you don't see me as the right one?'

'No. I see you as…'

'As what?'

'As… a bit of an idiot.'

'But we're all idiots,' Hunter protested.

'That's true,' she said, 'we are.' A customer approached and Vicky Park readied herself to meet them. 'But I've found, and often to my cost, there's very much a sliding scale.'

28

It was raining at Shudehill tram stop and Hunter, without umbrella or hood, was not under the protective awning, but out in the downpour, standing apart while a crowd took shelter.

The electronic board stated, Manchester Airport, 3 minutes.

Dry travellers bristled ready to enter the tram, all thought of politeness abandoned in their impending battle for a seat. The chill rain was soaking Hunter through, but he would be home soon enough. Back to the flat on Little Peter Street. Back to his upstairs neighbours as they clacked across wooden floors wearing what must only be clogs. Manchester Airport, 2 minutes.

Hunter would get home and towel the rain from his hair, drink plenty of water while he prepared some late-night snack – toast, perhaps, with a little jam if there were any in his cupboards – then attempt a good night's sleep and maybe, just maybe things, as Ahmed Said Ali had told him, would appear brighter in the morning. Manchester Airport, 1 minute.

On the opposite platform, Hunter saw movement. A sizeable

bird perched atop the ticket machine, a peregrine falcon struggling with the touch screen. Beak tapping glass to no effect, the bird gave a pained call and flew away.

Hunter glanced back up at the electronic board. Manchester Airport, 12 minutes.

The crowd under the awning had gone, and yet Hunter had seen no tram arrive and no one leave. The rain, however, remained and he still in it.

Hunter stared upwards to bellow profanity at the dark sky, only to notice a patch appeared darker still. A patch directly above him which appeared to be growing, growing and descending, descending upon Hunter. For a mind full of frustrations and alcohol, this could only mean trouble. Was this the Balloon Street discrepancy? Was Hunter about to be taken? Where would this evening end? Hospital? Heaven? Radcliffe was also a possibility. He tried to move yet found himself stricken. The icy deluge had him frozen to the spot.

Hunter attempted to decode this curiosity but with little success. This shadow appeared too perfectly spherical for a natural phenomenon and too mundane for alien technology. Only when it was almost on Hunter, when his life seemed about to end, did he recognise it to be a basket and above the basket a balloon which in time settled not on Hunter but before him and the platforms edge.

Inside the basket stood a man and with him, balancing on the basket edge, a cat. Hunter stared at the man, then at the cat, then back to the man. The man stared at Hunter but gave him nothing save a smile and a nod. The cat, also staring at Hunter, was rather more verbose.

'Are you getting in, or what?' the feline asked.

Hunter woke from the dream with a headache and a dry feeling in his mouth which no known liquid seemed to ease. Thirty minutes later he left for New Mount Street.

Thursday morning in the office began with a drumbeat playing on Hunter's door before the postman Claude stepped inside, extending his percussive barrage, first upon the filing cabinet, then on a rare open spot of wood on the cluttered desk. He added a little sideways shuffle as he reached into his satchel to pull out letters which were fanned out in front of Hunter like a winning hand of cards. Claude appeared, to anyone who knew him, unusually joyous.

Hunter ignored the letters and cradled his head. 'Can you not be so loud,' he told his friend.

'Can't help it, pal. I'm in a good mood.'

'That's obvious, but the thing is I'm not, so try and keep it down.'

The postman placed the letters slowly and silently on Hunter's closed laptop. He stood quiet for five seconds, staring at his friend. 'Are you not gonna mention the football?'

'I dunno,' said Hunter, struggling with even the most basic interaction, 'it's never usually a good idea.'

'To be fair, I think today it would be a wonderful idea.'

Hunter took a deep breath of stale office air hoping to offset the stale booze air which pervaded his system. 'Ok. What happened?'

By way of answer Claude Horn broke into dance and began to chant. 'Oh, Connor O'Connor. Oh, Connor O'Connor.'

Mentally, Hunter assumed the foetal position. 'Let's bring the volume down a bit shall we.'

Claude continued his gyrating but matched it with a whisper. 'Oh, Connor O'Connor. Oh, Connor O'Connor.'

Hunter looked blankly at the postman.

'You've not heard then?' asked Claude.

The last Hunter had seen United had been losing, as he had not checked the score after leaving the Bargemen. Following his rejection by Vicky Park he went to the Skull and Crumpet where he proceeded to drink himself into a state mere words could not describe.

'They were one nil down early doors,' Claude confirmed. 'Two nil at half-time, actually.'

'And this is a reason for song and dance?'

'It is after our mutual friend came on.'

Hunter lifted his head. 'O'Connor?'

The postman nodded. 'He only went and scored a bloody hat-trick.'

'Blimey,' said Hunter.

His friend watched him, waiting for more. 'Is that all you can say?'

'I'm at a bit of a low ebb.' O'Connor's success was pleasing to Hunter though he would have preferred a little of it to have rubbed off on him.

'Why?' asked Claude. What's up?'

Just as Hunter had not recounted his tryst with Estella, he did not now mention his failure with a lady last evening. 'Cases, that's all.'

'The dog?'

'The writer. I found him.

Claude became confused. 'But that's good, isn't it? Tell me, is he as hilarious off the page as he isn't on it?'

'Not intentionally,' replied Hunter before recapping the previous day's activity for his friend. The tailing of agent Estella. The confrontation in a swanky hotel room. The heinous plot at the heart of it all.

The postman blew out his cheeks. 'To be fair, pal. That's pretty audacious of them.'

Hunter could not disagree. There was an element of using humanity's flaws to further your own ends which he sometimes wished he could possess, or at least admit to.

'So, what're you gonna do?' Claude asked.

Hunter sat back and shrugged. 'I'm not sure what I can do.'

'How about putting it online?'

'The thing is I don't have any accounts and can't very well set one up as, with my zero followers, it would look as though I'd done just that.'

'I'd follow you.'

'Cheers, Claude.'

'Though, I'd probably mute you after a while, not that you'd know about it. But then that's the beauty of the mute.'

'Thanks for being up front about it, though.'

'No problem, pal.'

'Is there anyone you haven't muted?'

'If there is, I can't think of them.'

The outline of an idea began to form in Hunter's mind, and he leaned forward, elbows planted on Beckett's *The Complete Dramatic Works*. 'Has anyone muted you?'

'There'd be little to mute. I like and I lurk and not much beyond that. It wouldn't be worth anyone's time pressing the button.'

The idea was swelling now, taking shape, a shape that might lift Hunter out of his gloom and into clear blue sky. 'Yeah,' he said to himself and raised a digit in the direction of his friend. 'Yeah.'

'I don't like the way you're pointing at me. I've had quite enough of other people's fingers for one month.'

'*You* could do it,' Hunter told him.

'Do what?'

'Break this online.'

The postman's head shook. 'No, pal, I really couldn't.'

'Why not?'

'Because my social media accounts are carefully tended oases of calm. I mute, I block. I occasionally retweet pictures of animals or bands, or Salford and Manchester from yesteryear.'

'Come on, Claude.'

'No. I haven't the time for the day's controversies, I've a life to lead. You should go to the press. They love all that shit, and you've the contacts.'

'I do but I've tried them already.' Hunter sat back, his attention on the ceiling, his grand idea punctured, the once uplifting thought squeaking out like a long, slow fart. 'Apparently, I lack not just evidence but credibility.'

'Well,' Claude considered his words, 'to be fair, I'd say you're kind of fucked.'

The postman danced out the way he entered and left Hunter in delicate peace to think on his plans for the day. The Pyle issue, much like his chances at barmaid romance, he assigned to life's dustbin. The machinations of writer and agent were beyond Hunter now, their nefarious scheme unstoppable. He received a formal email from P&P informing him his services were no longer required and he would be paid his daily rate up to close of business yesterday. Hunter did not bother to contact Zora Liu nor even check his account. He had work to do.

Doctor Dickie Shrub was still missing, and Hunter had not spoken to Delamere Forest or her fiancé since the day of the séance. He had, however, heard from the dog-owning lawyer, a message the previous afternoon left in the ether of his office answerphone had first given him news her apartment was now free from the revolting poor and second asked that he contact her with an update. Hunter did not quite feel up to this task. He had nothing to tell her, even the supposed dognapper had not called back.

Looming beyond the missing canine was the DEATH cult. As it was Thursday they would meet again that very evening.

Height Library. 19:30. Refreshments provided.

Hunter would attend, though the thought made him nervous. What if someone should recognise him? What if they should figure out he was on to them? How might Hunter meet his end?

He tried not to picture himself set upon by cultists. Shot or poisoned. Cyanide, maybe, in the free weak tea; further reason never to accommodate such a beverage. Perhaps he would simply be being beaten bloody with a Thornton Pyle hardback or sacrificed ritually on the bowling green to the rear.

Hunter became aware of a light panting not his own and looked up to see Connor O'Connor in the doorway. His bearded face unobstructed by hood and in his arms a dachshund.

Something lifted in Hunter, his hangover took a bow and

receded to a far corner or more precisely a near corner, from where it could still poke him in the brain every now and then. Hunter stood and approached the unlikely pair as Doctor Dickie Shrub nuzzled his saviour's ear.

'Where'd you find him?' Hunter asked.

'He was outside,' the striker told him.

'Outside where?'

'Outside here, worrying a postman.'

Hunter pondered this turn of events while the footballer tickled the Doctor under his chin.

'Did he recognise you?' Hunter asked.

'This little fella?'

'No,' said Hunter. 'The postman.'

'Nah, mate. He was off up the street like a rocket.'

For the dachshund, Hunter took the Everton mug from his desk, emptied out the lone biro, and filled it with bottled water he had bought to rehydrate himself. For O'Connor he offered a low-sugar ginger crunch.

'I hear congratulations are in order,' Hunter said, taking a biscuit or two for himself.

The United player sat down, Doctor Dickie Shrub curled at his feet and lapping at the water. 'Thanks, mate. But I doubt I could have done it without you, really. It was you and your karma.'

As Hunter returned to his seat, he felt a feeling which was either a glow of pride or the spice of the ginger.

Across the desk, O'Connor crunched, chewed, swallowed, then continued. 'That first game I wasn't taking it seriously. I was thinking karma, but I wasn't *being* karma. You know what I mean?'

Hunter had no wish to spoil this beautiful moment.

'What it was, yesterday right I'm on my way to Old Trafford and at the bottom of our road I'm about to pull out and this taxi is coming along and usually I'd be in a rush, and I'd just be off, but I thought, no. Be karma. So, I just sat there taking a deep breath or two and let the guy go before me. Then, when I get to the ground and I'm about to race in the door before the kitman, I stop and think, no. Be karma. So, I hold the door for him and let him go first. I just stand there taking another deep breath. Then I'm in the changing rooms and the gaffer takes me aside and says, 'Sorry Connor, but you're on the bench tonight'. I knew it was coming, but I was still gutted. You know what I mean? Anyhow, I thought to myself, don't sulk, it is what it is, be karma, and I took a deep breath and was nice to everyone. Getting behind them, encouraging them.'

Hunter tried to match this relentless positivity with the face he had seen the night before on the pub screen, O'Connor looking sullen in a team puffer jacket. Yet it would have been the mark of a pedant to bring this up and Hunter let the striker continue.

'Anyhow, ten minutes into the second half Pablo does his hamstring, and the gaffer puts me on. We're two nil down by that point and I'm jogging onto the pitch and I breath in and think to myself, don't worry, there's loads of time left. All I can do is the best I can. So, in the next attack, Hermann, our right winger, has the ball and I see where he's gonna put it and I think if I run into that space and collide with the centre back, then go down, I could win us a penalty. But then as I'm running I take a breath and also see their keeper is probably going for the ball as well and I remember in the first half these two, the keeper and the centre back, kept getting in each other's way. I'd said to Pablo at halftime. 'Pablo,' I said, 'Estos dos no pueden comunicarse, Pablo.' Anyhow, I realised if I feint like I'm gonna run in but then hang back and let the ball come to me, I'll have an empty net to aim at. So, that's what I do. I feint and I wait, and I take a deep breath and I be karma, and it happens just like I saw. Their centre back and keeper get tangled up and the ball is loose and coming to me, and I set myself and I let go of everything that's been building up these past months, the missed sitters, the bruises, the mushroom, and I pick a spot in the top corner and just hit it.'

By now Hunter was on the edge of his chair, the drama sucking him in as he chewed a ginger crunch, the hangover a semi distant memory. Hunter put down his biscuit to ask, 'And it goes straight in the top corner?'

O'Connor shifted on the seat, bending down to stroke Doctor Dickie Shrub's back. 'No, mate. Bottom left, in the end, but they all count don't they.'

Five minutes after ending his drought, O'Connor had scored a second, an equaliser. Then, in the ninth minute of injury time, he added his third and a United winner. It was quite the redemption story. A resurrection, almost. Hunter watched O'Connor spread his hands, palms up. 'Be karma, mate,' the bearded figure declared.

Be karma, Hunter thought and smiled, glad now he had been unable to explain the concept more clearly to the footballer. He sat back, ginger crunch once more in hand, and allowed his attention to drift. Another two cases were now solved, and he had not even considered the striker's plight an actual case, though things had fallen into place regardless. Hunter asked if the striker would mind posing for a photograph.

'Sure,' said O'Connor. 'Send it me and I'll put it on my socials.'

The two men plus the Doctor assembled and Hunter, not usually one for a selfie, was arm out manoeuvring his phone to catch all three, taking a number of shots, the best of which he would send to his father hoping the old man would be impressed.

As he returned to his desk, Hunter pondered an Irish cream but decided against it. there would be time for such things later. He sat and scrolled through the selfies, wondering what cases might turn up next. The last fortnight had been a busy one and successful monetarily. The only spectre on the horizon was his date that evening with DEATH and if Hunter survived, perhaps he would take a holiday. That trip to America, or the cricket in Australia.

Be karma.

Hunter relaxed and reached for another biscuit. As he did so he noticed something in the background of the pictures. He had inadvertently captured the office window and in the window, what appeared to be a face. He zoomed in on the screen and saw a cat. His attention flicked to the actual window and there it was. A cat.

Yet situated on the second floor as his office was, Hunter did not see how this was possible. Had the feline shinned the drainpipe and taken up residence on a ledge? Did cats even possess shins?

His mind flashed with his recent Shudehill Sadler tram fantasy and a terrible thought overcame Hunter, that he was still on Little Peter Street, asleep and dreaming. Had this morning not actually happened? O'Connor's hat-trick. The finding of Doctor Dickie Shrub. Was this rush of glad news simply some fiction of the night?

To slap himself in company did not seem a proper course of action and so Hunter settled on pinching and twisting the skin on his forearm, pretending to be scratching an itch. The discomfort seemed real enough.

At that moment, Hunter saw the cat move and then something larger replace it, the face of a man Hunter vaguely recognised. The man smiled, raising a hand in salute, dirty yellow material clutched in his fingers, and then he moved, and Hunter caught sight of the feline face sewn on the window cleaner's sweatshirt. Hunter looked toward the footballer. O'Connor had missed all this; he was still petting the dachshund.

Be karma. Be karma. The words echoed in Hunter's brain, and he once more saw the cat in his window, and then something happened. A light went on in his mind and what he needed to do became clear. Hunter could not wait for the universe to settle its account with Thornton Pyle and Estella de Fenestrate. A solution had presented itself, had walked right into his office and was sitting the other side of his desk. Hunter put down his biscuit.

'What are you up to the rest of the day?' he asked.

O'Connor shrugged. 'Not a thing. The gaffer told me to rest up. We've got another big game this weekend.'

29

In a rare act, Hunter phoned Delamere Forest at her office during recognised working hours wishing to speak with the lady herself and not some pre-recorded duplicate. For his plotting to succeed, time would be an important factor.

'Waite, Tarry and Holding,' a familiar voice answered.

'Ms Forest?'

'Mr Hunter.'

'Ms Forest, I have wonderful news for you, but also a favour to ask.'

Delamere Forest was overjoyed at the return of Doctor Dickie Shrub and amenable to what some may have deemed a curious suggestion. With this part complete, Hunter's next call was to Ahmed Said Ali.

'Did your lads enjoy the game last night?' Hunter enquired.

'Never mind my lads, mate,' said the TV researcher, 'It was the best match I've seen in a long while.'

Hunter felt it best not to relay his tenuous part in O'Connor's rebirth and got to the point. 'Is your producer still sore over this Pyle business?'

'Very. Not that I'd ever call his demeanour upbeat at the best of times. Why?'

Hunter leaned back in his chair, landline handset resting between neck and inclined head, as he admired his recent photographic work on his mobile. 'Well, what if I had an alternate story for you to run?' One that would put you in his good books?'

'I doubt we'll be able to turn it around quickly enough. The Pyle interview is going out this afternoon. I mean, him and his agent are in the building, they're getting ready to record as we speak.'

'Balls to Pyle. I've everything you need right in my office.'

'Hunter, mate, I've been in your office so this doesn't sound promising.'

'It will do. I'm going to send you a photo and I promise you, you're gonna love it. Pyle is old hat, last week's news. The Opinion Sphincter Industrial Complex won't care any longer. But this story, it's a positive one just like you wanted, and it's happening right now.'

'Oh really?' Ahmed did not sound convinced.

'Well, last night and this morning, but still.'

'And what's it a photo of?'

'Do you know how they say a picture can paint a thousand words?'

'Fuck a thousand,' said Ahmed. 'You've got ten.'

Hunter's mind tried to boil down the scene before him, Connor O'Connor tickling Doctor Dickie Shrub under his ears.

'A classic tale.' Hunter counted to three on his fingers as he spoke. 'Adversity overcome.' That was five. 'Supreme act of heroism.' Nine. 'Dog.'

'Piss off, Hunter.'

'Plus, a celebrity.'

'That's now thirteen words. I'm ending this conversation. Don't call again.'

'Aren't you gonna ask what kind of celebrity?'

Hunter could have heard Ahmed's sigh even without the help of a telephone connection. 'I really don't want to know, mate.'

'You will do,' said Hunter, hearing Ahmed Said Ali's mobile ping with the text message he had just sent. 'Trust me, it's your favourite kind.'

Ahmed Said Ali arrived within thirty minutes. The story of the returned dachshund was to be a televised event. There was a full camera crew, mobile canteen and toilet, plus the shouting producer. Ahmed also brought with him a United shirt he wished Connor O'Connor to sign, apparently for his two sons though the sizing appeared somewhat on the larger side.

The impromptu set on New Mount Street inevitably attracted onlookers. Residents from the surrounding apartments. Workers from nearby offices and building sites. Passers-by lost in the maze off Rochdale Road. Joe Dimly leant against a lamppost, what appeared to be a football annual wedged under an arm. Rich Shrub was there, standing in his long coat off to one side, making hand gestures toward Hunter and mouthing a phrase he took to mean, 'call me, call me'. The medium Madame Bickerstaff stood with a younger female – all pixie haircut and sixties-style minidress – who the next time Hunter looked had disappeared.

The presenter Hunter recognised from the local news, a brunette with thick lustrous hair and a Salford accent. She was between Connor O'Connor and Delamere Forest, who carried in her arms the soon to be notorious Doctor Dickie Shrub, and in her eyes a look of appreciation and more for the bearded footballer. Lighting was directed upon this quartet; cameras began to roll.

'So, Connor,' the presenter began, 'First of all, congratulations on your hat-trick last night.'

'Cheers.'

'It's been quite the twenty-four hours for you. Could you tell us about what happened this morning?'

'Well, what it was, the other day I was in the office of my karmic guru and saw this poster about a missing dog. And I looked at the picture of this little fella,' at this point the striker reached out to stroke the canine, 'and I felt a connection.'

Later in his office, and with the day's excitement over with, Hunter sat at his desk ignoring his landline and mobile ring in tandem. First it would be the mobile – caller, Estella de Fenestrate – then the landline – caller, likely, the same. Then, the mobile again – caller, once more, Estella de Fenestrate.

It was currently his landline's turn and yet his mobile began to trill at the same time. Hunter checked the number, recognised that of Zora Liu, and answered with, 'The Society of Professional Mancunians, how can I help.'

The editor was in no mood for japery. 'Why am I watching some sports guy with a puppy and not Thornton Pyle grovelling?'

'It's not a puppy,' Hunter told her. 'That's as big as they get.'

'Why, Hunter?'

'I dunno, canine growth really isn't my field.'

The volume in his ear increased. 'WHY AM I NOT WATCHING MY AUTHOR BEG FORGIVENESS?'

'Zora, Zora, Zora,' said Hunter, tempted to stand and venture over to his filing cabinet, 'I don't know how much reach you think I have, but it doesn't extend to control over daytime programming. It was the producer who made the decision.'

'What?'

'Yeah, he just looked at how many hundreds of thousands of followers 'some sports guy' had on social media against your Pyle's big fat zero.'

'What is this shit? Is life a popularity contest now?'

'I also believe the sports guy and the non-puppy didn't fuck the producer over a week and a half ago.'

Hunter heard what sounded like a strained cry, then a chair move, followed by the disturbing of a cactus. 'Well, I did tell you Thornton Pyle was an idiot.' A cigarette was lit and inhaled. 'Have you heard from Estella?'

Hunter glanced at his landline, still ringing away. 'That's her now. She's been calling for the last half hour.'

'And are you going to answer it?'

'No chance. The case is over. I've filed the paperwork. She is now NLMFP, as we say in the trade.'

'NLMFP?'

'No Longer My Fucking Problem.'

Zora laughed and then coughed and then laugh/coughed. 'God, I bet she's pissed. I would so love to see her face about now.'

'I'm sure you'll see it soon enough. *At the Rising of The Cock* will be out before long, won't it.'

'Yes, but that will also be NLMFP.'

'What do you mean?'

'I'm about done around here, you know.'

'Really?'

'Yeah, I'm going home.'

'Back to New York?'

'This is not working out for me, and a chance has come up in my old office, they've found a recluse who needs an editor.'

'A recluse, like you've always wanted.'

'I know, right. No radio interviews to worry about. No random outbursts online.'

'Congratulations.' Hunter put his feet up on the desk. Things had turned out successfully for him as well. He would celebrate in some way later. Perhaps, a pint in The Skull and Crumpet or a nice takeaway or both. 'So, how're you gonna spend your last days in the capital?

'Carefully, that's how. I already wasted half a day at your Dylan needlework exhibition?'

'What do you mean, "wasted"?'

'Because it's full of fakes.'

'I know,' Hunter said and stared at the piece hanging on his wall. 'I told you it's not Dylan doing the sewing.'

'Not the sewing, the lyrics. They're not real.'

'What?'

'They're made up. I went yesterday after we spoke. Then had

my new unpaid intern send FYI Crisp a list of them and he got back to me this morning. FYI is like a Dylan maniac. I have his email printed out in front of me and do you know what he says?'

'Tell me.' Hunter said, making for the filing cabinet.

'He says none of them are actual Bob.'

'Not actual Bob?' Hunter pulled open the drawer.

'Not actual Bob, at all. In fact, all bogus Bob.'

Hunter twisted the cap off his bottle of Irish Cream. 'Bogus Bob?'

'Positively bogus Bob.'

'But I paid thirty quid for that.'

'Consider it a tax on your free trip down to London. Which, incidentally, if this had all happened next month you wouldn't have had to make.'

'Why?' Hunter asked, considering the faux Dylan on his wall, would he bin it or leave it up as an important lesson?

'The company's new offices will be open then. P&P are expanding into the north. It would have spared you a long journey for such a short meeting.'

The sound of Zora inhaling filled Hunter's ears as he poured silky liquid into a glass. He enquired where these offices might be: Sheffield? Liverpool? Glasgow?

Zora exhaled slowly. 'Someplace called Tottenham.'

30

Fridays on New Mount Street, as with most everywhere else, possessed a special quality. The sense of a working week near its end, two days of freedom approaching, and the joys of an early finish always a possibility. The latter was especially true for Hunter as his caseload was now empty.

Also empty was a space on his desk – Hunter had had a bit of a clear out, starting with his full drawer which was now only half full allowing him to move into it his puzzle books and his second comb, the original of which he had consigned to the wastebin, along with the now long out of date free newspaper. This desk space Hunter filled with a sacred triumvirate: Samuel Beckett's *The Complete Dramatic Works*; a tumbler of luxury Irish cream which Hunter had splashed out some of his recent pay on; and a stack of five low-sugar ginger biscuits.

Hunter picked up the book, found *Waiting for Godot*, and got as far as the words ACT ONE, when a rhythmic knock came at his door and there stood the postman Claude, letters in hand, satchel over a shoulder.

'Someone's looking very pleased with themselves,' noted the bespectacled mailman.

'And why not,' Hunter said, putting down the book, 'I've had a good few days and it's almost the weekend.'

He had enjoyed his morning walk from Little Peter Street despite the coldness of the air, had stopped in at a coffee shop and treated himself to a takeaway mocha, the cup warm in his hands as he had picked up a new free paper, the font-page story being: UNITED STRIKER FINDS FORM AND DOG.

'Are we having a pint tonight or tomorrow?' asked the postman. 'Or are you washing your hair again?'

'At least some of us have hair to wash.'

Claude adjusted his glasses with a ramrod middle finger and the pair made arrangements for Saturday evening in The Skull and Crumpet. With that sorted, the usual letters were handed over: a bill; an offer of credit; a further bill; and yet another envelope for Mr Elvis Love. On this last, Hunter crossed out the address on the front, circled the one on the rear, wrote in clear capitals, LOVE DON'T LIVE HERE ANYMORE, and then handed it back to Claude.

Hunter watched his friend's brow crinkle and waited for a chuckle that did not come. The postman began to shake his head. 'Doesn't work, pal.'

'Course it does,' said Hunter. 'It's my best one yet.'

'Doesn't work.'

'What do you mean?'

'Well, to be fair, "LIVE" would imply residential.'

'So?'

'Well, what you're in is business premises. So, unless there's something you haven't been telling your landlord, it doesn't work, pal.'

Hunter pressed the letter toward Claude, and the mail worker stepped back.

'I'm not taking it. Post it yourself. Anyway, how did you get on at the library?'

Hunter stared at his friend. *Library?* he thought. *Li-bra-ry?* It took a moment for comprehension to blossom in his mind – the DEATH cult. 'Oh fuck,' he said. 'I knew I forgot something.'

Hunter had been on the Height yesterday evening, though not at the library. He had ditched his other plans, the thoughts of a drink or takeaway and gone to his parent's house, mere streets away from the DEATH cult's meeting place. Hunter had watched television, eaten a pie like a normal person, and fended off enquiries from both his mother and father as to what exactly the job title "karmic guru" entailed. The water people had not surfaced even once.

The postman grinned. 'Just as well I didn't forget, then, isn't it.'

'You went?'

'Not a chance,' Claude replied, 'You know how I feel about group activities. My mam, on the other hand, loves that kind of shite.'

'You sent Mrs Horn to a DEATH cult meeting?'

'Mrs Euphonium, and yes and no. I didn't send her, I just happened to mention it and what with The Dog being shut, her and Jack have been looking for things to do of an evening.'

Despite the fact Hunter had now failed to attend two of their gatherings, he was curious about them. Who were these people and what foul business did they get up to on an otherwise quiet midweek evening. 'What did they find out?' he asked, sitting forward, his elbows resting on Beckett.

'Well,' Claude began, 'My mam was a little disappointed.'

'Why?'

'Because it turns out your DEATH cult is nothing more than a particularly enthusiastic mystery reading group.'

'What?'

'Doyle, Edgar, Agatha, Tana, Hammet,' said Claude, counting off each name on a finger. 'They talk about the books and read aloud certain scenes. It's half discussion, half amateur dramatics.'

Hunter sat back, his interest waning. 'No actual death then?'

'Only of the fictional variety.' Claude shifted his satchel ready to leave. 'They did, however, enjoy the free tea and biscuits.'

With the postman gone and Hunter distracted once again from his reading, he went to stand at the window. He checked for signs of imminent rain but found only clear dry blue and the bright lighting of the apartment opposite. Hunter decided he was done for the week. He slipped the reversible jacket on over his hooded top, opened the filing cabinet to collect a handful of ginger crunches for his walk across the city, and had just stepped toward his door, biscuit at his lips, when a sharp outburst from his landline stopped him.

Hunter glanced at his watch, it was not yet dinnertime, and the phone shrieked once more. He could leave now and enjoy his weekend with no thoughts of work on his mind. His answerphone would pick up any message and Hunter could begin whatever this was afresh on Monday morning. A third trill came, the noise now straying into the incessant. Hunter removed the biscuit from his mouth, returned to his desk, and lifted the receiver.

'The Fall fan club.'

'This is your last chance,' a voice intoned, and Hunter recognised the gravelly insistence of the dognapper.

'Last chance? I take it you don't keep up with the news?' he asked the man.

'Why would I? It's just opinion and speculation these days.'

Hunter lowered himself into his chair. 'Normally, I'd agree with you but every now and then careful attention is rewarded. But that's a whole other story, let's get back to my dog.'

'Five hundred quid,' announced the voice. 'Five hundred quid and the little fucker gets to come home. You remember the drop off?' Jiffy bag, bin near…'

'Yeah, yeah, jiffy bag, bin near Debenhams, I remember.' Hunter made himself comfortable, placing his booted feet up on the desk. 'Now, all things considered, five hundred isn't a bad price. The thing is, though, I can't help but think, given how keen you sound for me to take this fella off your hands, that you've got this the wrong way round.'

There was silence in Hunter's ear, followed by a question. 'In what way?'

'In the way that it's you who should be paying me.'

'That's not how this works. Trust me, I've done this before.'

Hunter sucked air in through his teeth. 'Trust is a dirty word round here these days. I have issues.'

'I couldn't give a toss. It's five hundred quid or bye bye Mr Wet Nose.'

'Ruggles,' said Hunter.

'You what?'

'His name's Ruggles.'

'Bye bye, Ruggles, then.'

'The thing is,' Hunter bit the corner from his biscuit, 'just because this kind of interaction has played out in a very linear way before now doesn't mean we can't mix it up a little.'

'What are you talking about?'

'Well, if things had never been tried differently, we might not be talking at all.'

'Eh?'

'Think about it. If whoever invented the telephone hadn't invented the telephone, this whole process would have to be done by mail, wouldn't it?'

'I don't see how this is…'

'If humanity had never pushed at boundaries, would I now be sat here eating a low-sugar ginger crunch? Would my jacket be a cotton polyester mix?'

'Look, can we just get back to the bloody dog?'

'Ok, Ok. I was just trying to make this a bit more interesting for the pair of us.'

'Five hundred quid…'

'Yeah, yeah, five hundred, jiffy bag, bin near Debenhams. Of course, it's not even Debenhams any longer, is it? It's nothing, just a shell.'

'Stop talking and listen to me. This is not a negotiation. This is me, telling you, and you fucking doing it. Got that?'

'Ok, right. I'm sorry.'

'Can we get on with this now?'

'Yes.' Hunter bit more of his biscuit and spoke around it. 'But maybe no. I think five hundred might be a bit much for me at the moment.

'What?'

'Well, it's been one of those weeks. A few unexpected outgoings have come in and I'm a bit skint. Now if you add little Ruggles to all that, I'll be even skinter.'

'That's not my problem.'

'No, but it's my problem and I am fifty percent of this, so hear me out.' Hunter took another chomp of biscuit. 'There's the upkeep to consider. Food, vet bills, the walking. So much walking. I know he's only got short legs but still. And then there's readjusting to having him back in my life.'

'What?'

Hunter stood up and made for the filing cabinet.

'In the time we've been apart I've grown as a person. As an individual. I feel more alive. I feel more… more me. I know it's only been two weeks and it's selfish, I know that. But there are times when you have to be selfish. To be true to yourself. To live the life you deserve. And I want to travel. Australia, New York. Maybe both, maybe neither.'

Hunter opened the top drawer and removed the bottle of luxury Irish cream and a glass.

'And I know what you're gonna say, I do, "dogs aren't just for Christmas", but that's not really applicable in this case, is it? It's not even Halloween.' Hunter unscrewed the bottle and began to pour. 'When it comes down to it, it's not him. It's not Ruggles. Ruggles is everything most would want from a canine companion. It's me.' Hunter lifted the glass to his lips. 'I just can't commit to giving Ruggles the life he wants, the life he deserves. You can appreciate that can't you? Hello? Hel-lo?'

Acknowledgements

I'd like to thank the following people:

To the early readers, Chris Grogan and Mike Smith, for giving their time, and Ian Hough for help with proofing.

To Graham Ennis of When Skies Are Grey fanzine for being my first editor, Ian Cusack for advice on publishing.

To my Royal Mail colleagues – especially Simon Barley, Mark Ormrod and Mike Tomlinson – for indulging my nonsense, and Abdul Saleh for Keeping Me Moving.

To John Hubbert and Jeff Wraith for the beers, company and laughs.

To my parents, Paul and Frances, who both loved to read, and my brother, Simon.

And to Nicola Mostyn, who inspires and amuses me daily.

Printed in Great Britain
by Amazon